The SEA is Ours
Tales of Steampunk
Southeast Asia

Acknowledgment for permission to reprint the following:

"The Unmaking of Cuadro Amoroso" by Kate Osias. First published in Philippine Speculative Fiction Vol. 9 (eds. Andrew Drilon & Charles Tan). July 2014. Reprinted by permission of the author.

Cover art and design by Shing Yin Khor

Rosarium Publishing
P.O. Box 544
Greenbelt, MD 20768-0544

ISBN: 978-1-4956-0756-1

The SEA is Ours
Tales of Steampunk
Southeast Asia

Edited by Jaymee Goh & Joyce Chng

Contents

Introduction

The Sea is Ours: Tales of Steampunk Southeast Asia came from a place of annoyance. As steampunk rose in popularity, as conversations on racialized representations and demand for diversity kept roiling in science fiction, as transnational writers struggled to gain recognition, we decided we needed an anthology that could speak to our frustrations with all these spheres, and thus The Sea Is Ours gained a glimmer of existence. It would take another two years before we found a publisher interested in the project. In the two years, the annoyance would turn into frustration, that frustration would turn into disillusionment, with steampunk, with diversity initiatives that always seemed to involve white voices calling the shots, with the continued hegemony of certain voices in science fiction and fantasy.

In our iteration of steampunk, neo-Victorianism and all its attendant issues are optional, even sidelined as we push back against this idea that we must acknowledge the superiority of the British Empire. As citizens of countries that were former colonies, whether of British or some other European power, we live with the history of imperial supremacy. If science fiction and fantasy is meant to provide us with alternate visions of the world, we felt we had to do it on our own terms, especially in the steampunk subgenre. Steampunk, in our anthology, is an aesthetic that combines retrofuturism, alternate history, and technofantasy, so we wanted to know, what do these elements look like from a Southeast Asian perspective?

Being a Southeast Asian can be odd in larger global contexts. In his anthology Alternative Alamat, editor Paolo Chikiamco commented, sometimes the Philippines is a footnote in global politics. One could say that about much of Southeast Asia as well. Our peoples tend to be unrecognized: Filipinos mistaken for Latin Americans; Malays mistaken for Mexicans or Arabs; few seem to understand that Borneo has the states of two countries on it, and one whole tiny country. We are associated with histories of refugeeism, with being undeveloped Third World countries with low living standards, with violent extremists and potential terrorist breeding grounds. In books on recent history, we are footnotes as the grounds upon which today's modern empires did battle in the name of democracy and modernity.

It was, and still is, imperative that we have volumes dedicated to our own voices, projects not of postcolonial melancholia, but of decolonial determination. Our psyches cry for justice for lost names, lost stories, lost histories, all lost to globalized, systemic racism, lost to imperial dreams imposed upon us too long. In the absence of time machines to recover them, we turn to re-creating, and creating anew. Thus, we use steampunk to have that conversation with our histories, our hearts and dreams.

We did our best to reach out to writers from Southeast Asia, and in some ways we have failed—several peoples of our incredibly diverse region are not represented in this volume, an emptiness which we hope to someday fill. We do hope we have had some small successes in other measures; if in the larger English-language science fiction world straight white men call the shots, then our anthology presents a range of authors and characters that is predominantly women, and hella queer.

The stories in this volume cover a wide range of themes and tropes, from delightful novelty, such as Timothy Dimacali's flying butanding (a general term referring to "extremely large fish," which we had initially read as "whales") in "On The Consequence of Sound," and long-time children's tradition, such as the fighting spiders in Robert Liow's "Spider Here." Ideology and technology spark off family conflicts, as in Laura Hill's "Ordained" and Paolo Chikiamco's "Between Severed Souls." Intense, passionate love affairs meet different endings: in Kate Osias' "Unmaking of the Cuadro Amoroso" with a bang, and in Nghi Vo's "Life Under Glass" with the discovery of a creature from a lost world.

Across Southeast Asia, our ties to local mythologies and legends remain steadfast, given a steampunk treatment in Alessa Hinlo's "The Last Aswang" which explores the indigenous aswang figure from an anti-imperial feminist perspective and Ivanna Mendels' "Petrified" which twists Indonesian history in the story of Malin Kundang, also known as Si Tenggang to those of us from the nearby Peninsular. Diaspora and forced migration, common in the movements of our peoples, are illustrated in Olivia Ho's "Working Woman" and z.m. quỳnh's "Chamber of Souls." Relationships of all kinds between women are a recurring thread throughout our anthology, whether between amoral pirates and righteous princesses as featured in Marilag Angway's "Chasing Volcanoes" or between cunning ladies, their handmaids, and daughters in Pear Nuallak's "The Women and The Insects Sing Together."

We give great thanks to our publisher, Bill Campbell of Rosarium Publishing, for the opportunity to share these incredible stories with you: Thank you, Bill, for your graciousness in sharing your platform with us, and thank you for your solidarity. We are also thankful for everyone who has supported this anthology, from the stage of ideas to the stage of fruition.

These waters which so many of us have traveled, upon and over, for fortune, for trade, for refuge, for livelihood—our ancestors' tears and sweat have been cast into the salt of the sea and we begin with the acknowledgement of their presence in our bloods, whether we break with tradition or re-cast it in the fire of the new worlds we have to build, proclaiming: THE SEA IS OURS!

On the Consequence of Sound

Timothy Dimacali

...and then there is the legend of the Bakunawa, first of all the sky whales. The Tagalog songs tell of a majestic beast as black as night, with scales that shimmered in the dark like stars, so big it could swallow the very moon itself.

Most Tagalogs believe that when Bathala created the world, he made seven moons of the purest bathalani to hold up the sky. So captivated was the Bakunawa, it is said, that it rose up and consumed all of them but one.

Some legends, however, take this instead to be true: that there was always but one moon; that the Bakunawa, as a creature of the sky, was a wise messenger sent by Bathala himself; and that it brought down from the heavens a piece of the solitary moon, which we know today as the floating island of Mount Taal.

—Damiana Eugenio, "Philippine Folk Literature: The Legends," 1993

~*~

The butanding is a curious creature, especially for a little girl who knew nothing about life outside the Walls.

I thought it was just a kite dancing in the wind, floating languidly on the morning breeze.

I think now that it must have been just a small juvenile, perhaps no more than 300 varas in length, but it was far bigger than any kite or bird I had ever seen before.

The blue-gray skin on its catfish-like body glistened in the morning sun as it glided calmly about, its fins catching on the wind as it swam.

The lone calf had probably lost its way from its herd and somehow wandered into the skies above the city.

The people below didn't seem to care. Stray whales were not completely uncommon, Papa said, and they never bothered the city or its inhabitants.

It swooped low overhead, almost touching our rooftop.

Its eyes shone like polished black marble, set against a gaping toothless mouth that trailed long gossamer whiskers in its wake.

It floated effortlessly above me, just out of reach.

Then, from far off beyond the Mariquina mountains came a low droning sound, a booming thunder that rolled across the sky.

Hroooooooommmmm!

That was an adult call, Papa said. Its herd was looking for it.

The pup opened its mouth wide and bellowed in reply:

Krooooooooooooooooooommmm!

The note echoed through the air, the vibrations sending shimmering ripples across the rows of blue-white bathalani crystals along the creature's flanks. Each wave of sound lifted it higher into the air.

The young sky whale twisted upwards in a gentle spiral.

Hrrrrrooooooooooooooooommmmm!

Krooooooeeeeeeeeooooooom! it answered back.

It shifted its fins, leveled out its flight, and headed home.

"What was that?" I asked.

"A choice," Papa said.

~*~

Intramuros! The old Manila. The original Manila. The Noble and Ever Loyal City... To the early missionaries she was a new Rome, but to the early conquistadores she was a new Solomon's Temple, filled with life and love—but most of all, with sound and music.

—Nick Joaquin, "Manila, My Manila," 1990

~*~

To live in Intramuros was to live surrounded by music.

I remember fondly one cold summer morning under a clear blue sky many years ago, when I was just a little child back in the old Walled City. My father, holding my hand, took me to our balcony to greet the new day.

I was too small to look over the ledge, too scared to look down. So I just closed my eyes and listened—to the dawn hymns of the monks singing in their chapels high up in the rascacielos, the clacking of horses' hooves on the cobblestoned streets far below, the throaty cries of the Sangley streetvendors echoing from the alleys, the rhythmic thumping of mortars on pestles as the day's rice was being prepared.

All around us, Intramuros was alive with the sounds of ritual and habit: a strong, steady heartbeat that had remained unchanged for centuries.

It was the sound of home, of life within the Walls.

Suddenly, Papa shook my shoulder.

"Look there, Aria!"

My curiosity got the better of me. I opened my eyes to find him pointing into the distance, out across the bay.

The Nuestra Señora del Cielo was a sight to behold as it came in to port.

The royal galleon's masts, each thick around as the torsos of seven men, seemed to defy the very sky itself. Her massive wooden hull, made from the most ancient and darkest narra wood and inlaid with gold and mother of pearl, cast a long shadow over the houses and churches beneath it. The whole city, it seemed, fell into silent awe at the sight of the great ship flying in from the sea.

A squadron of smaller, sliver-shaped escort ships flew in tight formation ahead of it, their linen sails billowing at full mast, white as clouds. Each escort glinted with its own complement of brass lantaka cannons extended in ceremonial salute.

The Navigators of the entire retinue, sight unseen, played at a steady tempo as they guided their ships on course. I will always remember the music of their viols descending from the air, a cascade of notes that swelled and receded in wave after grand wave of sonorous rapture, announcing the arrival of the royal galleon.

It was then that I knew I would become a Navigator.

One day, I shyly asked my father if I could learn to fly.

He was seated as usual at the head of the dining table, reading the day's issue of *La Vanguardia*. Mother had prepared him his usual cup of tsokolate with a side of buttered pan de sal.

I casually took my place beside him and reached over to the pile of hot, leaf-wrapped suman on the center serving tray.

I paused for a moment, wondering if it was a good time to disturb him.

"Papa, I want to be a Royal Navigator just like you!" I said in my tiny voice.

Papa burst into a hearty laugh. "And what made you think that, hija? A Navigator's life is hard work," he said, crossing his arms.

He spoke with authority on the matter as a First Order Initiate of the Cofradia de los Hermanos Alados, the Confraternity of the Winged Brotherhood—his emblem of office, a winged fist, proudly displayed on a pin that he always wore on his collar.

"Es que si... gosto co pong matotong lomipad," I stammered, hiding my face behind my hands.

He looked me sternly in the eye.

"And what would you do then, if you learned to fly, eh?"

"Gosto co pong homoli nang butanding," I giggled.

Papa shook his head.

"There is much more to being a Navigator than catching sky whales, my child."

He pointed out the window, across the cityscape, to the sky lanes filled with all manner of pedestrian craft. They flew in strict formation above the city, guided by their conductors.

A flock of carefree pigeons swooped and dashed about around them.

"Everything," he said, "has a price. One day you will learn what that means."

I giggled at the sight of the birds flitting about.

My father sighed and patted me on the head.

"Pero tiñgnan natin," he said. "We shall see."

~*~

Long ago, even before Intramuros existed, the inhabitants of Maynilad discovered the peculiar properties of gravidium ore—how it responded to sound, how vibrations of certain frequencies enabled it to Levitate and move about in the air. It was, then as now, thought to be a sacred link to the Almighty. Hence it was called bathalani, "God's Lodestone."

—Antonio de Morga, "History of the Philippine Islands," 1868

~*~

On the eve of my seventh birthday, my father presented me with a small, carved wooden box, no bigger than my two cupped hands. He undid a small brass fastener and produced what seemed to me a simple sliver of carved bamboo and a blue-gray crystal mounted on a silver chain.

"These are the most basic tools of Levitation. Anyone who wishes to be a Navigator must first learn to be proficient in their use," Papa said.

The kubing felt light in my hand, almost fragile. My father showed me how to place it to my mouth, to tap on its lamella to produce a single drone note.

"The hard part," he said, "is feeling the stone.

"No two are exactly alike, and you must learn to shape your notes properly to make it resonate.

"Go ahead," he said. "Try it."

I placed the kubing to my lips as he had shown me, and flicked it against my open mouth.

Twangtwangtwangtwangtwangtwangtwang...

The bathalani pendant sat quietly in its case, unmoving.

"Do not be afraid. Now arch your lips slightly, yes, and curve your tongue down. Yes, right. Like that."

Twoomtwoomtwoomtwoomtwoomtwoomtwoom...

I thought I saw the ore tremble ever so slightly.

"Expand your mouth more. Lower your tone."

Bwoombwoombwoombwoombwoombwoom...

The stone began to shudder.

"Good. Now feel the vibration build up inside you. Ride it, lend it your strength."

BWOOomBWOOomBWOOomBWOOomBWOOomBWOOom...

"Yes. Excellent. Dame mas!"

BWOOOMBWOOOMBWOOOMBWOOOMBWOOOM BWOOOMBWOOOM...

The stone danced, as on the edge of an invisible wave on an unseen shore.

"Watch its movement closely. Find its resonating point."

What happened next was one of the most exhilarating experiences of my life: the pendant raised itself magically up into the air, Levitating as if on a chain.

"Muy bien! You've done it, hija!"

Distracted, I lost control over the stone. It fell with a loud clatter onto the floor.

"That was good," my father said as he bent over to pick up the pendant.

"But you will need a lot more practice."

~*~

The kubing, or jaw harp, is an ancient musical instrument used in times of love and war, to woo and to slight, to court and to spurn. It is a simple yet elegant instrument whose sonorous qualities aptly lend themselves to the control of gravidium. Not surprisingly, it is the earliest known instrument that the ancients used for flight.

Similar instruments have been documented in other parts of Asia, suggesting that its invention may even predate the discovery and widespread use of bathalani for Levitation.

Despite the eventual development of the sturdier and more accurate Stroh viol and other instruments specifically for the purpose of Levitation, such is the simplicity and straightforward nature of the kubing that popular interest in the instrument has not waned in the intervening centuries.

—Dr. Jose Maceda, "Gongs & Bamboo: A Panorama of Philippine Musical Instruments," 1998

~*~

When I was old enough, my father gave me his heirloom Amati viol, an immaculate instrument with a lustrous dark brown varnish on fully aged wood. Its voice was like gold and it played like mercury, with rich deep registers that smoothly gave way to crystal treble tones.

It was perfect.

And so began my initial instruction in the finer points of Levitation.

I was taught how to strap the instrument to my shoulder, to accustom myself to the feel of it under my chin. Then came the finer intimacies of the fingerboard and the rigors of bow control.

Days turned into weeks into months. Solfegges followed scales followed arpeggios, and all over again. I learned to play etudes and caprices, practicing every day for hours on end with a set of bathalani geodes.

Papa would have me Levitate the stones in formation again and again.

My fingers ached all the time from the relentless drills.

"Mas rapido!" he would shout. "You're going too slow!"

One time, my fingers hurt so much that I cried.

"How can you expect to fly if you cannot even manage your own fingers?" Papa scolded me.

But he bent down and took my tiny hands in his and rubbed my palms.

He wiped a tear from my cheek.

"Start over," he ordered, and left me alone to practice.

~*~

During the latter half of the eighteenth century there culminated the long struggle for colonial empire between European states which we have been following. In the zealous movement for defense in support of the Spanish Crown that ensued, there rose to power the Cofradia de los Hermanos Alados, which bore as its motto the personal vow of its Navigators: "Totus tuus, Musica: Alis volas propria" —I am yours, O Music: You fly on your own wings.

—David P. Barrows, PhD, "A History of the Philippines," 1905

~*~

When I was deemed ready, I was taught to Levitate a cargo skiff. It was of a very humble make, with a low and somewhat flattened hull, meant as a light cargo pallet for shipping bulk items from one level of the city to another. A series of copper sound tubes extended out from the pilot's seat to the sides, where rows of gravidium pellets were bound tightly to the wooden frame with strong hemp rope.

As I watched, Papa placed his own viol under his chin and turned to face the skiff's sound cone.

"Watch closely," he said, and proceeded to play at a legato tempo. Slower than usual, so I could keep up.

He played a standard ascension arpeggio—a series of harmonic notes meant to Levitate a ship in a smooth, sloping upward trajectory.

The skiff's system of tubes carried the music to the crystals, which trembled and glowed at the sound.

The skiff rose up and away, just as intended. When he had reached roof height, he reversed the succession of notes, bringing the pallet gently back down.

"Now, you try it."

I took my place at the front of the skiff and strapped my feet into the pilot's harnesses. Papa stood just behind me on the cargo pallet, holding onto the side rails, closely watching my every move.

I made sure that my viol was strapped in and firmly wedged under my chin.

I pressed my fingers tentatively onto the fingerboard, trying my best to produce a steady liftoff scale.

"You're doing well, Aria. Just remember what I taught you. Steady notes, steady notes," Papa whispered into my ear.

It is always a scary feeling when you draw your bow across the strings and see yourself rising up into the air for the first time.

It is even scarier when you realize that the only thing keeping you from falling is the sound of your instrument.

My hands started to shake.

The craft listed suddenly to one side, almost throwing us off balance. I fought the urge to look back to see if Papa was alright.

"Careful! Be confident of your skills. Do not hesitate," he commanded me firmly.

I took a deep breath and played on, as calmly as I could, one note at a time.

The craft righted itself and floated steadily higher.

Through it all, I kept my gaze fixed forward. I had always been afraid of heights.

"No, no! You have to look down, Aria! Fight your fear. You need to know your craft's altitude so you can make adjustments."

He was right, of course. But I felt dizzy looking down at the floor.

"Don't worry, that's right. That's good. Now move forward."

I adjusted my stance and bowing as I had been taught.

I took a deep breath and steadied my hands. Thankfully, the skiff obeyed my notes.

At last, my father placed his hand gently on my shoulder, signaling me to descend.

The skiff touched the ground with a soft thud.

Papa helped me out of the harness.

"To fly," he said, "You must learn to surrender yourself to the music."

He touched a finger to my forehead.

"Trust the music. As long as you hear it in your head, you'll be fine."

~*~

It should come as no surprise that, despite their colonial trappings, the numerous lay aviation movements—of which the Cofradia was the most notable and widespread—were firmly rooted in the native spirituality of the peasants to whom the awe-inspiring butanding were but a commonplace miracle since before Hispanic times.

Fundamental to this spirituality was the concept of sacrifice, a virtue that the friars themselves fostered and propagated in ostensible emulation of Christ.

—*Reynaldo Ileto, "Pasyon and Revolution," 1979*

~*~

I was sixteen when I finally earned my wings.

"There is nothing more I can teach you," Papa said. "All that is left is for you to undergo your biñag, the rite of passage that we all must undertake before initiation into the Cofradia.

"But you need to be ready."

He sat down beside me and held my hand.

"There is a reason, you see, why so few are accepted into our ranks. Understand that, if I guide you on this path, you may not like what you discover. And there is no turning back, for both of us. Are you prepared for that?"

I did not hesitate. I nodded my assent.

"Very well, then. Tomorrow we travel to Mount Taal."

~*~

Little is known about the Philippine "sky whales" (Clarias volantis) or butanding, as they are called in the common tongue, other than that they are unique among the fauna of the world as they are the only animal yet discovered to have successfully made the developmental leap from an aquatic to an almost purely airborne lifecycle.

We also know that the creatures owe this singular existence to their heavy consumption of gravidium, which they scrape off the mountainside as a rodent would nibble on tree bark.

It is no wonder then that the butanding's habitat is severely limited almost exclusively to the island of Luzon, where the only known stores of naturally-occurring gravidium were a closely guarded secret of the Spanish government.

—*John Foreman, FRGS, "The Philippine Islands," 1905*

~*~

I had never been so far away from home before.

It was a pleasure watching the green countryside pass below us as the coach made its way through the rural arrabales of Cavite.

The conductor was very pleasant, a thin man with a well-groomed moustache, dressed in a formal barong.

"I wish I could take you farther, but you know that the civil government is very strict here," he said as we alighted.

"Don't worry, capatid, I know," Papa said, offering a tip to the gentleman.

"There's no need for that," the conductor said, smiling as he doffed his hat.

"Mag-yngat po cila," he told Papa.

"Yes, we'll take care. Maraming salamat," my father replied, shaking his hand.

He nodded to us again just as the porter dropped off our things.

With this, the conductor turned to the coach's attendant ensemble, raised his baton, and signaled for takeoff.

We watched as the vehicle rose up and away, leaving us alone by the roadside.

Papa's rank in the Cofradia meant that we had little trouble with the guardia civil on duty at the government checkpoint. The soldiers snapped to attention, saluting him as we passed.

Packs in hand, we made our way up to Tagaytay. It was a long trek uphill, with tall forest growth. Houses were few and far between.

Every so often, we would come across abandoned bathalani mines. And indeed, in these parts, gravidium ore was so plentiful that you could sometimes pick up shards off the ground.

But it was only when we reached Tagaytay Ridge that I understood why.

I had heard stories about it before, but seeing it for myself for the first time left me dumbfounded.

There, in the distance, was the majestic Mount Taal. It floated serenely in the distance like a mirage, an imposing island in the sky.

Rivers flowed from its peak down meandering streams to waterfalls that fed the wide lake below. All manner of birds flitted about the thick forests along its slopes.

There were plenty of sky whales there, too, flying about the island singing in a ceaseless cacophony.

And with each flutter and flurry, the entire underside of the immense mountain glowed a faint blue.

So the stories were true: Taal was the world's largest single known deposit of gravidium ore.

~*~

Since its discovery in ancient times, gravidium has found a wide range of uses apart from Levitation, particularly in the battlefield. Without a doubt, gravidium has proven to be an expensive but certainly durable long-term alternative to gunpowder and other projectile propulsion systems.

One need look no further than the fabled armaments of Panday
Pira, for example, whose brass lantakas featured gravidium-infused
breeches that proved to be cleaner and easier to load than their
European counterparts.

So effective was the design that it is still in use today as the weapon
of choice on Spanish naval decks.

—Austin Craig (ed.), "The Former Philippines Thru Foreign Eyes,"
1916

~*~

Ba-whoooooooooooooooommmmm!

From the north came a butanding herd. A handful of white-bellied
females and their calves, closely guarded by two or three black-striped
young males, flying in a tight formation that wended its way across
the sky towards Taal.

Ahead of the group was a large gray and white bull, its ivory sound
horn shining brightly as it caught the sun's rays. It was a large one,
certainly no less than a quarter of a legua in length.

The bull arched its back slowly, majestically, effortlessly gliding
through the air despite its massive size.

Such a full herd was a rare sight on the plains away from their
breeding grounds on the slopes of Mount Taal.

They were going to make a pass over the ridge, and we would have to
hitch a ride with them if we wanted to make it to the mountain at all.

I fastened our harnesses to one of my arrows and aimed squarely at
the belly of one of the trailing calves.

I pursed my lips and hummed.

It flew true, lodging firmly into the whale's thick hide, just at the
base of its right fin.

This did little harm to the creature, which seemed only mildly
surprised at the tiny creatures trailing down its side.

For a moment, it seemed to want to brush us off as a carabao might
shrug off errant flies. But it just turned its eye to us, shrugged, and
went on its way.

We clambered up the rope and onto the whale's fin. From there, it
was a steep climb to its broad back.

I reached down and patted the gentle creature, thanking it for
allowing us to join it on its flight.

Its skin felt warm and moist in the midday sun. I could feel its heartbeat under my hand.

The ground moved fast and far beneath us. In the distance floated great Taal, lush with life and forests, and rivers that streamed down its sides in great gushing waterfalls.

Our ride slowed as it approached its home, banking gently as it circled the mountain.

Papa turned to me. A wistful look came over him.

He pursed his lips and whistled an unfamiliar tune.

"That was a song my mother used to sing to me. It was the song I kept in my head during my own biñag."

"It's beautiful."

He smiled sadly.

"It's time for your biñag."

Balancing himself upright, he drew a long knife from his pack and placed it in my hands.

He indicated a point on the sky whale's hide.

"This is the base of its main nerve system. Any blow to this spot will render it mostly paralyzed, stopping its higher functions. The rest is easy: basic instincts will kick in, gliding it in to land.

"You see, anyone can learn an instrument and pilot a ship," he said. "But a Navigator's skill commands only the most sensitive and precise of musical instruments. So it demands no less than the finest bathalani, purified and concentrated deep in the body of a butanding.

"This is the Cofradia's greatest secret, one I am sworn to keep at all costs, should you fail."

Papa moved up behind me. I saw the shadow of his blade, raised high above my head.

"I'm sorry, my love. It is a price I hope I do not have to pay."

My heart raced in my chest.

Papa leaned in and whispered in my ear.

"Remember all that I taught you," he said. "Trust the music. Find your own song, and keep it in your head. Listen to it. Let it guide you."

I closed my eyes and tried to remember the sounds of home, of the life I cherished within the Wall.

I thought back to the little girl high up on the balcony that fateful day so very long ago. The chanting in the streets, the music in the skies. The plaintive cries of a lost sky whale. The laughter of a child dreaming of flight.

Papa was right: there is no turning back.

I tensed myself in preparation for the inevitable.

The blade came down, singing as it fell.

Chasing Volcanoes

Marilag Angway

The cracks grew wider beneath the ground, dispelling red, boiling liquid out in rage-like spurts. At any moment, the lava would spew into a violent eruption, and not even the magma suits would be able to protect the crew if they didn't act quickly.

Caliso barked orders as loud as she could, though this was done on reflex, not so much to tell her crew what to do. Volcano chasing was in their blood, and her crew members had remained with Caliso for so long that they could easily extract the earth's energy with their eyes closed and their hands guided by constant practice.

It would have been the third time in eight years that Bulkang Mayon erupted, covering the nearby areas with ash for weeks on end, the surrounding perimeter a gray and dismal bleakness. Yet even with nothing nearby, people flocked towards Mayon, some obsessed with studying it, others perceiving their journey as a pilgrimage to their raging God. Caliso had even spotted settlers at Legazpi, just south of the mountain itself, their village doomed from the moment the eruption clouds and earthquakes pervaded through the area.

The mountain itself was a symbol of natural perfection, a cone of aesthetic symmetry that pierced the sky in the middle of Luzon. It was a special volcano, a constant and volatile presence in the northern wastes of the Philippines.

To the crew of the Amihan, however, Bulkang Mayon's grandeur was nothing to be impressed about. It was like any other active volcano; it emitted a great deal of volcanic gas.

A hot rock whizzed past Caliso's helmet, her head just missing the grueling impact of volcanic debris smashing onto her clear and bendable malambaso visor. She ducked when another one followed, refusing to think how close she had gotten to a smashed and burnt face. Her gloved hands remained planted upon the rungs of a retractable metallic tube, its end fashioned into a syringe, all the better to suck out the gas from the softening earth. She hurried, knowing that at any minute, the gases would escape, and the floor below would be nothing but bursting magma and melting crew members.

"Casim's down!" the man beside her shouted. Caliso grunted to acknowledge her first mate's statement. Dato *would* be the one to worry. She, on the other hand, did not worry about Casim. Worry only led to distraction, and she needed her focus then and there.

"Hold her steady," she replied. Again, the ground rumbled, more rocks spewing from the pressure below. She heard two more screams behind her, but again she pushed her worries away. She believed in her crew.

The syringe made impact, and Caliso pushed. She felt the pressure almost as though the siphon had been a part of her body. She heard the suction and felt the slow vibrations of gas traveling along the tube that reached toward her ship. Below her, the unstable ground lost its violent nature, the angry welts of lava around her cooled and receded. What once had been energy seeking for escape had been lost, and Bulkang Mayon went from a burgeoning Strombolian tantrum to a half-hearted protest against a rock ceiling.

The flare went up above her. A second one followed, alerting her that they had company. Dato had seen it, too, and together, Caliso and her first mate spun the valves on the side of the tube, allowing some of the gas to dispel into the air, like rising steam in a hot bath. Caliso released her hold on the rungs, removed the steel bolts between the needle and the tube. She gave the hand signal to her crew, and they pulled.

"Come on, come on," Caliso murmured, her eyes following the tube's journey away from the needle and up toward the ship. Beside her, Dato motioned for two others to bring the siphon needle back with them.

When it was clear that the tube had made it safely toward the Amihan, Caliso let out a sigh of relief. The most difficult part had been over. Now it was just a matter of heading back, checking her losses, and hightailing it out of the volcano.

She climbed aboard her ship.

The floor that the volcano chasers had stood on below was swallowed up by the slow yet constant spew of magma. It was as though the rock had waited to retaliate only after Caliso and her team had evacuated the premises. Yet what was slow-moving magma to a crew with an airship? Bulkang Mayon would not explode with a degree of violence, but it was clear to the captain of the Amihan that her team had not siphoned nearly enough energy to render the volcano completely harmless.

Caliso removed her helmet and visor, which had become suffocating high above the volcano's mouth, her eyes immediately watering from the sulfur and other hot, volcanic fumes in the air. She murmured a word of thanks when Dato handed her a pair of brass goggles, strapping them over her eyes and pulling the nose filter down so as to dispel the fumes. When she was able to breathe, she nodded quickly at her navigator, who had approached her with a strange woman in tow. Caliso frowned.

"We're not at full capacity," Caliso said before the navigator could speak. "How are the injured, Gogg?"

"Casim's fine," the navigator said, "slight concussion, but he'll recover. We lost the Twins. They'd both miscalculated the crust's durability and stepped on ground that gave way to magma. Sorry, Cali, Atia and Ashi are dead."

She grimaced. Caliso had not lost more than five people within a given year, and for the most part, the loss had usually not led to fatalities. Two deaths in one volcano meant that her crew had become complacent, careless. They thought Bulkang Mayon was going to be an easy siphon. Clearly that assumption had proven deadly. "Dato, send what's left of their bodies back so their families can perform the proper funeral rites. Atia and Ashi have living parents. Make sure they get three times the funds that the Twins would have received in this mission, plus two energy canisters."

Dato cleared his throat. "Cali, for them, that's only two years' worth of energy. The Twins deserve more than that."

"It's all we can spare and the Twins would have known this," Caliso said. She held her first mate's glance and dared him to protest. When he didn't, she shrugged. "Two years is more than enough. Atia and Ashi knew the risks in this position. Neither they, nor you, took to this path lightly. Dismissed, Dato."

The man nodded grimly, saluted, and left Caliso's side.

Gogg cleared his throat.

Caliso had ignored the visitor at first, but once Dato had gone, she examined her. Gogg and the woman made a strange pair standing next to each other, her navigator bulky and as dark-skinned as a dried coconut, while the woman was thinner, taller, and paler than a regular sun-kissed Pinay. The woman's black hair was tied neatly back in a side tail that reached past her covered shoulder. She wore a baro't saya, the blouse made of white silk, the skirt wrap a long and intricate pattern of brown and silver. While Caliso and the crew of the Amihan sported scars and several burn marks upon their skins as byproducts of their tangles with volcanoes, the woman's skin was unblemished, clean. She belonged in a different world. She did not belong on that airship.

"What's a Cebuano doing here?" Caliso snapped. She harbored no hate for them, but Cebuanos tended to bring about trouble. Especially when more than likely, the government wouldn't be far behind. Volcano chasing was illegal in the south, and meeting up with a sheltered Cebu City woman might bring with it a fleet of soldiers waiting to confiscate what energy they'd siphoned. Hypocrites, the lot of them, Caliso thought.

"Not a Cebuano," the woman responded, amused by the assumption. Her voice was husky, deep, and her unwavering stare—though shielded by goggles—made Caliso shift with unease. "I came from Refugee Hills."

"You're as good as Cebuano then." Refugee Hills was part of the southern districts, three hours' travel from the nation's new capital. "Why are you so far north?"

"She comes for help, Cali," Gogg said. Caliso raised an eyebrow and shot a curious glance at her navigator. He rubbed his chin, a sign that he was nervous. Something told her that she wouldn't like what he was going to suggest. "We passed a nearby village—"

"Not our problem," Caliso interrupted, already guessing the rest of the request. She brushed past the navigator and the woman, heading toward her cabin. "Get rid of her."

"Please, I came all this way with the only floater the village had. They have no energy, no means of transport out. Wait!"

Caliso didn't. In fact, she would have slammed the door in her wake, had the woman not run after her, her smooth hands halting the door's movements. Caliso glared. "I'm no philanthropist, lady. Bulkang Mayon is a known active volcano. Why these settlers choose to continue to make homes in dangerous places is beyond mere stupidity. I don't do rescues."

The woman shook her head. "It's not—"

"Oh?" Caliso released the pressure on the door, and the woman almost stumbled in as a result. "Then prove me wrong. Tell me you're not on my ship to barter a village's passage from here to Refugee Hills."

"Well, I am, but..." When the captain made for the door again, the woman bit her lip, removed the goggles from her eyes, and said clearly, "But I can pay you. *Really* pay you. I can pay you whatever you want."

That got Caliso's interest. "Go on," she said, "I'm listening."

"Mixa," the woman said. "My name is Mixa."

A part of Caliso recognized the name. She paused and stared again, wracking her brain for the reason for its familiarity. Maybe she had encountered a person named Mixa before, some other volcano chaser or monger she'd dealt with in the past. Or maybe someone from a northern village she had recently visited.

What clued her in was not a memory of an encounter, however. Caliso scanned the woman's earnest face, her hard eyes, her smooth skin, and spied a tattoo engraved just at the base of her neck, half-covered by the white silk blouse. The blouse which, Caliso realized, was made of pricy silk from the western continent. The captain of the Amihan tapped on her own neck. "Let me see that."

The woman, Mixa, complied, pulling the fold of her blouse to fully show the tattoo, an outline of a two-horned bull mid-charge. A carabao. Caliso stiffened. She knew why she recognized the name, knew why Mixa appeared pampered and protected, almost hidden from the world. The tattoo of the nation's bull had been the very symbol that marked her as northern royalty, the last and only daughter of the New Manila monarch. Cebu City would pay tremendously for her person, and double that just for the whereabouts of the rest of the royal family.

Heck, Caliso might even be talking about getting *pardons* for the entire crew of the Amihan if she handed the woman over.

"You should have said so before." Caliso let her surprise give way to a smirk. "What can I do for you, Prinsesa?"

~*~

Mixa was not very forthcoming with the details of the evacuation. Once she had pointed out the location of Legazpi and agreed upon a price—an exorbitant amount by northern and southern standards—she had allowed Caliso's inner circle to plan the logistics of the matter. While she remained part of the officers' discussions, the New Manila princess had kept silent, choosing instead to stare out one of the meeting room windows, down toward the land masses broken apart by rivers and lakes and mountainous ranges.

Caliso did not blame the princess for being so drawn to the windows. Barring the view above the Amihan's open metal deck—which required the use of protective eye and nose-wear when traveling in the north—the meeting room provided the best view, with its full-length malambaso windows that protruded outward, allowing the viewer the choice of looking down and seeing more of the ground below. It was not something for people who had a problem with heights, or are uncomfortable with seeing nothing but glass beneath their feet, but if you were on the Amihan, you were accustomed to the sky—or you learned to get acquainted with it very quickly.

If the Amihan had been a battleship, Caliso would have covered the windows in metal panels and allowed enough space to prop cannons up on the sides. But she did not have to take such precautions. If the military ever came calling, her ship would easily outstrip a standard regulation battleship. The engines below were, after all, powered by volcanic energy.

"Don't see the point staring for so long," Caliso said, addressing Mixa. Her officers continued their conversation, though some of them turned their heads toward the woman passenger. Mixa gave no indication that she heard. "There's not much to see below."

Nothing but barren land and scorched earth. Nothing but cracked floor covered with hardened lava and ash and tephra. The rivers had become poisonous to its inhabitants, and if there was freshwater to be found in the lakes, it would have dried up by now. Even the skies seemed to add to the bleakness, for the sun was often obscured with clouds that rained acid and fog that seemed almost impossible to pierce unless one used a specific type of goggles. Northern Pinas had remained this way for twenty years, so ravaged by the continuous eruptions of its local volcanoes. Pinatubo. Taal. Mayon. The major figures that caused The Great Explosions of 1816, which led to the nation's Years of Ash Winter. Unlike the cold white snows of Wakoku and Zhongguo to the north, Pinas' snows were made out of broken rocks and ash, gray and dark and oppressive.

Ash and tephra brought no respite to the survivors, no matter how many times they returned to their homes in order to cultivate what could potentially be fertile volcanic soil. The constant volcanic flows never seemed to stop, and land covered in ash gave no economic value to New Manila, whose monarchic government opposed the powerful and affluent Cebu City.

Caliso knew Mixa would not be able to pay her for the evacuation. If the rumors were true—and her sources were highly reliable—the New Manila monarchy lived among the northern survival clans. Their king and heir apparent had been hidden away in some remote region, perhaps in Masbate, perhaps in the tephra ruins of Old Manila itself, but their whereabouts always changed, for it was said they traveled constantly, moving from one location to another. No matter the case, the fugitive royal family lived on the meager auspices of their loyal subjects, those who still believed in preserving the monarchic line by any means. There was no traditional money coming in, not for Mixa, not for her father.

"This is bigger than us, Cali," Dato warned her after everyone—including Mixa—filed out of the room. "You spent all these years building up a crew made up of northerners. What do you think most of them will say when you personally hand the Cebuanos their monarch's daughter?"

"I am not simply *handing* anyone over," Caliso said. "I'm willing to barter her for the right price. In fact, they should thank me. The money and pardon we could potentially get should set us up for life. We can choose which volcanoes to pursue, and we won't lose any crew doing so, carelessness and stupidity notwithstanding."

"It's not about the money." Dato propped his elbows on the table, rested his forehead over his palms. "Some of us still remember the Islands before the Explosions. Likely some of us want to see things returned in that way. For that to happen, the royal line *must* be preserved. And when the Cebuanos get a hold of the Prinsesa..."

Caliso shrugged. She had remained apathetic to the politics of the north and south, had always done so even under disapproving looks from her immediate family. To her father, mother, brothers, and iron-willed, traditional-minded grandfather, Caliso was too much of a disappointment, for she never spoke out against unfair village laws, nor did she seek to change anyone's welfare but hers. She was deemed self-serving, indifferent, entitled.

Politics was overrated, and so was her entire family. She had been only too glad to escape their expectations, and when she was old enough, she had stowed away upon a nearby airship, promising never to turn back, and never to take a side between the two clashing capitals. "If she's as valuable as you say, they'll hold her for ransom. And if she's of any value to the deposed king, then he will pay whatever price is necessary."

"You and I know the king would not be able to afford any price the Cebuanos set," Dato retorted. He glared at his captain. "More than likely the Cebuanos will parade her around as an example, and then kill her. I do not want this blood on our hands, Cali."

"Blood spilled won't be on our hands. The lawmakers of Cebu City are more than capable of taking that responsibility if they do away with her," Caliso said. She turned away and approached the windows. "You are following my orders and nothing more. If you're so queasy about this, I can drop you off at Refugee Hills with the rest of the evacuees. If I'm in a good mood, maybe I'll stop by the Hills and let you back on."

A long pause. Dato sighed. "I am of better use up here."

The captain glanced at her first mate.

He smiled grimly. "At least I'll make you feel guilty all the way to Cebu City. Perhaps I can even change your mind."

Caliso laughed. "You'd find it easier to move a mountain, but you can try."

~*~

Three hundred and thirty-two Legazpi settlers walked upon the retractable brass gangplank that rose in angle from the ground to the Amihan. With them came a few wagons of fruits, vegetables, and rice sacks, pulled along by carabao large enough to fit the width of the plank without tipping over. The same two carabao made return trips to bring more wagons, some that carried clothing, bamboo-woven baskets and hats, as well as woodwork and—more uncommonly—brasswork. Still others harbored the rest of the villagers, sixty-four of the newly-born and the nursing mothers, the sick, the pregnant, and the injured.

Caliso was determined to inspect every single entry, frowning all the while at the large number of occupants that would have to be cared for during the journey ahead. Her ship had retained a capacity large enough to house close to five hundred strong, but it was never meant to do so for actual people. The capacity had been created in order to make room for cargo and precious equipment. There had been an entire room of energy canisters, placed carefully inside boxes, which, after inspection, were stapled shut and wedged tightly in compartments so as not to run the risk of leakage and accidental explosions. This necessary precaution was what kept the ship intact for years. Caliso suspected that it was this lack of precaution that had ended the Legazpi settlers' ship Maganda, a mistake that brought them groveling to the closest airship captain mad enough to head north during an active eruption.

"You are sure all our equipment has been moved out of the way?"

Gogg stood beside her behind the bulwark overlooking the plank, his eyes raking in the passing villagers and wagons, his hand busy writing the inventory on a clipboard. "Packed away where not even the children can touch them."

"Which means we'll be unprepared should another volcano explode nearby," Caliso said. She watched disapprovingly as two children ran up the plank, halting the carabao's advance. "Back to your places!" she bellowed, while the children's mother murmured apologies as she grabbed the boys by their arms and dragged them back behind the carabao.

"We just won't stop until we get to Refugee Hills then," Gogg said, his smile more sardonic than optimistic. "Two days' trip at this rate."

Caliso stared. "*Two days?*"

"In theory, we could make it to Refugee Hills in less than a day." Gogg's fingers moved swiftly in the air, tracing numbers that he calculated mentally in his mind. "But that's with your fifty strong and a full supply of volcanic energy. The added weight of—ah—the passengers and their goods are going to slow us down, and we would have to go around Masbate in order to side-step the volcanoes running underneath."

She sighed. "Long trip, then."

Gogg seemed unperturbed by this. He quickly examined the next wagon—banana-leaf baskets filled with reddish-green mango and purple mangosteens—and waved them in, scribbling on the paper. "One thing's for sure. These settlers have the right idea, coming up north to work the soil. We'll be dining on the best fruits and vegetables the Pinas has to offer."

"Careful that it doesn't spoil you rotten," Caliso said, though the thought of eating ripe mango and rice was enough to lighten her mood.

~*~

It had taken a shorter time to settle the new passengers than it did to bring them into the ship. Caliso had the New Manila princess to thank for the efficiency; Mixa had joined her flock just before departure, had spoken to them about their trip to Refugee Hills and the safety that could be had upon arrival there. Her voice and words and eyes brought levity to the men and women, and they had remained anxious but overall obedient to the instructions that the ship's officers gave once the Amihan took flight.

Avoiding Masbate, however, was no longer on the agenda. The Amihan was a relatively-sized ship, a fast one run by a skeleton crew of fifty men and women. The Legazpi engineers added to the bulk of workers helping keep the ship efficient. And yet...

"We're losing air," Gogg said, his voice trembling in a mixture of frustration and worry. "There was so much to do, we forgot to refuel at Mayon. If we don't replace the canisters now, we'll not make it to the Hills. But if we land below, we risk the tremors and the volcanoes and—"

Caliso cursed. "How long do we have?"

"An hour, maybe less. It's just enough to hit the northern tip." The look he gave her was wide-eyed and full of fright. "The engineers are picking up disturbance in the waters, Cali. Do we risk the landing?"

"Yes." Many things that could go wrong usually did when risking landing near active volcanoes. But it was an even greater risk flailing in the sky with no fuel. Captains did not have room for doubt, and she would have to stick with her decision.

The Amihan descended onto the coast of Aroroy, Masbate's northernmost region, just upon a rocky outcropping near the sulfur-infested Burias Pass. Further out west, the waters mixed with the Sibuyan Sea, which contained blooms of poisonous jellyfish that had begun thriving once villagers no longer fished in the area. It would have been another beautiful place for people to soak in the sights, to jump from the high crags onto deep, pristine waters in order to cool off from the ever-present heat. But upon that point there was only a ship, its crew, two carabao, and three hundred-something passengers.

Caliso walked out onto the open bridge, peering down at the seemingly peaceful waters below. Dato had also stepped out, his goggles masking his expression just as Caliso's did hers. But when she looked at him, she knew her first mate's thoughts, knew that his forehead had crinkled in the way they would when he was worried. She turned her eyes back upon the water and waited. "There," she said, pointing toward bubbling waters almost obscured by a rocky arch. "Looks ready to burst any minute."

Dato whistled. "Want to get a crew down there to siphon?"

"Two crews. Either that or risk the entire rock area from exploding before any of our engineers can fuel the four corners. Gogg said the cracks ran underneath. Likely we've got a system of cracks below flowing with enough gas to blow this whole portion of the coast."

Her first mate shook his head. "Worse than Mayon?"

She cringed. "Much worse." She pushed herself away from the bridge's bulwark. "Better get to work."

Caliso paused at the entrance to the female changing rooms. One of Caliso's crew, Esta, had volunteered her extra magma suit, rubber boots, and a pair of thick, rubber gloves to Mixa, who had donned it in favor over her baro't saya. She'd swept her hair to the back and her tattoo was completely visible from the scoop neckline of a tucked-in yellow shirt. Caliso placed the royal woman's age to almost fifteen years her junior, not yet the proper debut age. Too young to be handling volcanized gas. Even the magma suit seemed to dwarf her.

"The Prinsesa insisted," a mechanical box said. The metallic nature of Esta's vozbox had lacked the tone of amusement, but Esta's face had told Caliso all she needed to know. "I informed her that volcano chasing was not for weak constitutions, but she's said she's done it before."

"Oh?" Caliso crossed her arms over her chest. "And what crew did you belong to that would give you such experience?"

"My father believes that understanding the power of volcanoes would lead us to a better way of life." Mixa had put the helmet over her face, and her voice crackled not unlike Esta's vozbox. "The way of the mountains, he called it. He placed me under the tutelage of my eldest brother Raksan."

Caliso resisted the urge to look impressed. Instead, she narrowed her eyes. "The captain of the Kalibutan?"

Mixa's helmet bobbed, indicating a nod. *Of all the luck*, Caliso thought. The Kalibutan had been one of the few ships that had never been caught by the Cebuanos after volcano chasing had been decreed illegal. It was also the only thing the New Manila monarchy possessed that could very well buy them a city. But even kings and princes have their pride and dignity, and the Kalibutan forever remained off the market and in the hands of the royal family.

Caliso shrugged. "Now is not truly the time to test your mettle." When it seemed as though Mixa was about to argue, the Amihan's captain raised her hand. "But we are three members down and I need people who *know* what they're doing to come with me. Esta, you, too. Dato has to oversee the refueling."

Esta nodded. She was a horse-like middle-aged woman decked in coveralls that seemed too big for her. Esta was mute and used the assistance of a vozbox in order to speak to anyone. Even so, she hardly utilized the mechanism, choosing instead to communicate with her long hands and fingers. Since Mixa did not know the hand-language, however, Esta's vozbox remained strapped to the woman's side.

Esta pulled another magma suit out, Caliso following in her wake. The two dressed silently, Caliso grunting as she pulled her boots over the thin, but cushioned armor. She'd always detested wearing such protective clothing, especially on a siphoning. No suit would be strong enough to protect anyone from a volcanic explosion. Sure, it would slow the magma from burning flesh, but there was no stopping the gases and ash from suffocating them in the suit. Not to mention the force of the blast, which could very well crush them in seconds.

Still, at least Gogg's new designs had made the suits more limber. Caliso stood.

"I do not need to tell you how dangerous an active volcano can be," she said. "If there is a possibility that it will erupt on your feet, you get out of the way as quickly as you can. Understood?"

The instruction had been more for Mixa's benefit than Esta's, yet both women's helmets wobbled in assent. If the New Manila princess had been nervous, Caliso could not tell. "You can stay with me, Prinsesa, at least then I can keep my eye on your safety."

"Ah, yes." Something in Mixa's voice hinted at wry amusement. "Can't pay you if I'm dead, I suppose?"

"Exactly," Caliso said. The Cebuanos would want the woman alive, and Caliso was loathe to disappoint them.

~*~

The climb down toward the water seemed endlessly long, and for a siphoning, this made all the difference.

"At this rate," Caliso grunted, testing the rocks for a foothold, "we will likely be dead before the siphon can get to the gases."

The bubbling waters, the slight shaking and breaking of rocks, the absence of jellyfish and other sea creatures, the increasing heat as they neared the bottom—these were what determined how close they would be to seeing an underwater mountain gush with powerful gases.

When both her feet found stable rock below, she waved to Mixa. The New Manila princess hunched over onto the rock wall, scaling down and following Caliso's path. Esta and several other engineers—Legazpi passengers and volcano chasers—took their turn as well, some following Caliso and Mixa's course, the others taking Esta's backup route. The captain's climb became more wary and over-cautious after each level of descent, and every few paces, she'd paused to gauge the wall's rumblings. Twice, she and Mixa had stayed still long enough to feel the rocks vibrate and hiss with flowing steam. Caliso had turned her head to the side to prevent the gases from blurring her vision.

Halfway down the long climb, Caliso slipped.

One hand clung desperately to the rock above, while the other clutched onto the thick, rapidly-fraying wire that connected her to the ship. Her feet flailed, and she felt her sweating hands slip slowly out of her rubber gloves. Caliso closed her eyes and breathed heavily through her mouth, misting her helmet. She looked down and her heart-rate increased. It was not the fall that had made her seize up in panic; if she survived the slip, she'd be killed by the rocks.

Mixa was at her side before Caliso's panic could fully take over. The New Manila princess held onto her wire, her feet steady and still, her other arm snaking over Caliso's waist, pressing her magma suit towards the rock with surprising strength. Caliso half-flailed with one hand and found a handhold close to her head. With both hands now clinging to rocks, she raised her body somewhat and felt below for something to steady her dangling feet. When she found herself stable again, she took deep breaths, calming herself.

"Thanks," she whispered. Mixa had already moved back to her position.

She slowed her climb to a crawling pace. By the time she hit the ground, she saw Esta already anchored on the other side of the bubbling water, just beneath the entrance of a cavern. Esta signaled above for the siphon and tube. She nodded once to her captain, then began to communicate with gestures and signals to the line of men and women who'd followed her route.

"Why the two teams?" Mixa asked as she landed next to the Amihan's captain. The two removed their wires—Caliso discarded hers with more contempt than necessary—and walked further toward the water.

"In case one doesn't make it back," Caliso said.

"Oh."

"Familiar with siphoning from an underwater volcano?"

"Different from taking gases above ground," Mixa said, crouching to look at the water. There were several large *pop pop pop*s in the water bubbles, then long periods where it merely splashed upon the rocks. The New Manila princess stirred her rubber gloves in and pulled her hand out of the water quickly. "Hot." She looked up. "It's one thing to siphon gas out of cracks in the rocks, quite another to extract gas bubbles out of water. Kuya Raksan had a deal of trouble using the accepted method."

She felt the princess hesitate, and Caliso frowned. "But?"

"We started using a filter and conversion system recently." Caliso detected a tone of pride in Mixa's voice. "So our water siphon works the same way as the regular siphon, except our tube gets fitted with several semi-permeable filter chambers that—" She paused again, as though she'd spoken too much on the subject. "The point is there's no need for the extra tubing."

Caliso fought to hide her grudging respect for the young woman.

Politics had been easy to ignore, and the begging and pleading even easier. Caliso had expected a pampered, smooth-skinned girl with idealistic ideas and no clue as to their implementation. What she saw instead was someone with exceptional talents, a girl who'd survived in a nation of explosions using her mind and physicality. She almost belonged on the airship as a volcano chaser, and it made Caliso begin to think that the price Cebu City had on Mixa's capture was too damn low. The end of the trip would be unpleasant at the least, with a tasteless betrayal coming soon to the talented young princess.

She stiffened. Since when had she begun thinking of her impending action as a tasteless betrayal?

"A pity then that we still use the *accepted* method," Caliso said drily. She waved to the crew at the top of the cliff. "But Gogg is more than happy to implement new upgrades, should you choose to want to divulge any designs."

Her crew had secured themselves on parts of the wall, either planting their feet safely on jutting rock, or strapping their waists upon the wires that held them together. When the crew member at the top saw her hand signal, he waved back, and two more people came close to the cliffs, lowering the tube and the water siphon.

The tube snaked its way from the edge of the rock wall, led quickly down by the crew members pulling on the metal rungs attached to the sides. The top-most engineers used a harness to send down the siphon needle, which—unlike the one they'd used at Bulkang Mayon—was a system of two glass vials, one closed at an end, the other open. The vials were connected to each other by a small passage in the middle. At the ends were two tubes, both made out of clear malambaso, more malleable than the vials, and certainly more movable.

Caliso's footing wobbled at the vibrating ground, and she steadied herself with the use of her wire. Before the siphon touched the floor, she reached for the tubes and began to move it towards the water.

By then another series of *pop pop pops* began, culminating in a splash so high that the water made it to the landing where Mixa and Caliso stood. Caliso had gotten out of the way, but Mixa took the hit of water, and she yelped.

"You hurt?" Caliso said.

"I—no," Mixa admitted. "Slight surprise, that's all." She grabbed the end rung of the siphon tube and pulled it closer to Caliso. She crouched low, easing the open end of the tube onto the glass siphons, making sure only the open vial was connected to the retractable tubing.

Across from them, there was a cry as more water began to splash upon Esta's group. Someone stumbled from their position upon the rock wall, and it took over a minute for another to help the fallen regain his footing.

The ground rumbled beneath Caliso, so hard and fast that she almost toppled over into the water. Thankfully, she had been grasping at the tubes, which kept her in her place. Caliso let out a series of curses, then shoved one of the malambaso tubes into the water. She nodded at Mixa, who flipped a switch just to the side of the siphon tube.

That was when the underwater volcano exploded.

~*~

The force of the water sent Caliso flying toward the bottom of the rock wall. The tubes followed her, and it took all of Caliso's energy to maneuver herself so that she got in between the glass vials and the falling rocks. A chunk of the solid landing had been pushed out by the force of water and gas. Caliso saw the debris scatter up and down, a threatening precipitation of rock. She rolled over to cover the glass vials, and had done it just in time to get struck by the large rocks. She groaned in agony and knew she would be sore later.

Mixa was no longer clinging onto the tube rung. There was a scream and frantic splashing, alerting her exactly where Mixa had gone.

Caliso felt the aching in her arms as she dragged the tubing with her, noting that it continued to suck in air. She struggled for a moment, then pushed one malambaso tube back into the water. She found that one of her engineers leapt from his position to hold onto the rungs to keep the tubes from flying out again. With a brief thanks, Caliso let go of the tubes. She searched the water.

The ground had fallen away from Mixa, and Caliso found her struggling to remain afloat in her magma suit within boiling, turbulent waters. Another *pop pop pop*, and Mixa yelped again, pushed further away out toward the open waters.

Strange, Caliso thought. The magma suits had been a light design, easy enough for anyone to swim back onto the shore, even in heated temperatures. Caliso began yelling for Mixa to swim back, directing her to the rocks, but found something wrong with the way Mixa flailed. It took a few moments to realize why she found this strange, and why she began to stare at the horizon in horror.

The New Manila princess didn't know how to swim.

~*~

The waters buffeted Mixa further out into the sea, away from what continued to be an erupting volcano. The ground and arching rocks continued to shake, like carabao shedding the excess water from their skins. Besides Caliso, the siphon sucked in the water and gases, dispelling the water back onto the volcanic top whilst taking the gases up onto the airship.

Captains did not have room for doubt. Yet Caliso stood there, staring at the horizon, at the struggling form of the young monarch, at the open sea filled with creatures poisonous enough to kill with a single, solitary brush of their skins. She stood, unable to make the decision to save or abandon. Mixa would not survive once she reached deep waters. If she didn't sink by then, she'd be taken in by the jellyfish poison. Getting her back was a measure of risk no skeleton crew should have to take.

Caliso remembered her fall only minutes ago, and the saving hand that guided her back onto the rocks. She saw in her mind the image of a young woman and the way she soothed a crowd of worried passengers. She recalled the conversation that passed between them, the young woman's voice filling with passion and brilliance, of ideas that could very well change the way volcano chasers worked their equipment.

"She's worth that great risk," Dato would say, his reverence of the royal family clear.

And perhaps he is right, Caliso thought.

It was a thought that brought her to a decision, so final and absolute that she had to stop herself from shaking, both with fright and anger. Fright for her life, and anger for being careless once again. She should not have brought Mixa down with her.

She leapt into the water, her magma suit altering its temperature to neutralize the heat of the volcanized water. She kicked forward and swam, stroke for stroke, her helmet swiveling from side to side as she continued toward Mixa's course.

The underwater volcano eased her swim, yet it was still difficult to move. The magma suit would only last so long before the heat would sink in. Caliso did not have much time before the real temperatures would hit her, but she pushed that thought out of her mind, swimming further and further, toward the woman who was beginning to sink.

She reached the fatigued princess and grabbed her by the waist, pulling her torso up so that her helmet was no longer half-submerged in water. Caliso heard the hard breathing and the panicked whimpers beneath the helmet, felt most of the fight leave Mixa.

"Keep awake," Caliso ordered, pulling at the waist and swimming with her other hand. "And *kick* the water back, you fool! Don't make this any harder for me than it is." It had been a stroke of luck that the captain made it to where Mixa had been. The New Manila princess was wading on dangerous deep waters.

Mixa did as she was instructed, kicking the water in silence as Caliso continued to swim with one hand. Several times, Caliso heard the young woman let out a sob, then a prayer, and finally, a series of thanks for saving her life.

Caliso winced, arm tingling from her sidestroke. "We're not there just yet. Save your thanks for later."

She headed toward Esta's team. The older engineer must have seen her captain move toward the water, for she had one of the crew members waiting there, hand outstretched, the other holding fast upon a wire. Caliso swam toward him, her strokes slowing, her breathing becoming more difficult. Just a little more, she told herself, just a little...

And the hand reached her arm, pulling, pulling. Then several hands, and finally, both women were out of the water and lying on the ground. Mixa removed her helmet, stumbled back to the edge of the rocks and retched. Caliso remained where she lay, taking deep breaths.

Her vision blurred. When Esta's helmet hovered over her, she saw not one, but two Estas side by side. She blinked several times to dispel the dizziness, but instead it resulted in a third head. She tried to move, to say anything. Nothing.

Esta had said something to cause the crew to stir toward Caliso. Two men came quickly to the captain's side. They lifted her body, strapped her with several wires, dragged her toward the rock wall. With her hanging in the middle, both men made their climb.

She felt the pain in her arm, sharp and fast and hot. She also felt the draft, and knew that her magma suit had been punctured at some point. Yet she couldn't remember when it had happened, or where. She slipped into unconsciousness, but not before she realized the cause of her debilitation.

Poison.

~*~

The Amihan felt peaceful, so much so that Caliso had not realized she was awake until she remembered the events that transpired before.

She tried to sit up, but found that she was too weak to do so.

"What..."

She heard someone move beside her, felt the cool touch of a hand on her forehead. "Fever, but it will pass."

Dato.

"What..." she repeated again.

Her first mate helped her up to a sitting position, and she grimaced when he lifted a cup of warm ginger-water to her mouth. Once she finished drinking, he sat back down. He leaned forward, shaking his head. "Jellyfish. The stupid things got to your suit. You must have missed the holes on your magma suit from your last inspection."

"I...I don't think that—" And then she remembered. The slip and fall, the way her hands flailed, scraping upon rock in the hope of getting hold of something, anything... "I slipped. Must have...torn my sleeve struggling."

"Nasty slip, that," Dato said, rubbing his nose and leaning back. "Esta and the Prinsesa told me the whole story. You got lucky. Esta recognized the symptoms right away. She'd seen people succumb to jellyfish stings quickly, but you must have had little enough dose that we managed to stop the poison from spreading."

"How?" Caliso had had no poison expert on the ship. There had been no reason to keep one. Except now.

He shrugged. "The Prinsesa asked the passengers for aid. One of them happened to be an expert."

"In poison?"

"In jellyfish."

The two lapsed into silence. Dato shifted. "We're hovering above the Hills now. Gogg's seeing to the landing. You and Esta managed to siphon enough gases to stop the volcano from sinking the coast. Well, long enough for us to refuel, that is. Likely the rest of the land in that part will sink to give way to a rising volcano. But that doesn't seem to matter now. The Prinsesa wants a word with you."

She inclined her head. "Not to deliver thanks, I hope?"

"Perhaps that. Perhaps more." Dato stood. "I better check on the engines, just to be sure." He headed to the door, stopped mid-exit, turned around. "Cali?"

She nodded, urging him to speak.

"No risk is worth more than your life. Never do that again."

Caliso watched him go, surprised at his words. Of all her crew members, she had not expected Dato to be the one to tell her to leave Mixa in the water. She sighed onto her pillow, her eyes roving the captain's room in order to stay awake.

The New Manila princess entered soon after Dato left. She had changed back to her baro't saya, her hair re-braided into one side, neat and clean. She had looked almost like the young woman who had traipsed in near Bulkang Mayon to proffer a deal. Smooth-skinned and pale, unblemished by nature. Almost.

Mixa caught Caliso's gaze upon her marked face and arms, upon the tattoo of the carabao, which had been boiled out of existence. The princess forced a smile to her face. "Dato says you call them trophies." She placed a hand reflexively on a peeling patch of skin on her upper arm and winced. "Your medic could only do so much to soften the blow, but I suppose there was still going to be some pain."

"The burns are a sign of respect," Caliso said. "The more unevenly colored your skin, the more telling your life."

"Then I will bear it proudly," Mixa said. She remained standing by the doorway. Some moments of silence ensued, then, "Why?"

The rest of the question was easy to guess. Caliso looked at Mixa, at the princess worth a hefty Cebuano ransom. Why indeed? Mixa had only been on the Amihan for less than a day, and yet she stood there as casually as though she'd been part of the crew for years.

She belonged on the Amihan.

Easy now, think it through, her inner voice said. But a captain did not have room for doubt. She did not answer Mixa's question. Instead, "I have a proposal for you."

Mixa nodded, walking inside, her hands resting upon the back of a high chair.

"You left out a few things about your work on your brother's ship."

"Sadly yes," Mixa admitted. "It is the curse of being the only daughter of a royal line. I am meant to be wed, not to learn tricks. Father wanted me to be aware of volcanoes, yes, but I did so in the safety of Kuya Raksan's cabins. I spent most of my time with the strategists and engineers. I most near lived in the boiler rooms where I heard stories of how kuya's crew siphoned gases from exploding mountains. I helped with some of the designs myself. But that does not seem terribly important anymore."

"Why not?"

"As you can see," the princess crooked half her mouth in a small smile. "I've left Kuya Raksan's care. I chose to help the settlers rebuild, to start a life beyond the one Cebu City offered northerners. My tatay and kuyas all believe that to beat the Cebuanos, one must retain the power of the volcanoes. It is why the Kalibutan chases eruptions so doggedly across the north. One day, they will amass the power they want. Perhaps they might even regain their rightful place as monarchs."

"But you don't believe this?"

The New Manila princess shrugged. "I think they forget how many people there are still trying to make ends meet. Not everyone lives in cities and airships. The Legazpi settlers have taught me that." Mixa removed her hands from the chair and sat. "They're back on the Hills now, and I've already said my goodbyes. So you can collect your fee any which way you want."

Caliso raised an eyebrow. Mixa must have known what she'd planned to do all along. "Did Dato tell you?"

"No," Mixa said. "But it was easy enough to guess. Everyone knows how much it costs to harbor northern royalty. It would be stupid not to hand me over. That was your proposal, wasn't it?"

It had seemed so long since Caliso's last good laugh. The sound had been hoarse, a result from the poison that had just been recently purged out of her system. But she laughed, much to Mixa's consternation. When she finally stopped, she wiped her tears with her thin covering.

"I'm so glad you find this amusing," Mixa said drily.

"I do," Caliso said. She smiled at the woman. "I'm here to offer you a job."

The sentence seemed to jar Mixa, to the point where she almost fell over backward on the chair. She stopped herself by touching the bedside table, and stared. "But I—you're not—what?"

"Your brother's loss is my gain." Her body still throbbed, but she knew the pain would go away eventually. She supposed she'd come out lucky in that regard. Normally, the only way to get rid of jellyfish poison was a quick slice of the infected body part. She could have lost an arm, but thanks to Mixa's rapport with the settlers, she didn't. "I could use a quick study like you, and I meant what I said about Gogg wanting to know about this filtering system you have. Work with me."

Mixa shook her head. "I...no. My work is for the settlers."

"And how do you figure you can go about helping them? Did you plan to forever risk your well-being by hitchhiking to every volcanized region as soon as an explosion hits? We'd get there faster, and you have seen how quickly we can mobilize. Take the job, Prinsesa."

"Mixa," she said, low and timid, as though she'd said it for the first time. "If you're going to be my superior, you had best call me Mixa."

Caliso grinned. "Welcome aboard, Mixa."

The two shared a smile, and the New Manila princess stood to leave. She reached the door and turned when she heard Caliso chuckle. To answer her questioning gaze, Caliso's grin widened. "Dato is going to kick himself sore. He's wanted to change my mind this whole time, and I told him it would be as futile as moving a mountain."

The young woman seemed to understand the joke, and she grinned, too. "Mountains move all the time in the Pinas. You just have to know where to look."

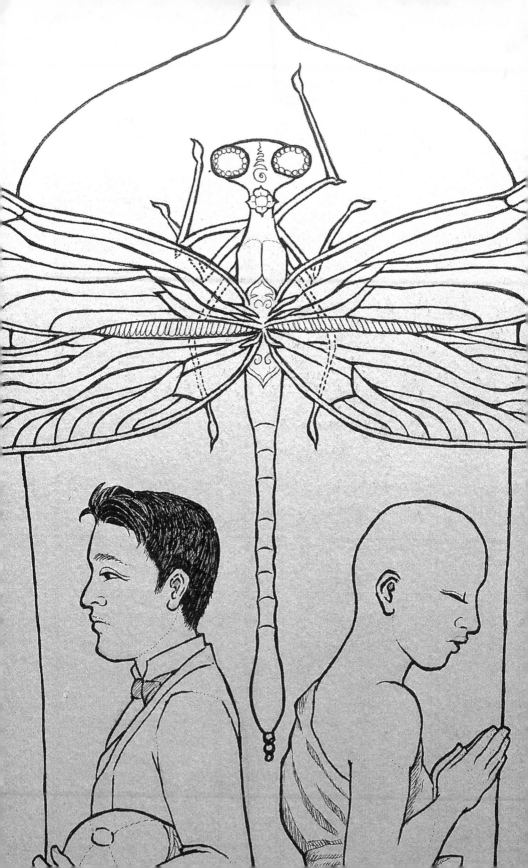

Ordained

L.L. Hill

Between a creased and callused thumb and forefinger, Preecha held the butterfly thorax. Three times he turned the legs in a full circle, hearing the gears grind the spring taut. With palms flat, he held his arms straight out at eye level. Stretched wings and poised legs faced the verdant green clad hills across the river. With a gentle brush of a thumb on a lever, the butterfly sprang away. From the base of his tongue, a solemn mantra followed the iridescent blue and green spotted insect into the retreating bosom of dawn.

Rapid wing flaps lifted the creature above the hills that stepped through mist above the brown slug of the Mekong. Energy run down spread wings spun in a gentle, glittering glide back to a perch on a polished ball of Pong Kham with other insects. Under the elephant head sized clear crystal sea of frozen vegetation, the black and red pits of another rock were magnified in their sealed sanctuary.

From his lotus on a bare grey rock set in a grassy meadow on a bluff over the river, Preecha selected a dragonfly from the orb and wound it. With wings clear, brown and ochre, it climbed furiously before sweeping down over his ochre robes to alight on the crystal.

An imperious toot preceded a small sailing paddle wheeler that thrashed the brown to white froth as it rounded a river bend. Not dropped, the sail billowed backwards in five cream waves. Pennants of yellow and blue marched in the rigging. Humid air stirred from lethargy by the impatient vigor entwined the smells of fruit orchards, forest and muddy water.

A spread legged man stood at the bow dressed in a European black suit under a tan pith helmet. Behind him, two attendants, also in stiff thick clothes, stumbled as the boat bumped into a short wooden pier.

Hands behind his back under short tails, the man stepped past scurrying crew onto the wharf and strode up on it. At the dark red patch in the rest trail leading up the steep embankment, he stopped and turned to his minions who scrambled off the boat and dashed past carrying a small wood bridge that they laid at their master's feet. A colorfully-clad woman hawking dried bark, roots and leaves from a canvas tarp next to the trail weied deeply and was ignored.

The trail disappeared into the foliage of a bamboo grove as did the black garbed man and his servants. As if alarmed by his energy, a gap appeared as the leafage parted above his passage.

Preecha deftly lifted the yellow and white butterfly from the frozen ocean and wound it for release to a clear sky. From the calluses raised during its making, the insect launched. Bright wings batted and flipped to a sweeping spiral glide over his shaved pate to dance stiff -legged on the hard sea.

A plaintive hum was left to step away on the green peaks of the giant staircase across the river as Preecha ended his morning ritual in meditation. Still cool damp air filled his lungs, slowly, each air molecule rejoicing to enter his sponges and meet with his blood.

Behind closed lids, energy spun and lifted him high above the brown artery that pulsed below. In his transcendental meditation, the worlds of myth and reality blended into one. Sinuous silver green nagas coiled and roiled near the Siam shore. Hanuman sat near the washed away chedi foundation, pale hands applauding another day; dog's face cheering, brown tail curled around his hairy rump. Brass greaves sparkling, a kinaree flew a low patrol on the shore line, blue wings alternating a beat and glide, gold eyes inspecting everything.

"Preecha."

In his name was command and condemnation. Breath bucked out of him in surprise. Jarred by the annoyance, his scant arm hair rose from their roots and prickles ran up his neck to the base of his bare head. Features impassive, he turned to regard the speaker.

Globules of sweat dripped from beneath the spiked black hair of the man in the tailored black suit as he stood with his pith helmet off. Irritated by Preecha's obvious indifference to the effort made to be present on the Mekong, Prasert exerted himself to maintain self-control and gain the cooperation of his brother. Behind him stood two acolytes who had abandoned their board game with pale and dark chips of wood at the trail junction and stood in flat faced silence.

"Prasert. Older brother. How are mother and sister?"

Prasert wiped sweat with one hand from his brow and flicked the drops away from long nails at the end of his pale fingers. In light tunics and short pants, the acolytes stood straighter and thinned their lips in disapproval. Prasert's thick lips split in a white toothed grin.

"Little brother, forgive the Western manners that our mother wished me to learn in Paris, and the medical training that our father wished me to protect the Thai people with. You have perhaps a drink of water for weary travelers?"

The acolytes waited for Preecha to give assent. The scent worn by Prasert began to overpower the musty odor of damp, decaying plant matter that coated the earth under the trees that encircled the meadow. A large black fly buzzed between the quietly standing men, and then flew to Prasert. Like a working saw it flew in and out around his head until an angry fist slapped it.

Morning heat radiated up from the bare blackened rock on which he stood with toes spread. In the afternoon, it would be too hot to walk on the weather-sculpted rocks and Preecha would retreat to study in his hermit's cave. Prasert would be gone by then. With a finger's twitch, one man turned stiffly away to a trail that ran beside a trickling brook and climbed higher into the clearing.

Prasert followed, his leather soled shoes slipping and clicking. With eyes straight ahead, Preecha walked the trail, weighing and feeling each step. Yellow and green grass stems swayed and swirled as he passed. One man was left as a figurative gatekeeper to this holy site. At a clear pool, fed by a welling spring and a tumbling waterfall, Prasert accepted the ladle of water.

Now in the shade of the foliage, relaxed after the exertion of his climb, near pool water that had quenched his thirst, Prasert's brown eyes gleamed at the rotating watermill. Held in a wood and metal brace, a hollow teak orb spun in the current that flowed from the waterfall. Inside the open frame, a hollow bamboo ball danced on the bubbling resurgence. Mist hovered over the rippling water, embracing the large green leaves that overhung the pool to escape dissipation by the sun.

Prasert started and dropped the bamboo scoop as his servant pair staggered up to the pool. They weied first and deeply to Preecha before doing so to Prasert. On their knees they pleaded with nearly dry skin and bowed heads to drink. Preecha nodded to his acolyte and turned away. Cold water splashed on his ankles.

Preecha turned off onto a faint side trail, used only by him. Between his toes squeezed mud, pebbles and grass. Behind him, Prasert stumbled and muttered about mud on his shoes.

The trail ended in a clearing of bare rock. Wrapped in ochre, the light brown veins and sinews of a gargantuan Bodhi tree towered over to footprints left by the Lord Buddha when he had stopped to admire the giant staircase across the river. Preecha knelt and prayed before the sacred relics. Each mud-caked indentation left would have cradled his lean and graceful body.

Prasert shuffled impatiently. "What is this?" he cracked like resin popping in burning pine.

"Can you see nothing?"

"I can see an ordained tree, one that has stood watch for years over two hollows that would be safe in anonymity if you hadn't followed your curiosity up from the river to worship its spirits."

Hand-sized wasps burred up and settled on spots ringed in black pebbles around the footprint. Each cleaned a long, coiled drill with yellow and black front legs. Then the amber drills unwound and began to bore through the rock. First one way, building momentum with speed then changing direction, until all the potential energy had been used. A novice scrambled around, winding the airborne digging crew. With meticulous precision, not one of the painted bamboo legs touched the pebble ring. One rectangular hole was nearly ready, the wasp miners drilling at their maximum reach and snapping the final pieces free.

Preecha wondered if Prasert was right: did he do this to bring honor to himself, or to the Lord Buddha? When he saw Prasert's smug smile, he knew that his left hand had been flexing spread fingers as he always had when a boy and faced with a moral conundrum.

Surely the skin that had sloughed off of the revered Buddha's feet needed to be saved, as he had very slowly been doing each morning while the novice worked the wasps around him. Each curl had been reverently placed in a brass tube and taken to his cave for safekeeping. Preecha knelt and cleaned the hole of debris before he slipped a bumpy stone out of a waist pouch and placed it in the center of the freshly finished excavation.

Prasert snorted loudly, a sound that he'd always made that combined a boar's snort with a bull's bellow. He knew that Preecha had reached a point of rationalization with himself.

"I know why I'm here, but why are you here?" Preecha asked in a slow, low voice.

"Since father died, Mother asked me to speak with you. With one son a doctor at the Rattanokosin court of his Majesty King Rama V, she wished to have her other son there as a monk, or as a courtier." Prasert's eyes slid to the side, and looked at the garlands on the tree behind Preecha's bare shoulder.

"A messenger would've been appropriate as well. Surely you're needed at court." Preecha resigned himself to having the truth about Prasert's needs and wants evaded by inspecting the work of the wasps. Each hole was filled with a hundred others.

"Your skills and knowledge of Issan herbs and healing has come to the Palace ears. The Abbott wishes you to teach skills to novices." With a mulish pout of resentment at almost telling the truth while excluding a fair segment of it, Prasert glared at his calm sibling.

Preecha sighed and walked away. It would be too much to ask Prasert or his mother to ever tell a complete truth. They appeared to only attain a state of near enlightenment if part of the truth was withheld or warped in some way.

A second novice rubbed a stele that a small crew of wasps also sanded and polished. Prasert barely paused to inspect the stone marker, concentrating solely on Preecha. He realized that he needed a stronger argument to make a convincing effort to recruit Preecha. Clearly, his younger brother was near entrenched in his emotional citadel. On the hillside ahead, the top of a cave mouth peeked above the roof of the novices hut.

"Perhaps another monk can be assigned to ensure the care of such a sacred site," Prasert observed in a crisp tone.

A smile twitched the corners of Preecha's lips. He wondered whether a miracle cure or a marvelous engineering feat had been promised by Prasert and to whom it had been promised. He opted to ignore his older brother and continue with plans for the day's work. Perhaps before his study time, they would both have reached a required decision.

"Let's wind the dragonfly for a test run," Preecha said to the young boy that worked with his head averted. He was rewarded with a round eyed smile. With fervent devotion, the pair had not left the clearing for a full month. The sacred place would remain clean and holy.

Almost as big as the boy, the dragonfly was hooked by its feet to the side of a papaya tree at the edge of the clearing. A sense of peace flowed through preacher as his fingers caressed the carved piece. Held together with the tensile sinews of bamboo fiber, this exotic tool weighed about the same as his arm. He and the novice arranged it on the stele, seeking a balance point. Prasert shuffled impatiently behind them as they murmured together.

With a legs anchored, the pair wound the body, each turn rising in pitch until it was almost too stiff to turn yet facing its target. Prasert blew his nose loudly, rocked from heel to toe and clenched a fist in a pocket.

"Ready?" asked Preecha, looking at the eagerly grinning face of the novice.

Released, the dragonfly's wings thundered, the clear silk fabric a tight tympanum that beat the air. As the stele lifted clear of the ground, one leg slipped. The novice wailed in anguish as the load swung. Preecha grabbed his arm and pulled him back, wondering what material would hold the rock more securely.

Prasert's lips were pressed as thin as he could make them. Never would he admit his fascination with Preecha's creations. He stood defiantly still. On the path at the edge of the clearing, torn between two worlds, his servants cautiously awaited his wishes.

A second leg broke free and the dragonfly wobbled again, the weight pulling it nearly backwards. Prasert stood defiantly before he started to duck, but the stone marker clipped him and sent him sliding down the bare rock, his pith helmet going past them all the way down to the net of vegetation.

Stunned, he lay in a muddy hollow. Laments of the novices rose to a keen that drowned the dwindling rumble of the landing dragonfly. Prasert's starched white shirt was now a gritty red, and his hands were scraped with most of his nails broken. Murmured requests from Preecha reduced the wails to whimpers and then silence.

A gust of wind shook the leaves of the Bodhi tree, swaying it back and forth as if laughing gales from deep in its spirit belly. It was as if the Lord Buddha himself was shaking in laughter at Prasert's predicament.

Terrified by the cries of the novices and the shaking Bodhi tree, the two servants at the bottom of the clearing tripped and fell over each other going back down in the trail. For days, weeks even, they would not be able to look at their master.

Slowly, Prasert rose to his knees where he scraped and flicked mud off. He was trembling, his face pomegranate red, when he finally stood outside the hollow. Without looking at anyone, Prasert stalked away as straight-backed as his muddy shoes would allow.

Stricken, the novices raised beseeching eyes to Preecha, wails silenced by his serenity. All the wasps had stopped their motion in apparent deference to the Bodhi tree. A fly walked from one novice's eye to the other without him blinking it away.

Preecha inspected the dragonfly, especially the legs from which the load had slipped. Giggles in small twigs of the Bodhi quivered to a stop. Splattered red mud was beginning to dry on the rocks as the sun rose over the river embankment.

"Sometimes, even the proudest people have to get close to the Lord Buddha," said Preecha, hoping to give peace to the young monks and wishing that they leaned less on his words. At least Prasert would not return to see him again, but he did not wish to say that.

The Last Aswang

Alessa Hinlo

Ever since the day she was cleaved, news came to Udaya in twos: bad later balanced by good more often than not. If she were lucky, both pieces were positive, but this was a rare occurence.

Neither of those situations happened today.

Udaya studied the swaths of jusi folded neatly in each of the women's laps. In turn, they watched her with expectant expressions on their faces. "What exactly is the issue?" she asked Lagnat, though she could guess.

Lagnat, her ever-loyal and long-suffering servant, had been put in charge of these women. In the past, the ones set with the task of preparing Kagubutan's gown hadn't needed such close supervision, but these seamstresses were new and younger. They lacked the proper respect for their benefactor. To them, Kagubutan was a name uttered as protection and curse, and not one of the diwata who'd saved them from the invaders who came bearing golden crosses.

Lagnat offered her a pained smile. "They cannot do it."

"Why not?" Her question came soft and quiet.

One of the women—a young and pretty thing with soulful eyes— shared glances with her companions before leaning forward. "It's unreasonable, this timeline you set. No one can embroider these patterns so quickly."

The impassioned words drew nods from the other women. Udaya was not so swayed. "Your predecessors did, with far less time, and the oldest of them was four times as old as the youngest of you," she said. "You are not inexperienced. You all came with high recommendations. I would not have chosen you otherwise." She dipped her head in regret. "A pity your previous employers were incorrect about you."

Her words quelled most of the women. Instant protestations spilled from their lips. Whether they respected Kagubutan or not, they knew failing her would leave a mark on their barely-made reputations.

The instigator, however, was not deterred despite the obvious loss of support. "I don't understand why it must be done by hand! Aren't there machines capable of aiding us? You're the local liaison! Can't you get one of them? Even just one would help us. What's the point of trading with España if we don't take advantage of what they offer?"

Udaya narrowed her eyes. This argument came up more and more these days—and not just from the mouths of seamstresses either. She'd let it pass without comment before, but perhaps that time had come to an end. "What is your name?"

Panic twisted Lagnat's face. What did her servant think she would do? Drink the woman's blood? "Mistress—"

"Answer me." Udaya ignored her servant's counsel.

With the aid of Kagubutan and her sisters, the datus and rajahs had driven the explorers and conquistadors from their islands. Even then, victory came with a price. The terms of the truce had been bitter, to Udaya and her fellow warriors especially, but the alternative had been worse. No one wanted a drawn-out war. So many lives had been lost already. In the end, the datus and rajahs had agreed over the objections of the diwata.

To think that España would try to find other ways to control them.

"Your name?" Udaya repeated a third, and final, time.

The seamstresses on either side of the instigator shifted away, not wanting to share in her ire. They were opportunists, Udaya noted with no small amount of amusement. Though they'd been complaining moments before, they now returned to work with fervent dedication.

Then, and only then, did the woman realize her position. Udaya could almost sympathize. It was hard being alone. The woman swallowed with visible difficulty and wet her lips. "Hiyasmin."

"Hiyasmin," Udaya echoed. The syllables filled her mouth, the shape etching itself into her memory. For better or worse, she'd never forget the young seamstress and no place on these islands would hide her from Udaya's nightly travels.

A commotion came from behind her. "Terrorizing children, liaison? So the stories my father told me are true."

Udaya turned to face the owner of that voice. And here was the other bit of news. Outside of the covered pavilion where the seamstresses worked stood a young woman. She held a parasol to keep the sun's rays from hitting her face. Strange to see the features so characteristic of her people set in such pale skin. Though it had been many years, Udaya recognized the young woman instantly. She always remembered the children.

"Ambassador," she greeted carefully. "When did you arrive?"

Maria Flora Agcaoili smiled. It was a beautiful smile.

It was also a dangerous one, and Udaya took warning.

Ambassador Maria Flora Agcaoli had come into the position

through an unusual string of events. Though she'd been born in Ilocos, she'd grown up in Americana Mexica where her father had been the previous ambassador. When a disease from those lands had struck him down unexpectedly, the vacant position left a gap of power. Rather than send someone else, the diwata had pushed the rajahs to appoint Maria Flora. On this point they agreed, and she'd become the youngest of the ambassadors, a voice for islands she could barely remember.

"Yesterday," Maria Flora replied. "I would have come immediately but the voyage tired me."

"It is a long voyage." Udaya understood the need for appearances. Then she noticed the ambassador's two companions and stiffened. "Why are you here?" she asked the old man in the black robe.

Maria Flora clucked her tongue. "Liaison," she said, "don't be rude. Father Ignacio has come a long way."

"I am sure," she replied with barely hidden hostility. First España sought to gain influence through trade and technology. Now they attempted again to insinuate their faith of a cold and distant god? Fighting a battle of blood and violence against armored men was simple compared to this.

The priest, for his part, took her greeting in stride. He bowed his head. "You serve the Diwata Kagubutan?" The syllables rolled strangely off his tongue, mangling her benefactor's name.

"I am her liaison," Udaya corrected. Her eyes fell upon the man next to the priest and stilled. He might not wear armor and he might not bear sword, but she knew his kind on sight. She had fought many and killed more in her time. Once, he would have been a conquistador. But now— "This is your bodyguard?"

A frown flitted across the priest's face. "Javier is here to ensure my safety."

Udaya smiled. Though time had dulled her senses, she still loved the taste of fear. "You do not trust us?"

Her question made the old man uncomfortable. The not-conquistador scowled. A keeper of his thoughts, he was not. Good. Udaya preferred straightforward men. It made them easy to predict.

Maria Flora's laughter rang through the pavilion. "My father's stories about you were indeed correct. I am glad. I worried that you might have changed and I'd have nothing familiar with which to ground me." She grew puzzled. "Odd that you look so young. It's been many years. Many doñas would kill for your secret."

Udaya merely tilted her head. The ambassador had been gone a long time. No matter how good her intentions, growing up on foreign soil changed you. It couldn't be helped, and Udaya bore no ill will towards Maria Flora.

But some things should remain unsaid.

"Why have you come? As you can see, we are busy with preparations for the ritual." She gestured towards the gathered women, who bent over their embroidery with intent focus. Udaya harbored no illusions. She knew they eavesdropped and she knew this encounter would be the subject of tonight's gossip over supper.

"Yes," the ambassador replied with a nod. "The pagdiwata. When Father Ignacio heard that my visit would coincide with the ritual, he asked to come. I warned him the voyage was long, but he *insisted*."

The emphasis made Udaya narrow her eyes. Neither the priest nor the not-conquistador noticed the change in inflection, but she did.

"I see." She addressed the priest. "Have you need to speak to the dead, priest? I thought you already had your crucified messiah?"

Maria Flora winced, and the bodyguard called Javier stiffened in offense. Udaya ignored them both. Their reactions did not interest her.

Father Ignacio's calm remained unperturbed. Udaya would be impressed, if he weren't a representative of that accursed religion. "I know the history between our peoples is contentious. But I believe we can find common ground through understanding and compassion. I came here merely to learn."

Udaya had heard similar words once, and the results of *that* were carved into her belly. She shrugged. "If you wish." She nodded at Lagnat before turning to Maria Flora. "If you have time, I can take you to Kagubutan now."

The suggestion startled the ambassador. "If... if you are sure." Maria Flora glanced sidelong at Father Ignacio and Javier.

"Of course you are welcome as well." Udaya tipped her head at the two men. Ignoring Maria Flora's covert signals to stop, she spun on her heel and left the pavilion.

They would follow. They always did.

~*~

Maria Flora breathed in wonder at the sight of the stunning balete. "Diwata Kagubutan lives here? Amazing!"

Udaya hid a smile. "You came here once as a child." At the other woman's questioning look, she nodded. "You were very young. I suppose you don't remember."

"How are we supposed to get there?" Javier cut in rudely.

Disapproval radiated off Maria Flora, and she cast a sharp glance towards the man.

"It's a fair question," Udaya said. It felt strange playing peacemaker.

A chasm ringed the balete, making it impossible to reach by anyone other than those most trusted by Kagubutan. It hadn't always been that way. Once you could walk straight into the balete's shadow.

That changed when the datus and rajahs began to demand more and more of the diwatas after the war with España ended. The peace, however tenuous it might be, had made them bolder and forgetful of their place. Datus and rajahs lead, but they are not goddesses who walk on earth.

Udaya knelt by the bamboo key-cage and opened it with care. A small snake, constructed of molave and animated by a diwata's pure will, uncoiled itself and slithered into her waiting hands. One of the first casualties suffered by the islands during the war was the loss of their serpents and crocodiles. Though España understood little of their islands and the people who lived there, they quickly grasped that these creatures were sacred and served as messengers for the diwata. The poisons they'd unleashed had been cleansed by Kagubutan and her sisters but not before they claimed their targets.

She blew into the little wooden snake's face. "Tell your mistress that I come with guests."

A tiny tongue, made of a sliver of palm, flickered as if tasting the air before the snake slipped down her arm, then torso, then leg. It moved through the grass and over the edge of the chasm.

Maria Flora was delighted. "How brilliant! I've never seen such a thing. I hear the automatons in Europa are made of metal."

"Metal is not alive," Udaya murmured. "It lacks a soul."

Javier was considerably less impressed. "That doesn't solve the problem of us crossing-"

A loud crack interrupted him. Before them, a delicate bridge of narra constructed itself, one plank and cross-beam as a time. Udaya noted with amusement that the design was more ornate than usual. The duende were showing off. Not a bad idea, considering her companions.

"Come." She gestured to Maria Flora and Father Ignacio and stepped into the bridge. She walked slowly, allowing the structure to form. The others followed behind her but their uneven footsteps revealed their trepidation. "It is stronger than it looks. We won't fall provided you don't outpace the building."

"How is it staying up?" Father Ignacio asked.

Duende ingenuity. "Magic." Her mouth curved as the reply only further fueled their curiosity.

As always, some things were best left unsaid. Unlike the tikbalang, duende were small. For all their brilliance, their appearance did not strike fear. No need to inform outsiders of their existence.

~*~

Udaya led them into the balete. For her, the trailing branches parted. After a brief touch, they did the same for Maria Flora. Father Ignacio navigated with difficulty, but he too eventually made it past the obstacle. Even so, she noticed the way the branches hovered after him as if waiting. An unclear judgment.

Javier, however, could not pass. Udaya stared at the bodyguard, ensnared thoroughly by the branches and hissed softly, baring her teeth at him.

Maria Flora looked at her in concern. "Should we help him?"

"No," she replied flatly. "The balete has judged and found him lacking. He waits outside."

"Oh, but—" The ambassador glanced in worry at the priest.

Father Ignacio shook his head. "It is all right. If I wish for there to be true peace between our people, I must show trust." He sighed at his bodyguard's predicament. "I wish others would follow that example."

Pitiful Javier. Even his charge disapproved of him.

Udaya led them inside, abandoning the bodyguard. He'd be there when they returned. The balete would take good care of him.

Several gold-framed boxes lined the spiraling walkway that descended into the balete. Translucent, they displayed their contents clearly in the mid-afternoon sun.

Maria Flora touched one. "They're cold!"

Father Ignacio peered at the contraption. "These are similar to the transport boxes carried by the Manila galleons, aren't they?"

"Yes, the Kalakalang Galyons," Udaya murmured. "They are modified and made larger though." Nothing the archipelago and Americana Mexica traded required such large containers.

"Fascinating." The priest adjusted his spectacles and studied the contents. Each box held the figure of a kneeling woman, her head bowed and eyes closed in repose. Clothed in simple garments that left the shoulders and backs bare, a single gumamela decorated their neat, tidy buns. "You made them into receptacles for art. I see the Diwata Kagubutan is a lover of beauty."

"She loves natural beauty, yes." Udaya met Maria Flora's eyes behind the priest's back. The other woman left smeared fingerprints on the cooled surface, the only sign of her fear. The ambassador may never have seen one, but she knew what these were. No matter where in the world, every child of the islands grew up knowing the word aswang.

"This way." She gestured. Maria Flora leapt at the chance to leave the boxes and their precious contents. The priest was slower, but he followed shortly thereafter.

"So many," Maria Flora whispered as they continued towards Kagubutan's reception area, more gold-framed boxes stretching before them.

When they reached the end, Father Ignacio pointed at the last one. "This is empty."

Udaya shook her head. "It's not." It was, after all, filled to the brim with chilled vinegar.

Kagubutan waited for them, lounging on her rattan throne. Next to her a boy prepared buko to drink, the bolo slicing through the air with practiced care. By her feet dozed a wooden crocodile, lids low over capiz eyes. She brightened at their arrival. "Marikit, you've grown! Come closer. I want to get a good look at you."

Color bloomed on the ambassador's face. "My name is Maria Flora."

Kagubutan laughed. "Perhaps in that land across the sea but here, you are Marikit. I named you." Her tone offered no room for disagreement. The diwata sighed dramatically. "Why do the ambassadors always change their names? As if that will make anyone forget who they are. We cannot hide. We bear the marks on our faces and bodies."

Visibly discomfited, Maria Flora approached Kagubutan and curtsied. "Did your gifts arrive?"

The diwata frowned and ignored the woman's question. "Raise your head. I said I want to look at you." The frown deepened as she took in Maria Flora's gown. "You must be sweltering in that. Udaya, bring her proper clothes."

Father Ignacio paled in alarm. "No!" Udaya had no doubt what he protested, judging by the glances he gave her bare shoulders and back.

Kagubutan arched one graceful brow. Stronger men than the priest had broken beneath that upward sweep. "It is your choice to wear that frock, foreign liaison. I will not have one of my daughters wear such a ridiculous thing. Not during the height of summer."

"Diwata Kagubutan," Maria Flora said. "It is all right. I am comfortable in this gown, and it is also hot in Americana Mexica although the heat is dryer further inland rather than wet. I don't require new clothes."

Skepticism painted itself across Kagubutan's face. She obviously believed the decision to choose layers of stifling fabric over the lightweight halter and wrap-skirt was foolish. "Very well," she relented. "To answer your earlier question, I did. I've never seen such jewelry before. Who made it?"

"They are presents of goodwill from the Maya. I've had the opportunity to speak with their nobility and they are interested in fostering a relationship with the diwata across the sea."

"Are they?" Kagubutan asked, her gaze sharp and clear.

Udaya bent her head. Ah, so Maria Flora hadn't come to view the ritual at all. That explained much. "Noy," she called to the boy who was arranging the buko for their refreshment. "Will you please take Father Ignacio on a tour? I doubt he will have many opportunities to walk inside a balete."

"Indeed you are correct, liaison."

After they left, a prepared buko in the priest's hands, Udaya turned to Maria Flora. "Why are you here?" she asked in Cebuano.

"Udaya," Kagubutan chided.

"No," Maria Flora shook her head, her brow furrowed. "I want to. Just... talk slowly. I don't have much opportunity to practice."

"We can send a girl back with you," Udaya said. "You mustn't forget our tongue."

"I'd like that," the ambassador accepted, her words stilted and slow.

"Well," Kagubutan said, playing a lock of her floor-length hair. "Answer my liaison's question."

"The Maya wish to request aid. More of their cities have fallen under España's rule. They have fought long and hard but—"

"They are the last ones left, aren't they?" Kagubutan tapped her lip. "I believe the other tribes have fallen long before now."

Maria Flora nodded. "The Aztec and Inca fell before I was born."

"And if the Maya fall, there will be no one else." The diwata sighed. "It is hard instigating a revolution." Udaya watched as her solemn gaze fell upon the dual rows of gold-framed boxes. A smile bloomed across Kagubutan's face. "But I do have a suggestion."

~*~

Udaya tapped her foot. Where had the priest gone? "I shouldn't have trusted Noy to keep an eye on him. He's a good boy but easily distracted."

Maria Flora lifted her shoulders in a graceful shrug. "Perhaps he went back outside." She was in far better mood after having listened to Kagubutan's plan.

"I hope not." Udaya ascended the stairs, touching one gold-framed box after another. "It's easy to get lost here."

"The way looks simple enough. One way in and one way out. The same way, no less."

Udaya smiled at the young woman. "That is only because I am with you. You wouldn't have been able to make it inside by yourself."

Unease filling her face, Maria Flora changed the subject. "I thought the aswang were supposed to have been destroyed."

Udaya snorted. "As I told the priest, Kagubutan likes natural beauty."

"The aswang are natural?"

She'd strike another person for asking such a question, but Maria Flora was genuinely curious without a hint of malice. "Of course." Udaya glanced at the ambassador. "I thought your father told you about me."

She expected the other woman to ask about the lone box that stood empty, but the ambassador kept silent. Perhaps Maria Flora was beginning to learn what needed to remain unsaid.

They reached the entrance in considerably less time than it took for them to walk to Kagubutan's reception area. An ominous discrepancy and one Udaya knew the meaning of all too well. But how it would manifest—

There, at the entrance of the balete, lay the body of Father Ignacio. Udaya exhaled at his nearly bisected torso. In another life, Javier would indeed have been a conquistador. Udaya cared little for those who bore crosses as symbols, but she hoped the priest would find peace in the arms of his stern and distant god. Living goddesses who walked through forests and across mountaintops had nothing to spare for dying men.

As Maria Flora screamed, Udaya met the eyes of Javier. She glanced around and saw the cut branches that had been hacked to pieces. Then she spied the matching scratches across his face, the way his clothes hung ripped and torn. The branches had lost—wood such as this had little hope of defeating steel—but not without a fight. "You shouldn't have fought. You should have stayed."

"Javier!" Maria Flora shouted. "What are you doing?"

The genuine shock in the ambassador answered Udaya's question at least. She hadn't known or expected this. Good. Kagubutan had conspired with the ambassador, after all, and Udaya hated to see her diwata's trust so misplaced.

Javier lifted his bloodied sword. "I apologize, ambassador, but this is for the glory of España."

Udaya pushed Maria Flora behind her. "Let's see. A priest and an ambassador come to watch a ritual in good will. I imagine Maria Flora is well-loved in Americana Mexica? Her death would be met with anger and the priest's with outrage. Add in a diwata and a balete tree? It makes for a neat trap." Not just trade and faith then. España had indeed wanted to renew the violence, this time testing the islands' magic-fuel tech against their steam-powered machinery.

Who would have won? And how long would it have taken to determine the victor, no matter how many lives were lost in the process?

Udaya glanced at the sky. More time had passed than she'd thought. The sun had begun to set, and shadows gathered thick under the balete.

"How dare you?" Maria Flora snapped. "I will have you tried for this!"

"How?" Such arrogance in Javier'[s voice. "You will be dead."

"No," Udaya interrupted. "She will not."

She placed a hand on Maria Flora's breastbone and shoved. The ambassador hit the ground as the sun fell below the horizon. "And a trial won"t be necessary for you." She pressed a hand against her belly, which had begun to burn as it did each and every night the sun set.

Javier sneered. "I will be glad to kill you, woman—"

He trailed off into silence as Udaya's knees hit the ground. But only her knees—her head and shoulders did not sink. Pulling the gumamela from her neat bun, her black hair streamed down over her shoulders and bare back. It slipped over the entrails that hung freely from beneath her rib cage.

"I was a babaylan before your people came to these shores," she told him. "Men like you came, bearing steel and crosses. They attacked my village and killed everyone. A man like you cut me in half much like you just cut your priest down. But Kagubutan found me and saved me."

Horror transformed Javier's face. Fear, the great equalizer. "You're one of them."

"You made us. You went after babaylan like me because you thought removing us would make it easier for your priests. But the diwata would not let us die. And so we became like this." Udaya gestured to her floating torso. The skin over her shoulderblades itched. Soon the wings would burst forth. Below her, the bottom half of her body knelt in graceful stillness.

"You made us," she repeated. "Spare me your regret. If we terrorize your dreams from across the sea, it is your fault."

She attacked him.

The blood of adult men lacked the delicacy of children or the sweetness of unborn babies, but a liver torn from the body of a warrior tasted of victory all the same.

~*~

Udaya cracked open the gold-framed box. She jerked back as a feathered serpent poked its head out, its tongue flicking at the air.

Kagubutan descended from her throne and joined Udaya's side. "A snake?" The childlike wonder in the diwata's voice gladdened her heart. It had been so long since a living snake tasted the islands' air with its tongue.

The little serpent wavered between the two—the aswang and the diwata—before making a decision. It used Udaya's arm as a means to reach Kagubutan, where it coiled around her head like a crown. "A present from the Mayan nobility, or so Maria Flora says." She handed the accompanying letter to the goddess.

Kagubutan smiled indulgently. "So they liked my gifts."

"They'll like it even more at the solstice. Though the Spaniard spectators less so." Udaya regretted the fact she couldn't be there to witness it, but one must always remain by Kagubutan's side.

She looked at the spiraling steps that led to and from Kagubutan's reception area. The gold-framed boxes that had once lined them were gone. Carried away on a Kalakalang Galyon, now they were in the possession of a certain ambassador, with tikbalang in kamagong armor protecting them all.

Only one box remained, but that one had always stood empty saved for the chilled vinegar that filled it.

Udaya's eyes fell upon Kagubutan's next project. It was yet in the beginning stages so only materials had been gathered: narra for the body, rose vines for the entrails, gumamela blossoms for the hair. But these were the easy pieces. The trick, as the diwata had explained to her, was figuring out what material to use for the wings—figuring out what would allow her new aswang to fly.

Kagubutan hummed. "I did promise Maria Flora that she'd have someone to practice her mother tongue with."

"So you did."

And the diwata always make good on their promises.

Life Under Glass

Nghi Vo

When I opened my eyes, the air was cooler and damper than it had been when I went to sleep the night before, as if the wind had brought the chill of the East Sea along with it. It reminded me that the monsoon season was close, and that my time in the Trường Sơn Range was nearly up. Before next week, Linh and I would have to send up the sky lantern that would signal the ranger station at Hải Vân Pass for a pick up by air. After that, it would be a careful trip by rail to Saigon where we could get to work unpacking our rare cargo.

Our terrariums, some the size of my fist and a few that stood waist-high, were full of sleeping animals and insects, held in suspended animation until they could be released into the Trường Sơn dome at the Universal Exposition in Saigon. Between my sister and I and the five years we had spent on expedition in the Trường Sơn Range, I would guess that we were responsible for at least a quarter, if not more, of the flora and fauna in the Trường Sơn dome. There were going to be eight domes altogether, three from Vietnam itself, and five replicating biomes from around the world. The world was coming to Saigon in a year, and Linh had observed wryly that we wanted the world to know that we could keep it under glass if we wished to.

Our return to Saigon was going to be modestly successful, but the thought of coming out of the mountains, back to the university, made my stomach clench. My memory is very good, a benefit when I was memorizing taxonomy and anatomical structures, and a nightmare when it came to personal failure. I shook aside the ghostly memory of a slender hand holding mine and sat up in my cot.

Linh had let me sleep late. Outside my tent, I could already hear her talking with the young boy who had been coming to our camp every few weeks.

"No, we need more than just one," she was saying in Cham. "It's a beauty, but if you only have one, we might as well leave it here."

Curiosity piqued, I pushed aside the mosquito netting and pulled on my trousers and my tunic before stepping into my shoes.

"What's a beauty?" I asked, coming out to join them, and the boy turned to me to show me what he held.

It was a frilled lizard barely longer than his palm, and it sat still as a statue as I examined it. The scales were small and fine, giving it a jade-like translucence, and the frills around the lizard's head and running along its back and, most exceptionally, its tail were just a shade darker. I could see how the mixture of light and dark green would allow it to be nearly invisible in the dappled light under the canopy, and when it opened its eyes at me, I was delighted to see that they were a deep amber flecked with black.

"It *is* a beauty," I agreed, and on impulse, I dug into my bag for money to pay.

"Oh, Thi," Linh said disapprovingly, "You know we can't just bring back one."

Saigon was thinking ahead. It wanted the domes to be more than just tourist attractions for the year the world came to call. The domes were experiments in sustainability, an attempt to create functional environments in glassed spaces as large as small towns. Everything we brought back should ideally not only live out a natural span, it should reproduce and thrive. Unless the little frilled lizard happened to be parthenogenetic, like the whiptail lizard that An had brought back from her internship at the Hopi preserve in North Americas, there wasn't much point in bringing it back.

I frowned, not wanting to think of An yet again. She was like a sprained ankle; just when I thought I'd healed, I'd have a memory of her hand on my face or the smell of her hair at the nape of her neck, and I'd stumble all over again. I dropped a few bhat into the boy's hand and he dropped the lizard into my cupped palms. It was a calm little thing, and I wondered if, like some of the animals we had collected, it was so unused to humans as to think we were merely part of the landscape.

The Cham boy turned to go, but I stopped him.

"Tell me where you found him, and I'll give you more," I said, and he nodded, sticking out his hand. When I gave him a few more bhat, he pointed.

"North, past the rock that looks like a man, and after that west, following the stream. There's a pool there."

"Are there others like this one?" I asked, and he shrugged. I sighed and sent him off.

I avoided Linh's gaze as I carefully closed the little lizard into one of the terrariums. It was small enough that the lizard had to curl its elegant tail around its feet, but when I pressed the button that activated the soporific gas and dropped the temperature, it blinked, yawned hugely, and curled up. It would rest peacefully until we began the process to wake it up in Saigon. The terrariums were simple enough when dealing with reptiles, but some of the larger ones and the ones designed for dealing with mammals and birds were more complicated. I busied myself checking the other terrariums, where various lizards, rodents, and birds slumbered until they could be released into an area that would hopefully be indistinguishable from home. I paused over our real prize for the trip, a quartet of striped rabbits sleeping in a pile, and at that point, Linh lost patience with me.

"We're going to spend today locking things down," Linh said. "We don't have time to go running off after a single lizard."

"It's not that late yet," I said, still avoiding my older sister's glare. "You can stay and start locking down, I'll go out and look. Maybe I'll bring back some other things too. It's gorgeous, chi Linh, and the department's going to love it to bits."

"We're already going to be somewhat late getting back to Saigon, and I don't want to make it very late."

She paused, and I got a puck of glutinous rice and mung beans wrapped in green leaves to slide into my bag along with a few of the small terrariums. I might have managed to get out of camp with only her disapproving glare weighing me down, but she shook her head.

"This is about An."

"Not everything is!" I snapped, and her elegant eyebrow arched in disbelief.

"I didn't say everything was, I said that this was. You know you're going to have to come home eventually, and she's going to be there too, sooner or later. The department isn't that big."

"The world's plenty big," I protested, knowing even as I did that I was fighting a losing and fairly stupid battle. "Maybe I'll transfer up to Thăng Long. Maybe I'll decide I want to take that teaching position in Hue. Maybe I want to just stay here."

"First, the world's smaller than you think it is, second, you hate northern food, third, you hate teaching, and fourth, I'd like to see you stay here when the monsoons come in and you're still hiding in your little canvas tent."

I glared, and she glared back. My sister isn't a soft woman, but she's a family woman through and through. She may not have understood my relationship with An, but my older sister had my mother's firm belief that taking charge or feeding me would fix it.

"Stay here. Help me lock down, and we can send up the lantern tomorrow night. We can be back in Saigon before the end of the week, and you can figure out that no one at the university gives a damn about your little romance, *em*..."

"It *wasn't* just a little romance!" I shouted, and I chewed my lip in frustration when Linh only nodded.

"Come on. Come help me with the terrariums. We'll be in Saigon before the end of the week. I'll buy you an oxtail curry, and maybe you can lose your head over another girl."

I might have done it except she mentioned another girl, and I stomped off down the northern path.

"You have to come back eventually, em!" she called after me, and just because she was right didn't make me happier.

~*~

The forests of the Trường Sơn Range are as unlike southern Vietnam as night is to day, or, as Linh would have said, as different as a moist broadleaf forest is from a verdant river delta. The air was cooler, the colors different, and even the buzz of the insects was lower. I caught myself humming as I walked along the wild pig track that Linh and I had been using to go north, and when I stopped, there was something strangely soaked about the silence. The air was sullen with the promise of the monsoon to come, and I shivered to think about how much inhospitable the forest would become drenched in bucketing water.

The Cham boy had mentioned the rock that looked like a man, and I knew what he meant, but when I passed it, it occurred to me that it didn't look like a man at all. It was a jut of old stone, smooth and gray in the forest's green, and though I could see an indentation that looked like a pair of legs, and a bend of the stone looked like a man's curled arm, I could think of it as nothing but a lizard, sitting up, alert, and ready to flee or bite.

I patted it on the head as I walked by, and it reminded me of An and I picnicking together as undergraduates at the university. She had gotten me in the habit of patting the stone lions that guarded the university gates, and I had never quit.

I walked faster, following the stream as the boy had directed. If I walked faster, perhaps I would be able to out-pace the memories that seemed to crowd close whenever I thought of An and of the six years we had spent together. The memories weren't as sharp as they were, but as my father had always told me, dull knives are the most dangerous.

I had been stupid, I had been naïve, and worse than that, I had been in love, though by the end, I realized now that it was less love than habit. My family had been understanding, but confused, both when I brought An home and when we broke up, and soon, I knew, they would start the round of introducing me to friends' sons and grandsons and nephews, and perhaps I would meet someone interesting, someone funny and kind, and then An and I would just be a memory.

I walked faster, and then I made myself slow down. It was dangerous to walk so quickly in the forest, and Linh and I had had more than a few sprained ankles to tell us that.

The stream grew a little broader, and I followed its edge closely, watching the shallows where the sunlight pierced the water with aching clarity. I saw a few lizards, several that we had already collected, but I couldn't find a match for the little jade beauty that was sleeping back at camp. It was a lovely thing, but if I couldn't find it at least one mate, Linh was right, we were better off leaving it in the mountains than bringing it to Saigon

The stream continued west, but I veered towards a protected sandbar that created a grotto underneath the shelter of the evergreens. It was the pond that the boy had told me about, and I could see small fish breaking the surface, and as I watched, a laughingthrush fluttered down to the water to drink. It would usually have been a dim little spot, but there was a bright ray of light coming through the canopy, lighting up the water and bringing it to life.

I squatted down close to the edge of the pond, pulling out my collapsible net. I could sit like a stone for hours if that was what it took, and I relaxed, scanning the water and keeping my eyes on the shallows.

This type of observation and collection was almost meditative, but what I was meditating on, unfortunately, was An. Her speciality was on the deserts of North America, and she was spending the next semester in Hungo Pavi as a resident professor. When we had first met, she was fresh from her successful internship there, and now that we were over, she was headed back again. I wished I could ascribe her trip to a broken heart, but I knew better.

I couldn't remember whether she had broken up with me or I had broken up with her. It's strange that the important parts of the end were so muddled when the insignificant parts were so achingly clear. I remembered the last night we spent together before the break up, and then the awkward nights after that, when I was sleeping at Linh's and being fed bowl after bowl of clear soup and Chinese buns. I remembered coming across a pillowcase that still smelled like her in my things, and I remembered the first disastrous time I tried to go out on a group date with my friends. It had gone so badly that I slipped away in the middle, tired and miserable in my brand new orange áo dài.

My mind chased after the familiar thought that I would do anything to have her back, and then I realized that instead, I was thinking how wonderful it would be if I could just lose the grief, regardless of whether she came back or not.

The thought was so startling that it sent a shiver down my back, making me straighten up, and that was when I realized that I was being watched.

Across the pond, sheltered by the enormous trunk of an ancient evergreen, I could see a frilled head the size of my torso, a long and elegant neck, a body that was almost snakelike and behind it all, a tail that was surely at least three meters long.

The lizard was enormous, and though later on I would think of the Komodo dragons of Indonesia and the nearly extinct aiolosauruses of Mongolia, right then, all I could think, all I *knew*, was that I was looking at a dragon.

The dainty frills of the lizard I had bought that morning were fully realized into crests of spines that lined either side of the dragon's face, and I stared at the animal that had surely had the myths of a civilization built on its smooth back. For better or worse, my stillness and silence is probably what drew the dragon closer.

In a single bound, it leaped across the edge of the pond, landing on all four feet. I couldn't help but notice the twisting of the long body, a gait suited to an animal that was as comfortable slithering close to the ground as it was springing on prey. Up close, I could see how lithe it was. Its body was slender rather than dense, and there was something crocodilian about its face. The eyes were amber flecked with black, and I thought blankly that I had gone looking for a match for my lizard and that I had found it.

The dragon opened and closed its mouth rapidly at me, and its frills expanded in what I realized in sudden stark and primitive terror was a threat display. I could see needle-sharp teeth, noting somewhere in a corner of my brain that there were two full rows, one behind the other. I remembered how the bite of similar animals turned septic inside of a few hours.

I stood stock still, and the dragon came closer yet, splashing water as it went, and dropping its head to look at me. The black slit pupils contracted and expanded, and I could smell its musky dry scent. Those scales that were so small on the hatchling were still small on the adult. The effect was an animal carved from jade with darker veins underneath, and for one single, insane moment I wanted to reach out and touch it.

The dragon huffed at me, almost catlike, and then abruptly, deciding I was neither food nor threat, it turned. I saw its body tense for a split second before it sank to the ground, its neck stretched out and level with its torso. I watched in fascination as it slithered into the underbrush, both snake and lizard, and it wasn't until its tail tip vanished into the forest that I slumped back on my rear. I gasped out my panic and terror, and what they left behind was a nearly frantic exhaustion and a whirlwind of thoughts.

There had always been stories of large crocodilians and monitor lizards in the mountains, but dragons were another thing. People hunted them the way that they did thunderbirds in North America and bunyip in Australia, and while there was always the odd footprint or scale to set off a new fervor, there had been nothing like this.

The Trường Sơn Range was vast, however, and I wondered if recent mining on the Laotian side of the border had brought it out of hiding, or if it was merely that there were so few of them that a sighting was impossibly rare.

I thought of population densities, about how close I had come to getting my throat ripped out, and about what it would take to bring a dragon back to Saigon, and suddenly, as suddenly as a dragon coming out of the evergreen trees, I started to laugh.

For the first time in a long time, I wasn't thinking about An. That was when I could see the beginning of the next part of my life, and it was all about dragons.

~*~

By the time I got back to camp, it was already dusk, and Linh had most of the equipment secured. She would need my help to take care of the rest, but instead of coming to harry me to work, she handed me a bowl of warm egg soup instead. There were a few species of wild fowl that were tame enough we thought that they had simply gone feral, and we'd been thieving from their nests off and on for the last few months.

I drank the soup quickly, feeling the warmth sink through me and the richness of the egg yolk giving me strength. Linh sat next to me on the log we'd pulled up next to our camp fire, sipping delicately at her portion. She'd always been thinner than me, but our months on the Trường Sơn Range had made her gaunt. Tuan, her husband, would tsk and make her caramelized pork belly and every other dish she loved to fatten her up again, and she wouldn't have to cook at all until she was back in the mountains with her stubborn sister.

"We're sending the lantern up tomorrow night," she said, a note of warning in her voice. It said that she didn't want to fight, but she would if she had to.

"Let me change your mind," I said, and before she could protest, I started to talk.

~*~

We went back to the pond the next day, but though we looked, we saw no sign of the dragon or the hatchlings. Then, no matter how much we wished otherwise, we needed to pack up, because the morning had brought with it the first splatters of the monsoon rains. We were going to be really late rather than somewhat late, and packing up camp and securing our living freight took most of the next day.

We waited for dark, and we pulled out the sky lantern. It was a lovely thing made from white oiled paper on a frame of treated wood. When it was lit, the hot air caused the balloon to rise, and when it reached its apex, the fuel reserve would cause the lantern to hang in the sky, burning brightly so that the rangers watching for us at Hải Vân Pass would see. Unlike the antique paper lanterns of the past, this lantern would burn until nearly all of the fuel was gone, and then begin a quick, nearly vertical descent. The cool air extinguished the flame as it fell, and soon the only remnant of our message would be a few charred sticks of wood.

The white lantern floated up in the indigo sky and burst into brilliant chemical flames, hovering high above like an amber eye.

"I'm glad we're going home," Linh said softly, and I linked my arm through hers, standing close.

Linh and I were coming back to the Trường Sơn Range, and next time, instead of running away from a love affair, I would be searching for something beautiful and strange.

We stood in the dark, watching the red fireflies flicker through the trees. The cold wind was going to bring rain by morning, there was a dragon hatchling sleeping in our cargo, and we were going home.

Between Severed Souls

Paolo Chikiamco

A memory of voices, raised and reverent:
To those who emerge untouched...
We give greetings. Hmmm...
We give respect. Hmmm...
May our words not become unpleasant.
To the watchers of the world.

~*~

April, 1762.

"I come bearing a gift!"

The voice boomed from just beyond sight, funneled down the gash in the rock that was the only access point to the cavern that served as both workplace and sanctuary for Domingo Malong.

"Then you may leave with it as well," said Domingo, but he knew better than to think his words would so much as slow his brother's pace. Dominador Malong had difficulty grasping the notion that his little brother might have desires that weren't completely in accord with his own.

So Domingo was unsurprised to hear the echoes of his brother's heavy footfalls playing out between the rock walls. What finally made Domingo turn away from his work was the realization that he didn't hear only one set of feet.

"Damn it," Domingo growled, as his eldest brother came into view. "This is my workshop, not a plaza."

In better days, it would be easy to see that Dominador and Domingo were siblings. While Domingo had inherited the slim build of their mother rather than the solid frame of their father, he and Dominador shared the same heavy brows, the same low cheekbones, the same stubborn jaw, all features that had long identified the Malong clan. But Domingo hadn't bathed in weeks, and his hair was so thick with sweat and dirt that strands could serve as nails for his machines. An over-sized camisa de chino hung to his knees when he stood, covering worn trousers that looked old enough to have sailed to the islands with Magellan.

Dominador, on the other hand, dressed in accordance with his perceived place in the world. He wore the breeches, stockings, coat, and waistcoat of a European gentleman of means, a sword at his waist and a cane in his hand. He gazed out at his brother from behind green tinted spectacles, an irritating affectation he'd brought home from his sojourn at the University of Glasgow. For a time, he'd even taken to wearing a wig before...

A memory rises, riding the gaps between heartbeats—

A suppressed giggle, the feel of her warm palm over his own mouth. The scent of burning hair and the reflected light in her eyes.

This is the sexiest thing we've ever done, Dom.

—it's gone, pushed down deep. The absence was both a salve and a wound, and Domingo found himself short for breath, barely catching the tail end of his brother's words.

"—would imply that actual work was being done here, bunso." Dominador looked around the large domed cavern, wrinkling his nose at the stench. Above them, a colony of bats dozed away the daylight, while regularly expelling the remnants of last night's bounty onto whatever was unfortunate enough to lie below them. The elder Malong stepped around a few larger deposits of guano, and stopped before a pile of machine parts.

"I had to call in a lot of favors, fill a lot of pockets, to get working parts of a Newcomen clockman," said Dominador, scraping a copper elbow joint gently with his cane, tracing a spiral pattern in the accumulated dirt and excrement. "If this is some new method of reverse engineering, I must say it is a remarkably slow one... But of course, that too, would imply some sort of progress."

Domingo said nothing. He turned his back on his brother, hunching over one of the workshop's smaller carving benches. For a few minutes, there was no sound in the cavern other than the whisk of a blade biting into soft wood, and the curses of Dominador's men as they navigated the broken rock of the cavern floor. From the scuffling of their feet and their labored breathing, it was clear they bore something of significant weight.

Domingo resisted the urge to turn around and look. It didn't matter if Dominador walked an entire army of the English machines through the door. "So it's to be another lecture then, I take it? Tell me, if I list the accomplishments of every Malong for the past hundred years, will you spare me your exhortations? What about if I named every family that's broken their oaths to us since the Grand Revolt? I know how old grudges keep you warm at night."

Dominador struck a brass plate with his cane, and it took a full minute for the echoes of the sharp clang to fall silent. "Don't mock our heritage," said Dominador, his voice as light as his meaning was plain.

Domingo felt a pang of guilt. His heritage... Domingo's entire life had revolved around the obsession of his family with the fact that, for five months, their ancestor had once been King of Pangasinan. Since then, everyone with Malong blood was expected to do their part in recovering the family's lost "kingdom", and in punishing all those who had benefited from their downfall. Each Malong was expected to give his all for the great Cause.

Domingo had never possessed the same fervor as the rest of his brothers. Hell, even Clarita showed more fire for the Cause. Years of education in the Fleet of Wisdom had made Domingo's wife more sensitive to the daily affronts and indignities of Spanish rule, things that many Tagalogs took for granted.

And now, Clarita was dead.

"Considering what that heritage has cost me, I—"

Domingo felt the carving knife spasm in his grip. A delicate incision became a cut too deep to salvage. With small, controlled movements, Domingo set the knife down. For his brother's sake, he set it down far enough away that he'd have to think twice about reaching for it once Dominador started in on the inevitable tirade.

"What do you want, kuya?"

Dominador sighed. "You never were a very good listener. Particularly when I'm the one doing the talking."

Here it comes.

"One would think I was due a bit more courtesy, all things considered. Tell me, brother: Have you visited Cynthia lately?"

Domingo grit his teeth at his daughter's name. Daughter. He could hardly make sense of a world where he had a daughter, even more than a year after she was born. But then, he could hardly make sense of anything after Clarita's death. It was why he'd left his daughter's care to Dominador's family. It was what was best for her, he told himself.

Hey, I don't mind taking all the credit for the squiggly little grub. Allah knows I don't see your breasts being masticated... But she belongs to both of us, Dom. Our greatest creation. Well, until we build her a city. Now why don't you give us both a kiss, hm?

Domingo shook his head, and realized that his brother was standing beside him, looking down at the pieces on his carving bench.

"Of course you haven't," said his brother. It took Domingo some time to realize that Dominador was answering his own question. "You've been occupied with... other matters."

Domingo felt his cheeks heat up. He quickly covered the unfinished figures with a threadbare cloth. They were all in various states of completion, pieces using a wide variety of woods and techniques, but they did share two things in common: the likeness of the model, and the fact that Domingo had given up on each of them. The last thing Domingo wanted was another heart-felt talk about how it was time to move on, how none of this would bring her back...

Dominador placed his hands gently under Domingo's arms, lifting him to his feet.

"As I said..." The older Malong turned Domingo around. "I come bearing a gift."

The smug self-satisfaction in his brother's voice didn't even register into Domingo's mind, so enraptured was he by the smooth, almost black, tree trunk that two of Dominador's men had just deposited on his workshop floor.

Domingo had been carving wood for as long as he could remember. Before he'd learned how to use wood to make men fly and soldiers fall, Domingo had been an accomplished carver, bringing out the beautiful figures that lay dormant beneath the grain.

Of course, some wood was so striking that it seemed sacrilegious to make it seem anything but itself. In his years of working wood, first as a carver, and then as an engineer, Domingo had seen timbers so exquisite—burled molave, spalted ipil, narra with quilting that would put a Buhi weaver to shame—that he had refused to work them. Some beauty was best kept free of human artifice.

But this... What Dominador had brought him was like no wood he had ever seen before. It was a deep, deep brown, the color of banalo at the bottom of a well, or kamagong at moonless midnight. What's more, it had no fragrance to speak of, even when Domingo let his nose touch the bark. The wood was smooth too, smooth as marble, but retaining the warmth of wood. He could almost feel it breathing.

Domingo wrinkled his nose, then backed away. He circled the trunk warily, an enforced skepticism keeping his wonder at bay. He ran through a catalogue of specimens in his head, both foreign and local, but none of them fit, none of them were right.

"What...?"

"They call it Molaui. This one is out of a forest near Cebu, but it's something of a legend across the islands, apparently. They're rare, and as a rule, these trees are left alone because the wood is unusable."

Domingo placed a palm against the Molaui, trying to ignore the uneasy feeling creeping up his arm. He dug a fingernail into the bark, felt it yield gently. "Seems otherwise to me."

Dominador nodded toward the Molaui. "You see what this piece resembles of course?"

Domingo said nothing, taking two full steps back from the wood.

"Every piece of Molaui seems to have some inherent... form. The carvers say that if they seek to shape the wood in any other way—to make a fine chest, an elegant oar—it simply falls apart at the next new moon. There have been those who've attempted to bring out the native figure, of course, since the legend goes that only then will the wood retain its strength. The carvers I've met say that no one's succeeded thus far. I told them that my brother had yet to try."

Domingo backed up to his carving bench, his right hand reaching for one of his straight wedges. But the moment he touched the hilt, Dominador's hand closed around his, holding it fast.

"Shall we say, three days for a working Newcomen scale model?"

Domingo looked at his brother, then at the Molaui trunk, unworked, possibly unworkable. Without even trying, his gaze traced the contours of a woman, strong, regal. It felt like she was looking back at him. It felt like...

Domingo swallowed. "You'll have them in two."

Dominador ruffled his youngest brother's hair. "That's my boy."

~*~

The memory of reverence fades.
Existence itself is forgotten.
Then, unfurling, a sound.
Chk. Chk. Chk.
Metal biting into wood.
Chk. Chk. Chk.
A pressure. An itch.
A voice, susuring.
Adoring.
The watcher begins to wake.

~*~

June, 1762.

Domingo didn't know how long she'd been standing in the doorway to his workshop, a disapproving frown on her face, the fingers of her right hand tapping a staccato rhythm on the left, on the brass of her artificial forearm. Domingo didn't even know what day it was, or how many hours he'd slept.

But he knew that if Nur bint Jamal Hassim al Maguindanao was paying him a visit, he was in trouble.

"Wipe the spittle from your face, Tagalog."

Domingo scowled, but complied. He rose to his feet, resisting the urge to massage the small of his back. It was a point of pride on his part not to show weakness in front of Nur. He did, however, check her for weapons as surreptitiously as he could. She wasn't visibly armed, but Domingo knew that didn't mean much—if there was one thing Domingo had learned in their time together, it was that when Nur wanted to hurt someone, she'd find a way.

If there was a second thing he'd learned, it was that Nur usually wanted to hurt Domingo. And that had been before he'd gotten her first love killed.

"Haven't seen you since the funeral," he said, hardly stumbling over the word this time. He was making progress. "Didn't really expect to."

"Believe me, this isn't my idea." Nur stepped into the cavern, boots making scuffing noises against the now even floor. Domingo had cleaned his workshop once he'd begun to do work for Dominador again, gotten rid of the bats, and even gone so far as to install some contraptions of his own devising that allowed him to do sophisticated work in this most primitive of locations.

Still, he didn't expect Nur to be much impressed with what he'd done with the place. Personal issues aside, Nur was a teacher, a Çelebi, on the Fleet of Wisdom, the foremost institution of learning in Asia— if not the planet. Two years ago, Nur, Clarita, and Domingo had been three of their very best engineers. Now, Domingo had heard, Nur was being groomed to take over as head of the War Masters, the school devoted to making mechanical implements of war. If he and Clarita hadn't left, Domingo supposed they'd be in similar positions in their own schools.

A lot of things would have been different if they hadn't left... but even he, the least enthusiastic of the Malong clan, had been unable to ignore his father's dying wish.

And what the old man had wished for was war.

It was not going well.

Now, the Malong forces were hiding in a chain of islands in the Gulf of Lingayen, north of Pangasinan. Dominador had assured everyone repeatedly that he was on the cusp of an important alliance that would turn the war around, but in the meantime, all they could do was lick their wounds, and pray that their location remained a secret from all but their few allies.

Nur spared a glance for some of Domingo's quarter-scale models, a batch of the earlier modified Nucomen prototypes he'd produced for Dominador. If she was at all curious about the modifications he'd installed in each variant, from continuous track "wheels" to several attempts at flight-capable frames, she didn't let that interest show on her face.

Domingo consciously avoided looking at the work-in-progress at the center of the workshop, the "personal piece" covered by a large water-resistant canvas.

"You've put me in something of a difficult situation," Nur began, her eyes still on the prototypes.

"Wouldn't be the first time," Domingo said. He crossed to a corner of the room, trying to draw Nur's attention with him.

"I guess not. But I'd hoped that, after Clarita's death, we'd be through with each other."

Now Domingo was worried. Nur was usually as indirect as a bullet fired straight down. She didn't do preambles, or retrospection, or small talk. At least, not when she had a job to do. Which was clearly the case today... so what kind of job would give her pause?

Domingo felt the world sag from under him. "He's sent you for my daughter."

Only then did Nur meet his gaze. She gave him a grave nod.

Pierre-Henri Leschot was one of the most influential men in the Qudarat Sultanate, no mean feat for a Frenchman, even if he had converted to Islam. It helped that Pierre-Henri was an automata expert in Jolo, a city obsessed with the mechanical.

"I've just been to see your brother," said Nur, "and I must say that Clarita's letters understated his degree of... snake-ishness."

"Cynthia is my daughter," Domingo said. "Not his."

"And my message was for your brother, not you," said Nur. Her expression soured. "The Fleet would like the Malong patriarch to know that it supports Leschot's claim, and that if I do not leave in possession of the child by the twelfth of the month, there may be a sudden and drastic decrease in the amount of ordinance you'll be receiving from the Fleet."

Clarita's father had studied, not at the Fleet, but in the workshop of the famed Jacques Vaucanson. At Jolo, Pierre-Henri had made a fortune and a reputation replicating Vaucanson's automata servants for the Sultan and his court. Pierre-Henri had used his position to encourage the Sultanate's support of the Fleet of Wisdom, a favor which had not gone unnoticed amongst the Çelebi. Pierre-Henri's influence on the affairs of the Fleet was substantial, if rarely used.

But now it seemed he was calling in every favor he was owed, in order to take custody of his granddaughter.

Domingo balled his hands into fists. "The twelfth... Two days away. How generous of him to give me time to say goodbye."

"The twelfth was when I was supposed to arrive." Nur adjusted her kombong fastidiously. "I... made better time than expected, that's all."

Domingo stared at her. "Nur. Thank—"

"Don't. I'm not doing this for you." Nur opened her mouth, then shut it again, brow furrowing. Finally, she said, "If all you use this time for is a drawn out farewell, you're a weaker man than even I thought you were."

Domingo gave her a hard look. Nur was an intimidating woman, even without her brass limb. She had the fit slimness of one who treated exercise as calibration and food as an unfortunate necessity, as well as the bearing of one who surveyed the works of nature and felt that, at best, it was a good start. But Domingo had grown so used to Nur's harsh judgment and barbed tongue that the insult barely registered, in the face of the message that lay beneath.

She thought he was going to take Cynthia and run.

Domingo sat down heavily on a nearby stool. "Maybe it's for the best."

Nur's jaw slackened.

"I've been too busy to attend to her, and if her grandfather is willing to go to these lengths, then I'm certain he'll spare no expense in—"

"What happened to boldly proclaiming she was your daughter?" Incredulous scorn. "You'd throw out Clarita's flesh and blood?"

"Too much of that blood has spilled here already!"

"Which is why I have given you a chance at escape!" Nur slammed her brass fist onto the work bench, which gave an audible crack as it buckled beneath the force of the blow.

"Escape? Don't you see?" Domingo crossed his arms to keep them from shaking. "If I turn aside, if Leschot makes good on his threat, if we lose this war... Then she died for *nothing!*"

"She did die for nothing Tagalog—she died for *you*." The words came out as a growl, heavy with rage and pain. "But when you stopped being a husband, you didn't stop being a father!"

He didn't have to listen to this. Brusquely, Domingo pushed past her.

Nur caught his shoulder with her good hand. "We're not finish—" but before she could finish speaking, Domingo whirled, grabbed her by the opposite shoulder, and flung her away. Nur cursed as her back slammed against the canvas-covered piece.

"You..." Nur growled, but seemed unable to find a strong enough word. Instead, she twisted the wrist of her brass arm, and a long, razor-sharp blade emerged from the forefinger.

"Do it," challenged Domingo. "She's not here to stop us anymore."

Domingo could see the muscles in Nur's jaw working, but then she lowered her blade, though it remained unsheathed. Nur grabbed a handful of canvas and pulled herself to her feet. "She made her choice long ago. And unlike you, I won't soil her memory even by erasing her biggest... her..."

Nur stopped as the canvas fell to the floor, uncovering its secret. The woman who had once sunk a Spanish galleon single-handedly began to shake.

Domingo had never before worked with a wood as strange, as... independent, as Molaui. He wasn't sure how much credence to give the stories of sudden disintegration, but the wood did seem to have a preference, for lack of a better word, in how it was to be worked. When his carving and chipping served to highlight the contours of the woman he saw in the wood, then the Molaui was responsive under his tools, soft and yielding, allowing him nuances and subtleties he'd never before been able to achieve—each visible strand of hair on the carving's head seemed to distinct, reacting in its own way to an unseen breeze.

Deviate from that form, however, and the Molaui suddenly and inexplicably became hard, or brittle, or began to excrete a malodorous resin that risked marring the entire work. After ruining his third compass saw and fifth gouge, Domingo had given up on attempting to carve clothes on the figure, resigned to a later use of glue and a lesser wood.

But her face... perhaps it was because the muted features of the implied figure, or because Domingo was that much more dogged, but with persistence, patience—and regular tool replacement—he'd coaxed and coerced the Molaui into a visage achingly familiar. It was still unfinished of course, but only in the sense that Domingo wasn't convinced it was perfect. To the eyes of any other, to someone who knew her, it was simply Clarita Leschot Esteybar reborn.

Nur clutched her chest with her good hand, and made a faint, painful noise.

And then she cut the carving in half.

~*~

The voice has become a beacon.
A cord of birth.
Sustaining. Connecting.
Even as the sound shapes.
Chk. Chk. Chk.
As the sound creates.
Chk. Chk. Chk.
A dream of flight.
Chk. Chk.
Chk.
SHUNK
—separation
release—
-identity-
-I-

~*~

Even much later, Domingo wasn't sure who noticed it first. One moment he and Nur were at each other's throats, shared pain and loss bringing them together and tearing them apart...

... and in the next, they were staring, speechless, at the upper torso of the severed carving. At the head. The face. Clarita's face.

Looking.

Blinking.

The scream now, *that* came from Domingo, as he backpedaled into a shelf of wood samples, toppling codo-long pieces of polo-maria and lanete as he scrambled away from the... whatever it was.

"What have you done, Domingo?" Nur placed herself between him and the carving, which was now beginning to jerk and tremble on its own power—not just the upper torso, but its lower half as well. "What jinn has left its mark on you?"

"It's just a carving," Domingo hissed, insulted in spite of the situation. "I'm a man of science, not spirits!"

The carving's lips trembled, and a low rumble issued from the solid wood where its throat would have been.

"You'll excuse my skepticism here," Nur said. The War Master held her blade up in a guard position. "That hardly looks like science to me."

Not...

Both Nur and Domingo were startled when the sounds from the creature began to form into words.

"Does that sound like Tagalog to you?" Domingo asked.

Nur looked at him askance. "It's clearly Tausug."

Not... finished...

"'Not... finished?'" Domingo quoted the creature.

Nur's eyes narrowed. "It's not speaking out loud. It's in our minds."

Your work... is not... finished... Man...

Nur's eyebrows rose. "It's speaking to you, apparently. Perhaps I should leave the two of you alone?"

Domingo hushed Nur distractedly as he moved forward. "It's not Clarita," he said, his voice husky with relief.

With the initial shock fading, and certain that he had not somehow done something unspeakable, Domingo found himself absolutely fascinated by what he was seeing. His mind rapidly proposed and rejected hypothesis after hypothesis as he slowly approached the upper torso.

"Have a care, Domingo."

He motioned for Nur to keep her distance. Domingo knelt down beside the carving's head, unable to keep a shiver from running up his spine as the unpainted wooden eyes moved, impossibly, up and right, tracking his movements.

He steeled himself, then grabbed the torso by the shoulders. He almost dropped it—the Molaui was warm to the touch, not quite flesh, but something quite other than dead organic matter. He set it down carefully on the stump of its waist, and knelt down before it so that he and the carving were roughly eye to eye.

"What are you?"

Not... finished...

"What are you?"

The eyes blinked. Shifted.

Alive. Aware.

The torso began to tremble again, and Domingo could hear the wood grinding as different sections strove to move in different directions.

Trapped. Trapped. Tr... ap...

The voice in Domingo's head began to fragment, and he winced as a wave of panic and horror washed over him. Behind him, he heard Nur curse.

"Calm down! Calm down!" He laid a hand against the quivering wood again. "I'm a... a carpenter. I can help you. We can help you."

Nur shook her head emphatically as Domingo turned to her. "Oh no, Tagalog. I came here on a mission."

"One you never had any intention of fulfilling," Domingo said, his mind already busy with plans. "Don't you see? Something like this could change everything. Change..." He stopped, remembering one thing he hadn't taken into account.

"We can help you," he addressed the creature. "But without your help in return, all of us here are doomed, and in short order."

The answer came in a term that Domingo was only vageuly familiar with.

Anito, the creature repeated. *We are... were... anito.*

"What does that mean?" asked Nur, leaning down next to Domingo.

"A guardian," Domingo said, starting to smile. "One who once watched over those who were born in these islands. And with our help..."

Clarita's eyes stared into his, aware but unblinking.

We will watch over you anew.

~*~

"Let's build a city."

"You were serious about that?"

"I'm always serious when it comes to building."

"But... why a city?"

"I miss having a home. A place where I belong."

"You belong—"

"I don't. You don't either, not really, whatever your brother says. But we're builders, Dom. If we want something that isn't there, we make it."

~*~

August, 1762.

"Wings?"

From her seat on the display pedestal, the anito watched with interest as Nur and Domingo reacted to her request. In the days since the Carpenter had brought her to full wakefulness, she had begun to relearn the complexities of human faces. Domingo seemed troubled, Nur merely puzzled. Little Cynthia, from her traditional position slung across Domingo's chest, merely babbled.

"They are part of my... natural form," the anito answered in halting Tagalog. It had been easy enough to learn the common languages of this era, but it had taken a long time to convince the two humans to go to the effort of giving her an audible voice.

The project, like much of her new body, had been undertaken with a mixture of sound theory and complete guesswork. They'd hollowed out much of the wood that was host to her consciousness, and used the pieces to create elaborate mechanisms, mechanisms that took advantage of the fact that she was able to move individual pieces of the Molaui, with varying degrees of force and agility. The exact nature of the movement varied: for example, she'd been unable to bend her fingers at all until proper joints had been installed, but she was able to blink and rotate her eyes as though she were still a being of flesh and bone.

Nur and Domingo had finally given her a voice through a combination of artifice and the anito's control of the Molaui, tubes and elastics complemented by an approximation of a bellows constructed from a continuous shaving of the host wood, which the anito was able to inflate and deflate at will. The human pair argued for days over how to replicate the function of a tongue, but the solution proved impossibly simple: once the Carpenter had hollowed out the anito's mouth, and carved a tongue distinct from the rest of the mouth, the anito found that she could move it naturally, as if a muscle. She had resisted the urge to test the tongue out to its fullest extent—the human engineers, as they referred to themselves, had been required to make a great many alterations to their world view already—but her wings were non-negotiable.

"First this self-segmentation business," Nur said, running a hand across her brow, "and now wings. You're sure you're not just taking this opportunity to add a few improvements..."

Nur trailed off, then tapped a finger against her brass forearm. "We really do need to call you something, anito."

"My memory of the past is still... fragmented," the anito replied. "But I do know that names are important. Whether I recall what I was once called, or settle on another, it must be something that is... natural."

"Nothing about any of this is natural," Nur replied, before feeding Cynthia some lugaw from a pewter pap boat. "What do you think, Tagalog? Maybe repurpose one of the Auto-birds?"

The Carpenter seemed distracted. "Possible, if the rotation of the..." He stopped, then shook his head once, authoritatively. "No. Never."

"What's gotten into you now?" Nur said.

"Put on an Auto-bird. On, on..." he gestured toward the anito's face. The anito had noticed that the Carpenter rarely looked her in the eye any more. "She died, wearing that machine."

The anito now knew that there was only one person Domingo referred to in that tone of voice. The human woman whose face she now wore.

Nur sighed, and massaged the seam where brass met flesh. "It wasn't the fault of the Auto-bird."

"You know that's not the point."

"For someone who went to great lengths to create a replica of his wife," Nur began, irritation seeping into her tone, "you've suddenly become damn allergic to anything that reminds you of her."

Domingo grit his teeth and slid his gaze to some unseen horizon, something the Carpenter did when he was being irrationally stubborn. It was something the anito had become familiar with.

This time though, after a deep breath, Domingo looked straight at her. The pain behind his eyes was muted, but still evident, and something about it made the anito distinctly uncomfortable.

"I'll give you your wings," he said. "In return, you'll let me erase your face."

The workshop was suddenly filled with the sound of wood on wood, the sound of cogs and gears echoing inside the anito's hollowed out wooden body as she rose to her full height. She wasn't sure what expression she was making with her borrowed face, but it was enough to make Domingo take a step back.

"You presume too—" the anito began, but a voice from outside the workshop unified everyone within it in a common panic.

"You'd better be in there, bunso," said Dominador Malong. The sound of a group of people traversing the cavern floor began to make its way into the workshop. "You and your little Moro friend."

Without even exchanging looks, the anito and the two humans sprung into action. Domingo quickly closed the anito's torso plate, which they'd had open for maintenance. The anito quickly took a standing position atop the pedestal, resuming the repose of the Carpenter's original carving. Still, to play it safe, Nur threw an opaque canvas over the anito's form, as some of their alterations to the wood would become immediately apparent from up close.

Dominador Malong seldom came down to the workshop, but she'd heard enough from beneath her flimsy camouflage to agree with Domingo's decision to keep her existence a secret, at least until she had been fully restored. From what she'd gathered from Dominador's visits, the war with the occupiers was not going well, and attempts to recreate the machines of other foreigners had been too costly. Each visit had seen the Carpenter's brother grow increasingly more agitated and impatient with Domingo's failure to find a cheaper way to replicate these Newcomen.

But today, Dominador had not arrived to speak to Domingo.

"You're coming with us, Moro," said Dominador.

The anito heard the sound of a struggle, and then that of a human crashing into one of the carving benches. Most likely someone who had tried to lay hands on Nur.

"You'll need more men, Dominador," said Nur.

"Are you insane?" Domingo's voice was high with outrage. "You're attacking a Çelebi of the Fleet of Wisdom!"

"Am I?" Domindaor's own voice was trembling with anger. "Ah yes, the same Fleet that, according to your friend here, sent word that they would no longer require me to send Pierre-Henri Leschot his granddaughter, as long as she was here to 'monitor' you. So imagine my surprise when I received a message from that very same Fleet this morning, telling me that they considered my refusal to return the child *and* my illegal *detention* of their Çelebi to be an act of aggression, and further—"

"Brother," Domingo began, but Dominador cut him off viciously.

"—and further, giving me an ultimatum, that if I do not send this child back with their messenger, immediately, the Fleet will give us no aid against the Spanish attack."

"Wait, slow down," said Domingo.

"What atta—" Nur began to ask, before a loud explosion shook the cavern, sending bits of rock and other debris raining down.

Dominador cursed loudly. "You three, grab the Moro. Domingo, bring your daughter."

"You can't seriously believe," Domingo said, in a low, dangerous voice. "That I'm going to bring my daughter out into a fire fight."

"You can't seriously believe I won't do it myself if I have... oh, by the Spanish God," Dominador said, as the sound of breaking wood heralded the failure of more of his men. Then the anito heard a strange sound, metal on metal. Cynthia began to wail. "Put down the blade, Nur, or I'll shoot my brother where he stands."

A beat of silence. "Go ahead," whispered Nur. "Never cared for him anyway."

"Don't insult my intelligence," replied Dominador. "And don't take another step. Blade down, I said! This is bigger than you, this is bigger than family. Your mutual stupidity has come at the worst possible time. Yesterday, I received confirmation that my negotiations have borne fruit—the British should be knocking on Manila's doors in a month. Don't you see? We can bring about the end of Spanish rule! But if we die here, then the Cause dies with us. And if you don't think I'd shoot anyone, even my brother, to keep that from happening y—"

But by then the anito had heard enough. With a lurch, she threw off the canvas, and, as Dominador's eyes widened in horror, she relieved him of his strange weapon, then hurled him into the cavern wall.

The anito turned quickly toward Nur, but the woman had already dealt with her two opponents, and was busy claiming their weapons for herself. "Cat's out of the bag," she said. "If Leschot has given the Spaniards the location of your little secret base, now's the time to take Cynthia and run."

"You may have another option," said the anito. She marched purposefully toward Dominador, who cowered away from her as if he saw his death in her wooden eyes.

"How many humans are in the occupier's force?"

"Wh-wha-wha..."

The anito let her wooden tongue flick out.

"How. Many. Invaders."

"Two... three ships... a-around four... four hundred men each..."

If they were on ships, the number of men didn't matter. The anito turned to the Carpenter.

"Give me my wings."

This time, his condition was different.

"Only if I come with you."

~*~

"A city."

"A city. Our city."

"And hers."

"And the squiggly grub's too."

"Seems irrational to think about the future when we're in the middle of a war."

"Dom. The future's the only thing worth going to war *for*."

~*~

"On your left."

"I have sharper eyes than you, Carpenter. I see them."

Anxious as he was over his first flight—his first battle—in over a year, and for the safety of Cynthia and Nur in the workshop far below them, Domingo couldn't help but marvel at the grace with which the anito operated the Auto-Bird. The anito's demand that she be able to fly with only her upper torso had cost them precious minutes as Nur jury-rigged the controls to allow solely for hand control, but after a short time acclimatizing herself to the controls, the anito flew better than Domingo ever had. Even better than Clarita had, he was forced to admit.

When he'd been a child, Domingo had heard stories of the manananggal, of the sort to frighten children—how they were demons that took the form of women, whose torsos flew off at night to devour infants with their monstrous tongues. He wondered how anyone could mistake the anito for a monster. He wondered what had happened, to cause them to inhabit the Molaui.

"Are you sure these weapons will work?" The anito pointed one of Nur's prototype rockets worryingly close to her face. Domingo resisted the urge to put some distance between them.

"If you want to suggest otherwise to Nur, go ahead," Domingo said. "As for me... there are no guarantees. They haven't been properly field tested yet, but that's why we won't fire them until we're right on top of our targets. Whatever problems there may be in the propulsion, each is full of old, dependable, gunpowder. Won't take much to set them off."

"You'll need to explain this 'powder' magic to me in more detail."

Domingo heard a chorus of cries rise up from the ships. "All you need to know is that 'powder magic' is about to shoot twenty-four pound iron balls at us right about... now."

Domingo and the anito veered away from each other as they dodged the canon shot, Domingo with a jerking zig-zag, and the anito with an aerial dance that would put eagles to shame. Slowly, but steadily, a smile grew on the anito's face, Clarita's face, and Domingo had to bite his lip hard.

Will you please loosen up? We're flying, Dom! We're flying!

"Quickly, while they're re-loading," he said, his voice rough. "I'll take the leftmost and you take the rightmost."

"Wait..."

"We don't have time!"

"Some of the men on those ships look like our people, Carpenter. Brown people."

For the first time, Domingo heard suspicion in the anito's tone. He chose his next words carefully, as Dominador would. "Most of their army is recruited here on the islands. Not all of us wish to be free of the leash, anito. That is their choice. But if they seek to keep the rest of us collared, they are unworthy of mercy."

"I'm not sure a warrior's words suit you, Carpenter."

"I'm—"

But the anito was already diving down toward her target, a strange cry issuing forth from her wooden lips. Domingo wondered how much panic her appearance would cause amongst the men, but he didn't have the time to watch. He could see that the crew of the ship he'd selected was already well into their reloading regimen. He'd have to survive another barrage before he was close enough to light his rocket.

Stop worrying so much. I'm here. We'll watch out for each other.

For the first time in a year, those remembered words didn't feel like a broken promise. Domingo cinched the straps of his Auto-Bird and swooped down at the Spanish ship with uncharacteristic abandon. Like the other two the Spanish had deployed against the Malong forces, it was a Rayo-class ship-of-the-line, with eighty guns total, including several of the modified obús that allowed the Spanish to bombard the Malong's island bases from long range. The ships were still far enough away that if they were sunk, the Spanish and their allies would be unable to continue toward the islands—at least not and be in any shape to fight. This was the time to strike.

The second barrage of fire shot toward Domingo just as he'd halved the distance between him and the ship. This close, the gap of time between the canon blasts and the arrival of the cannon balls was much shorter, so instead of zig-zagging, he retracted the Auto-Bird's wings and allowed himself to drop straight down. It was a maneuver that could only be done once before a wily foe took measures to vary the angles of their canons—but once was all he needed. As the final cannon ball soared over his head, Domingo unfurled the Auto-Bird's wings, and made his final approach.

He was within range of normal firearms now, but barring a very lucky—or unlucky—shot, he could take a hit and still continue with his mission. With one hand he took a rocket from its holster—one of two each that he and the anito had taken—and with the other, carefully, took a sulfur stick from a pouch. As he flew over the deck of the ship, Domingo lit the stick, then the fuse, and dropped the rocket straight down.

Domingo had already moved his attention to the middle ship when the explosion that ripped through his target sent him spiraling out of control. Desperately, he retracted his wings once more, waiting for the shockwave from the blast to wash over him before he again unfolded the delicate membranes. He'd expected Nur's weapons to be effective... but not quite that effective. If the anito and her wooden body were anywhere near a rocket when it went off...

As soon as he'd regained his equilibrium, Domingo looked toward the rightmost ship. Like his own target, it was aflame and sinking fast, but he saw no sign of the anito.

Stop worrying so much.

Domingo didn't have time to anyway. With two ships down, the crew of the final ship was taking no chances, varying their rate and angle of fire, and mixing cannonade and musket shots. Domingo managed to duck and weave his way to within striking distance when a bullet hit him in the hip—and more importantly, passed through the pouch containing his sulfur sticks, igniting them instantaneously. Cursing, he managed to fling the pouch into the sea—just as a cannonball struck his left wing.

Domingo landed hard on the deck of the ship, the frame of his Auto-Bird bearing the brunt of the impact, but also sending sharp pieces and splinters of wood into his flesh. He coughed blood, his ears ringing, struggling to free himself from the remains of the machine before the Spanish forces could finish him off. But his head was spinning, and his body didn't seem inclined to obey his instructions. He shook his head, trying to clear it, but all he succeeded in doing was blurring his vision as he saw the silhouettes of soldiers approaching him with drawn weapons.

I'm here.

An inhuman screech stopped the soldiers in their tracks, and blanketed the ship in an unnatural silence. Then... THUD. The eighty gun ship rocked as if it had been rammed by a whale.

THUD.

THUD!

KER-RACK!

Soldiers scattered as the deck of the ship buckled outward and up as something emerged from beneath, to hover between Domingo and the ship's crew. From behind, it took Domingo several moments to recognize the anito, so transfigured was her form. Wooden stalks extended from her segmented waist, writhing like tendrils from some creature of the deep. Her arms seemed unnaturally distended, as if the wood been distended on a rack, ending now in hooked claws where once there had been slender fingers. She was no longer even controlling the Auto-Bird, Domingo realized, at least, not with her hands. Instead, the wooden frame of the machine seemed to have somehow grafted itself to the anito's Molaui body, the wings responding to some mental command, stroking up and down like those of a monstrous bat.

One of the Spaniards made a break for the side of the ship, screaming. The anito turned, following his path with her eyes, and that's when Domingo saw that unlike the rest of her body, her face was, disconcertingly, unchanged.

That is, until she opened her mouth, and an undulating tongue shot out over four vara to spear the young man through the chest, just as he vaulted over the rail. For a moment, he just hung there, suspended on the anito's tongue, before a disinterested flick sent the corpse into the sea.

That was too much for the Spanish forces. A mad scramble overboard ensued, and this time the anito let them. Soon the upper deck was cleared.

Slowly, Domingo approached the anito. She watched him approach, chest heaving in a facsimile of breathing, her expression guarded.

I'll protect you.

"I lost my second rocket," she said, before he could speak. "I didn't know if this... if I could still take on this form. It was the only weapon I had left."

Domingo reached for one of the writhing tentacles, but it flinched away. Domingo looked into her eyes and held her gaze as he moved his hand back toward the tentacle. It was warm to the touch, pulsing, alive.

"Tell me there's more of you," he said.

Once more, she withdrew.

"And if there were? What would you have of us?"

Domingo looked out at the chain of islands that had served as the last refuge of the Cause. A place of pain, of desperation, of need. He thought of late night talks with Clarita. He thought of her father, watching, waiting. He thought of his daughter and how many times he'd almost lost her in one year alone.

"A city," he said.

For the second time, there was silence on the deck. Then, laughter, surprisingly deep and unrestrained.

"Now those... those are words which suit you, Carpenter," she said. The anito too looked out at the islands. Domingo wondered if she saw the same things he did. But whatever she saw, it seemed to please her, and Domingo realized that was enough.

"If you free the rest of my kind," the anito said, "many may choose to help you. Others, however, will ask for a price."

"And what's yours?"

She told him. And when the name left his mouth, a name as familiar and as different as the face she wore, they both knew that it was a natural fit.

The Unmaking of The Cuadro Amoroso

Kate Osias

The four of us found each other in the Facultad de Ciencias; four so very different people in our approach to scientific exploration, and yet the core of our passions so very much the same, that we bonded quickly and irrevocably.

There was Cristan, a gastronomist, with his distinctive arsenal of flavors made unique by the quintaesencia of nontraditional materials. There was Maren, a machinist, with her coiled toroid constructions which simplified and amplified the flow power in the galleon de cielos that adorned the skies. There was Hustino, a pianist, who sought elaborate melodic solutions to the mathematical theories embodied in the Cancion del Universo. And then there was me, a dancer, who aspired to defy the prescribed laws of fisica through self-augmentation and movement.

We were considered prodigies of our generation, young stars set on a trajectory to become greater than the esteemed catedraticos of the colonia, and thus we were accorded favors that our less-accomplished peers could only dream about, from workshops equipped with tools of our craft, casas that protected us from the prying eyes of contemporaries, to indulgent allowances for our sometimes volatile eccentricities. By day we would study and experiment and teach and learn and rail (against the finite nature of time, against the limitations of flesh, against the vast swaths of knowledge we had yet to conquer despite our superior intellect). At night, we would spend our remaining stores of energy in a mesh of limbs and tongues and moans, a careless prayer to motion and taste and sound and interlocking parts combining to become whole.

We pretended to comply with the conventions of the common, but beneath the glamour of our triumphs, inside a hidden sanctum where censorious eyes could not find us, we rebelled against the strictures imposed on us by the sons and daughters of la Madre Patria. And in our foolishness, we even gave our clandestine relationship a name: Cuadro Amoroso.

"Oh, Zolen. Could we have not selected something more sophisticated?" the ghost of Maren asks, as she drifts beside me on my right, appearing like a dark-skinned Madonna with her long, flowing hair.

"Nothing wrong with the name," the specter of Cristan says, as he floats to my left, the scent of spiced bread settling about him like a fragrant fog. "By twisting a popular idiom, we imply a question which is answered by the nomenclature itself."

"Says the man who convinced us to take it on in the first place." But Maren is laughing and Cristan laughs as well, as he has become less solemn in the afterlife, and they continue to talk and tease each other about names and choices and the questions we never really asked ourselves because it did not matter in the greater landscape of our emotions.

With deliberate strokes, I dab and smear and blend paint on my face, my focus seemingly centered on my reflection. But as Cristan and Maren punctuate their banter with laughter and flirtatious caresses, my copper-springed heart cannot help but rejoice, cannot help but break a little more. I hear them, but they are not truly there. They are wisps of memory, mere phantoms conjured to give me courage for what I have to do, for what I will do.

The glimmer of Hustino comes just as I complete my mask of pigment and dye, the pulsing lines beneath my skin well-concealed. Maren and Cristan welcome him with smiles, easily folding him into the embrace of their conversation. Despite my resolutions to ignore the apparitions, I take an unnecessary pause. When Hustino puts his hands on my shoulders, I close my eyes. Intoxicated by the smells and sounds of the past, I let myself sink deeper into the illusion of his fingers, his clever, elegant fingers, tapping a familiar sonata on my skin.

"Come, Zolen," he says, his voice resounding from deep within me. "It is time."

Soon, I say by leaning back against thin air, deeper into the mirage-Hustino's embrace. *Let me finish this*, as I draw Hustino's ghostly hands over the flesh that shields my copper-springed heart. *For us.*

I linger for one more moment. Then, I stand up and walk out the door to my final performance.

~*~

Our end began not with the unwitting discovery of our secret, but with music.

Hustino had just committed himself to unlocking the 27th

movement of the Cancion del Universo, a year after his debut performance of the Cancion's 32nd. The rest of us only had a fledgling understanding of the mathematics involved, but what we knew, what everyone knew, was that maestros spent entire lifetimes attempting to recreate a single part of the Great Song. Few succeeded; fewer still emerged triumphant with two movements under their belt. No one but the first Maestro Matematico—whose archaic musical notation was the basis for all modern interpretations of the Cancion—has been known to execute the impossibly complex piece in its entirety, and even then, the retellings of his performance had the sheen of myth rather than the clarity of fact.

Still, Hustino was Hustino. At eighteen, he had succeeded in solving the mathematical mysteries of the 32nd movement in front of the colonia's elite which included the Gobernador-General, her coterie of paramours and advisors and her small legion of guardia sibil; the embajadors of Tsina, Hindustan, Inglatera and Mejico, and their respective babel of translators; high-ranking doctors of faith from the rival Facultad de Certeza; and us, Cristan, Maren and myself, under the guise of like-minded peers to appease narrow-minded conservatives. The performance was widely acclaimed not just because of Hustino's age—although certainly that, in itself, was already a noteworthy accomplishment—but also because he had caused a rare and sought-after effect: the alma parpadear.

At the climactic crescendo (after the lengthy introductions, after several opening sonatas, after one loud cantata) every one of us who was then present—from the lowliest starch-collared bureaucrat to the bejeweled, acting sovereign of the colonia—felt a sharp shift in the ground beneath us, an internal trembling so intense that it seemed as if our hearts had ceased to beat and our minds had conceded all rational thought while our souls, our traitorous souls, in sublime accord, laid bare our most guarded, our most terrible of secrets to unite us with the music as it surged and swelled and assaulted and claimed and sundered and soothed and triumphed and faded and thundered again. When Hustino's performance finally ended—as it had to, eventually—we all were left feeling raw but cleansed.

An alma parpadear is a consequence of the Cancion done right, but no maestro, and especially not an aspiring one born in one of the colonias, would have attempted to affect so large a crowd. Hustino, being Hustino, explained the science afterward, when we had sufficiently recovered, when he had begun conversing again, when he had stopped wielding his genius through melody and when we, his audience, had been mollified by the realization that we remembered very little—and certainly none of the details—of our unwitting mathematics-driven confessionals.

"Resonant frequency, nothing more," he said, obviously pleased with the destruction he had wrought to our inner workings. "We all have our own unique internal frequency, but like all sound, it can be calibrated, adjusted, reset. The Cancion was written to unite people in a single wave. Theoretically, if you solve it and play it correctly, the music will create an encompassing language that is bereft of deceit and subterfuge; a language free of bias; a language to bind us all into one thought, one voice, one sound."

The carefully-worded invitations—written in florid script and invoking the beauty of the universe as preordained by the Arquitecto Sagrado—arrived shortly after Hustino announced his intention to work on the 27th movement.

Hustino, as was his wont, ignored them. Sound was an unforgiving mistress, and most of his days were spent analyzing velocity vectors, even going as far as abandoning his other fields of study. The catedraticos were lenient because of what Hustino had accomplished, even without the titular designation of maestro.

The missives, however, were less merciful, more insistent, as unrelenting as a noonday sun. With each letter unanswered, there was a proportionate increase in the rumors of heresy practiced within the walls of the Ciencias. Everyone knew the supplicants of Certeza perpetuated these false tales. Everyone knew that the malicious gossip would not stop until Hustino agreed to meet the doctors of faith.

It was an exceptionally humid night, the air thick with the promise of rains that would not come, when Cristan finally spoke out.

"Hustino. Can you not spare the time to meet with these self-aggrandizing fools? Perhaps they merely want you to play them a minuet; perhaps they merely want to congratulate you on your success. As it is now, they are taking your refusal as an insult to not just the healing arts, but also to the faith." Cristan stretched out past Maren to stroke Hustino's bare thigh, his fingertips grazing the sensitive inner part in a slow caress to take the sting out of his words. "Hearing them out can help relieve the tension."

We had just been reborn from the encompassing consumption of lovemaking, our skins gleaming with sweat, our eyes heavy-lidded. Despite our bodies' relaxed states, tension was quick to bloom, then twist out from Hustino. Connected as we were in a complex embrace, it was difficult to miss the pianist's discomfort.

"Now, now, my love, none of that," Maren said, smiling against Hustino's skin. "You know an encounter with the odious healers would be inevitable after your incredible success with the 32nd."

I concurred by letting my legs tangle with his, executing a gentler version of enganche to articulate my support while still arguing for the only rational course of action.

After a moment, Hustino laughed, effectively dispelling the awkward moment with his good-humored surrender. "Who am I to go against the will of the Cuadro Amoroso?" Then he turned to accept Cristan's open-mouthed kiss and I saw, from the way he shifted his shoulders to the way his muscles contracted, that he was no longer thinking about doctors and inconvenient invitations. No other discussion of the coherent sort occurred again that evening.

And so it was that Hustino took time away from calculating fractions of octaves to meet with the doctors of faith from the Facultad de Certeza. When he returned, he was irritably upset.

"They want to use the Cancion's alma parpadear to make sheep!" Hustino all but shouted. "The bastards are claiming the Arquitecto Sagrado wills it so. The fools."

Hustino plunged himself deeper into his craft, rebuffing all further requests from the good doctors, turning a deaf ear to the increasingly violent altercations that erupted between the students of science and faith. When he was not in his workshop testing the tonality of string, he was translating musical notations, transposing keys, trying out solutions that sounded bitter and dissonant. It was obvious to us that he was distressed, that there was an unpleasant aftertaste he was trying to wash out of his system with his work. Often, his raging emotions came out as furious, wood-breaking, paper-crumpling frustration; sometimes, it came out as genius, as he made considerable headway with the 27th by exploring musical avenues that he would have disregarded in more pleasant times.

Cristan, Maren, and I dealt with Hustino's ill-temper in our own inimitable ways. Cristan worked on constructing a modified ash-furnace that could distill not just ordinary ingredients, but metals as well, reflecting Hustino's determined efforts to build a set of ivory keys with perfect tonality. Maren, on the other hand, adjusted and dissected and tinkered with the coupling gaps of coiled transformers, as though Hustino's manic compulsions to measure and re-measure amplitude against frequency fed her own. While I, who trafficked in the unspoken, who was fascinated by the pianist's frenetic grace, attempted to interpret Hustino's motions by adjusting the kinematic chains on my arms and legs, loosening certain joints for a certain degree of freedom, imposing a slider where it was unexpected, to better mimic abrupt movement.

Before Hustino's encounter with the doctors could blend into a harmless, blurred memory, colorfully-attired dignitaries of various origins began to visit, carrying with them their strange accents and their strange smells and their strange tributes, tainting the quality of the air in Hustino's workshop even long after they had left and their offerings been thrown away. Hustino refused to meet with any of the embajadors, regardless of their representatives' nuanced greetings or the exquisite detail of their gifts. During this period, the import and export of goods with the colonia's neighbors became more restrictive, more bureaucratic. Everyone believed that the so-called friends of la Madre Patria were the cause of the sudden difficulty in trade. Everyone believed that Hustino alone had the power to appease.

A storm was spewing large, angry raindrops outside when Maren broached the subject.

"Oh, Hustino. The embajadors are silly inconveniences, are they not? But we may wish to travel to their lands someday, to see their sun, to see the way their stars glisten in their skies, to feel their winds that make their features so," Maren said, punctuating her words with feather-light kisses down Hustino's neck. "What harm can a courtesy call do?"

It had been an exhausting day for all of us, and the night had almost yielded us nothing in terms of gratification, as our usual foreplay did little to whet our appetites. Eventually, however, like tightly-coiled spring that was suddenly unwound, we found a release so intense we were left bone-weary and empty. Collapsed as we were in our last configuration—with me and Maren draped over the torsos of the men—it was easy for us to sense Hustino's immediate resistance.

"Do not say no without considering the resources we may not have access to," Cristan, always the serious one, said. "The best ebony cannot, unfortunately, be found in the colonia."

I stated my case by letting my palm glide down from Hustino's chest to his hip bone and up again, a torturously slow caricia that tells him that he was free to do as he would, but there were consequences he had to be aware of.

Hustino drew a deep breath, then slowly exhaled it. "Anything for the Cuadro Amoroso," he said, smiling tenderly as he brushed a wayward wisp of hair away from Maren's face. When he settled his weight more deeply into the bed, I knew that he had already forgiven us for our meddling.

And so it was that Hustino took time away from projecting the undertone blend of key musical sequences to meet with the each of the embajadors in their marbled palaces. When he came back from his forced tour of the houses of Tsina, Hindustan, Inglatera and Mejico, he was deeply troubled.

"Weapons," Hustino said, almost tonelessly. "They want to make a weapon out of the Cancion. They did not believe me when I said— and will say—no to all of them. They are thinking of nothing but war."

Hustino turned further inward, eschewing company that was not absolutely necessary for his work, completing his transformation into an irritable recluse who cared little for the complaints sounded by local and foreign merchants, or for the palpable animosity between the students of Certeza and Ciencia. His mental anguish inevitably rippled its effect outward to us, but where his creative endeavors suffered, ours thrived.

Cristan used his refashioned ash-furnaces to distill the quintaesencia of gold, which he further laced with the calx of wine, letting the precious metal's subtle tones elevate the addictive qualities of the alcohol, even as Hustino reverted to previously mastered scales. Maren constructed a galleon de cielo large enough to carry four, a steamless beast made of wood and metal, powered by dynamos and an apparatus of coils that transmitted blue pulses from one end to the other, even as Hustino wrote and rewrote rudimentary harmonic equations. I began performing the choreography Hustino inspired, my movements harsh one moment, smooth and languid the next, and pained, always, always pained, because creativity was an agonizing exercise of loneliness, even as Hustino diminished in mass and in spirit, becoming a frail approximation of the man he once was.

We did our best to bring joy back to our Hustino, but despite tasting Cristan's blissful concoctions sprinkled with gilded wine, despite riding on Maren's steamless galleon, despite seeing so many weep at my depiction of his artistry, the pianist remained inconsolable.

We were converged in our secret retreat, letting the cool breeze tinted with hymns and carols do what it could to soothe the red slashes on our skins, when I finally articulated my thoughts.

Hustino, I said by caressing the pianist's waist with my leg, a simple piernazo to call his attention and to prepare him for the rest of what I had to say. *The Gobernador-General herself will ask something from you. You will not like it.* I execute a gancho by hooking my leg around his thigh, then slowly letting it slide in a graceful lustrada, expressing through the trap and release motion the truth of our situation.

Say yes, I begged by pulling him into a closer embrace, *or, if you are truly unwilling, let us escape. Let us find a new beginning away from here.*

Hustino had not been Hustino for weeks, and the tenor of our nightly carnal pursuits had changed in the absence of the man we knew. It had become more violent, his expression of the act almost cruel, often brutal, sometimes unbearably vicious. But there was still sexual satisfaction, even a painful variant of pleasure. But perhaps the most important reward occurred afterward, when the ropes had been untied, when the whips had been set aside, when the gags had been thrown away, and Hustino returned to being Hustino, all the anger drained out of him, leaving only a pensive type of tenderness. It was the unguarded look in his face, along with the loving way he caressed the welts on my wrists, that gave me courage to speak.

But Hustino's answer was as adamant, as immovable, as unyielding as the grave, and it was immediate.

"No," Hustino said, as he turned away from me.

"Hustino, perhaps you do not completely understand—" Cristan began.

"I understand." Hustino stood up. "I understand perfectly."

"My love, please—"

"In this, the Cuadro Amoroso has no say." And then, he left.

The guardia sibil came for Hustino the next day. Dangerous-looking, heavy-coated men with their elaborate swords and oversized pistols, they knocked on Hustino's door, parroted the command of the Gobernador-General, and asked him to accompany them to an undisclosed location. Hustino did not struggle; instead, he relented with the grace of a doomed man. And we, purportedly the ones who loved him the most, could only watch from our respective windows, unable to help, unable to stop them, unable to do anything but wish things had gone differently.

Hustino was gone for seven days; when he was returned, he was barely alive.

We did our best to medicate him, but though Cristan distilled the healing essences of herbs; though Maren revived his heart numerous times with sparked coils; though I added mechanical joints and replaced broken bone with sturdy metal, there was not much improvement in Hustino's condition. We were scientists, not doctors, and the sum of our brilliance could not equal the healing arts practiced by the faithful. And if there were lore in the neighboring powers that could have helped in Hustino's recuperation, those doors were closed to us as well.

In the end, all we could do was stand vigil.

How I wished Hustino could have spoken; how I re-imagined those times to be filled with tender goodbyes or sunset-tinged rememberings instead of mournful quietude. But Hustino was unable to express anything in words, and his fingers were too irreparably broken to express his horrors in music. Whatever the Gobernador-General had the guardia sibil do to him, it was, in many ways, worse than immediate death. It was as if Hustino had gone through the antithesis of an alma parpadear where, instead of being united into a greater thought and a grander dream, he was instead disassembled and methodically dismantled, until his heart was just a cluster of malfunctioning valves, his mind a maze of shadows and nightmares, and his soul a tattered assembly of memories. Near the end of his days, Hustino became increasingly silent, worryingly still, as if his core had drifted into a vacuum where no sound could exist, terribly alone, terribly beyond our reach.

When he died, Cristan, Maren and I began to plan.

~*~

The first part of the scheme was all about me, because I needed both their expertise, because I was unsure as to how to go about it, because for all my self-surgeries, I had never attempted to change any vital organs with artificial ones and was thus less confident of my recovery rate.

The second part was Cristan, partly because he was impatient, and partly because his was the easiest to execute. Poison required only the most basic alchemy. The real challenge was in being able to outwit the doctors of faith, for once symptoms started to show, it would just be a simple exercise of their arts to heal themselves.

Instead of crafting fast-acting venom, as other deviants had done in the past with varying degrees of success, Cristan chose to go slow. The quintaesencia of lead tasted sweet, or so Cristan told us. It was only detectable when it was too late, when the metal had rooted itself deeply into the bones, when the abdominal pains had already gone past excruciating, when the dementia had taken hold.

And so it was that during the celebration of Eostre, Cristan delivered several boxes of fragrant rice cakes to the good doctors as an offering to the Arquitecto Sagrado.

Then, he waited.

We were not fools enough to believe that we would not be caught, for certainly if we were geniuses in our fields, there must be corresponding intellects of the same degree working as guardias or as doctors or as detectives. But Cristan had wanted to see if his mad plan would work; he wanted to revel in the chaos it would cause. And so it was not until three weeks later, just hours before the detectives had solved the mystery of the dancing demented doctors, that he took his own life using the most traditional of poisons: arsenic.

As a parting gift, Cristan created a sumptuous feast for the detectives who would barge into his casa to arrest him. Survivors would later inadequately describe the majesty of the assembled towers, made of spun sugar, marzipan and confectioner's paste, generously gilded with silver and gold and lead and powdered wine; they would use ill-fitting words to articulate the tantalizing scents of the ornately plated cakes and tarts and pies, mysteriously still warm as if Cristan had just taken them out of the ovens moments before they arrived; they would ineptly recount their despair at taking one bite, then another, and another, unable to stop, unable to deny the orgasmic glory that came with tasting each perfectly crafted gastronomical delight.

Only those of the weakest constitutions died; many survived the ordeal, only to be haunted by a craving Cristan alone could satisfy.

The detectives were persuaded, with the help of a carefully crafted letter echoing the sentiment of heretics, that radical thought served as motivation for Cristan's crimes. Thus, the Cucinero Peligroso, as Cristan would later be called, enjoyed the reputation of being a deviant in the eyes of the colonia and a martyr among revolutionaries.

~*~

The third part of the plan was Maren.

Her challenge was to be able to gather the embajadors in one area, when the resulting economic bullying had forced these officials to be at odds with not only the colonia, but each other. To accomplish this nearly impossible feat, she took her small galleon to the road.

At first, only a few of our peers, mostly catedraticos who thought kindly of her and her flirtatious smiles, came and listened. But as her invention took flight, as more people saw the flow of currents inside Maren's metallic beast, as more of the citizenry began to experience firsthand how it was to ride a ship without steam, more important members of society began to take notice.

It was during the monsoon season that she was finally able to attract the attention of the embajadors, who all came en masse because of their fear of being outdone by the other. By then, Maren had mastered the art of presentation, adding exciting flourishes and embellishments to what should have been a simple, scientific lecture. The most awaited moment of her demonstration had ceased to be the galleon de cielo itself, but rather Maren, beautifully attired with long flowing hair, entering a metal cage which was then subsequently charged with large volts of lightning from her coiled constructions.

"Esteemed guests, see how the bolts arc outside this metal compartment but leave me, inside it, unharmed? Earlier, I showed you how a small amount of current was sufficient to fry an egg. Yet here I am, perfectly well, and conversing with the distinguished gentlemen and beauteous ladies with nary a burn," Maren would say, as she manipulated her inventions from within. "This is why, despite the metal casings of my galleon, despite the massive amounts of current it will need, it can and will carry its passengers safely to their destinations. It will be different matter, however, if my device was not used. Why, it is more dangerous than any known weapons la Madre Patria has been able to develop." At this point, Maren would extend a hand to her captivated audience. "Now please, come closer, see for yourselves how harmless it is."

I was not at her last presentation, but I have often imagined how silly the embajadors must have looked as they approached the lightning cage; how their eyes must have widened with greed being so close to something so powerful; how exquisite Maren's smile must have been as she switched off the mechanism that controlled the electrical charges; how chaotically beautiful everyone must have appeared, limned in metal-tinged blue, stripped of their artifice and their false etiquette and their elegant veneers, unable to flee, unable to find respite, unable to go beyond the reach of arcing volts and coruscating electricity and instead, were redeemed, and at the same time, reduced through Maren's act to being a mere component of an all-consuming force.

The detectives concluded, not convincingly, that it was an accident; an unfortunate accident that took the lives of the ambassadors of Tsina, Hindustan, Inglatera and Mejico, their babel of translators, and the promising machinist who would go down in history as Senora el Relampago, the Lightning Lady.

~*~

I am the last bolt to slide in place, the last piece on the puzzle of revenge. It took me months to recover; a year to rebuild my reputation as a dancer of note; a couple more pass before I finally piqued the interest of my target.

My challenge is to murder the acting sovereign of the colonia. The Gobernador-General is protected by guardia sibil, some of who have their own augmented limbs, to enable a more effective defense. The key is to do something no one has done before, to truly rebel against the laws of fisica, to fly higher, move faster, so that I may be able to penetrate the wall of men and women that surround the Gobernador. To do that, I need power.

The copper-springed heart was my idea, but I needed Maren to build the mechanism that would operate it, and I needed Cristan to distill me the medication I would need to survive the transplant. We knew there was a possibility it would not work; we knew I could die for, just as with Hustino, we were merely mimicking the healing arts.

But my body proved once again its resilience. It accepted the change and became stronger for it. And if cerulean pulsing lines often appear under my skin, and if I hear the whirring sound of turbines instead of the steady thrum of a heartbeat, and if I see phantoms of my dead lovers conversing, laughing, asking me to come with them, all of these combined is still a small price to pay for what, in turn, I am able to do.

I see Cristan and Maren and Hustino take their imaginary seats among the selected guests invited to the Gobernador-General's soiree. The audience is small, even accounting for the guardia sibil, the stage they allotted me, large. In my starting position on the raised platform, the endless opportunity of space beckons to me, calling to me to fill its emptiness with the caress of my arms, the harsh flicks of my feet. I delve deep within myself to stay still. Only when the melancholy music begins do I move.

I drag one leg, then the other, in time with the subtle base, tapping my foot lightly on the wood, letting the exhausted sadness of my movements flavor the ambient energy. At the unexpected melodic crescendo, I execute a sharp roto trasero then proceed to a slow slide, as if the harsh interruption never happened.

I am lost, I tell the audience as I interrupt the sway of my hips with a jump and twist in midair. *I am broken*, I say as I harshly stop the gentle flutter of my arms with a drop on the floor. And I repeat this again, and again, with broken salidas, and disrupted ochos, and a sudden stop to a languorous pirouette.

When the music fades I begin to turn.

The 360-degree rotations of girasoles encadenados require balance and concentration, but it is my copper-springed heart and not my mind that holds me steady. I am reliving the last years again, temporarily immune to friction and gravity and the failings of mechanical joints and mortal limbs, free to dwell on images of Hustino, laughing as he explained the alma parpadear, and Cristan as he served his decadent flavorful masterpieces, and Maren, as she navigated the winds in her marvelous, powerful galleon. With each completed revolution, with each spin that defies the laws of fisica with its almost infinite source of angular momentum, I feel the stress inside me building, growing, increasing to the point of sublime pain, until the images themselves cease to be illusions, but take on weight and mass and volume (and texture and scent and sound) so that I am surrounded by the Cuadro Amorso, turning to the music of a thousand precious memories, even as a miniscule part of my artificial heart loses its place, leaving a dynamo to course its power without a circuit, intensifying the pain a hundredfold and momentarily blinding me, until finally, eventually, inevitably I stumble to a halt.

And my chest explodes.

My last image is of my heart, impossibly slow to my eyes, traveling a straight line toward the Gobernador-General, to its unavoidable end.

Working Woman

Olivia Ho

It was about three o'clock in the afternoon when the hearse ran away.

This was one of Singapore's very hot days, when the heat sat in thick layers upon the dust of the streets and people moved as slowly as they could so as not to attract its attention. The hearse, one of the newer auto models, had been moving slowly. One moment it was trundling demurely along in the funeral procession, puffing gently; the next, it was shrieking down Victoria Street trailing clouds of steam and bruised mourners in its wake. A yawning fissure in the road skewed it a sharp left, and it ploughed through streets of terrified carpet merchants and songkok makers. Nobody tried to stop it, of course; any engine on wheels was liable to explode these days, and hearses were particularly contentious since the health of their passengers was no longer a standing issue. Instead, the runaway hearse went on gaining speed and losing pursuit, shedding flowers and tassels, until it crashed to a stop in the Malay cemetery.

By the time the funeral party caught up, the hearse was lying on its side, gaping, empty. The mourners looked to their leader, who swore violently in Cantonese, paused for breath and added, "It can't have gone far."

"No," said another, "it's a body."

Still panting, their leader surveyed the wreckage of the hearse, the gathering crowd, the growing unease that traditionally followed the incursion of large groups of Chinese men into a Malay neighbourhood. How long did they have before the police showed up and started asking difficult questions? He weighed his options.

The hearse solved this dilemma for him by emitting an ominous whistling noise, and then blowing up.

The ensuing chaos meant that nobody noticed when, a few streets away, a door flew open, a dish smashed and a woman screamed.

~*~

"Weapons," said the man at the door.

Ning Lam raised an eyebrow. She pushed her loose braid back

over her shoulder, reached inside her paper cone of kacang puteh and popped a boiled chickpea into her mouth. This she chewed deliberately.

"Weapons," growled the guard again. "You're not going in to see the old man armed to the teeth. And throw away that stupid snack."

Ning rolled her one good eye. The other merely clicked in her head, a gleaming clockwork eyeball, and remained pointing straight at the guard, a trick that most found disconcerting. Indeed, the man almost flinched, only just catching himself. Ning winked at him with the good eye, unclipped her butterfly knives from her belt and laid them on the table, followed by two boxes of bolts. From her back, she unstrapped her crossbow. 'This I'm keeping,' she added, waving the kacang puteh.

The man made an ill-advised grab for it. Ning tossed the paper cone to her left hand; with her right, she grabbed the oncoming fingers and twisted them halfway around. The man let out a yelp. Ning released him and strode past, fishing in the cone for roasted nuts.

She heard him spit in the doorway after her retreating back. "Fucking hybrid."

Ning made her way across the gambling floor, past yelling men in singlets jostling elbows with bored housewives at the chap ji kee tables and the brassy new slot machines. The room beyond was dim and low-ceilinged; she had to stoop as she picked her way across the mess of thin copper pipes that snaked across the floor and curled up besides the shadowy figures lying prostrate on low bunks, sucking dreamily at the opium smoke flowering from the gutta-percha mouths of the pipes. Down another corridor, another man standing guard at the end. This one asked no questions, merely looked her up and down in her coolie trousers and her dirty kebaya that was once a light green, now loose and unbuttoned over a samfoo top. He held back the red beaded curtain for her to step through, saying as he did, "Miss Ning, Grandfather."

"You are early, Miss Ning," said the head of the kongsi. "If you will excuse me my unfinished business, I will be with you in a moment."

He turned back to the table he was examining. On the table lay a carved tray carrying thirty or so fingers. Some of the fingers had gold rings on them and some had long scars. None was from the same hand. Ning popped kacang puteh into her mouth, discovered it was a dried pea and spat it out.

"Make sure you wrap them nicely before they go to Penang," Grandfather said to the waiting men. "I want the Hakka scum who fester there to be able to tell which is whose. Let them think twice before they interfere with our shipments again. Not that one," he added, pointing at a finger in the corner which had had its nail gnawed something dreadful. "That one is from Eng Siok, whom I once thought of as a son. Send it to his family in Keong Saik, to show them he has spit on our sacred oaths. Perhaps it will help them remember to whom their allegiance is owed."

The tray of fingers was whisked away, replaced by two cups of steaming tea. "Forgive me the display, Miss Ning," said Grandfather. "It is distasteful. I am but a humble businessman, trying to help my people get by. Unfortunately this makes me enemies, and they have— shall I say—forced my hand."

Ning crumpled up the empty paper cone and sat down. "Longjing," she remarked of the tea. "You honour me, Grandfather."

"I have it shipped straight from Zhejiang," replied Grandfather. "You have a good nose for teas, Miss Ning."

"I have a good nose for many things." Ning picked up the teacup, passed it delicately back and forth beneath her nose.

"So we hear." Grandfather did the same. "We have need of such a skill now. There is a missing woman. Chinese, tall, heavily scarred about the body; you'll know her when you see her. She was last seen near Kandahar Street."

"Ah," said Ning. That explained some things. She was fluent in Malay and familiar with the Kampong Glam area; few in the kongsi could lay claim to either. "That hearse business, that was your doing."

Grandfather raised an eyebrow. "Quick of you, Miss Ning. Yes. The hearse was ours."

"Now I don't pretend to be an expert on hearses," went on Ning, "but usually the folk inside them, they're dead."

"Shut your mouth!" came a voice from the back of the room. "No more of your lip to Grandfather, hybrid."

Ning glanced at the man hunched in the shadows. Chee the Younger, Grandfather's great-nephew, slouched on a stool picking his nails with a pocketknife. "Someone's touchy," she mused. "Let me guess. The hearse was your idea. Takes a genius brain like yours to balls up an errand that simple. But what do I know, I'm just a simple working girl."

Chee leapt off his stool, came into the light. "Grandfather, I've said it already, there's no need to bring in outsiders on our business, let alone a half-woman with no clan to her name, I said—"

Grandfather slammed his fist down on the table. The teacups sloshed. "You've said enough, is what you've said! I've lost enough men on this fool's venture." He sighed heavily. "Bringing all these machines into the business. It'll be the downfall of us all. In the old days you threw an axe at a white man and he went away. None of this mechanical devil-shit."

Ning sipped her tea and did not point out that throwing the axe at the British head of the Chinese Protectorate had indirectly resulted in the violent crackdown on the Chinese secret societies, under which business had suffered since. Eventually Grandfather continued. "The woman you are to look for is not...all flesh."

"A hybrid, then."

"So to speak." Grandfather paused, then added, "More hybrid, in fact, than anyone you will ever have seen."

"Where'd you take her from?"

"None of your business," growled Chee.

"It is my business," retorted Ning, "because whoever that was, they're going to want her back. And I need to know if they'll get in my way."

Grandfather said, "She was government property."

Ning whistled. "Cheeky. You know I charge extra for tangling with British."

"You'll be paid for your time," snapped Grandfather. "And for your discretion. If you are compromised, nothing is to come back to us."

"What do you want her for, anyway?" Ning demanded. "If she's got that much gear in her, there's not a decent engineer in Chinatown who'll know how to sort out her insides."

"Now *that*," said Grandfather, "is none of your business. Deliver her, that's all you're to do."

Ning held her tongue. It was not hard to envision what the kongsi might want with a top-secret government experiment. The British crackdown had significantly crippled their activity; they were still searching for ways to hit back. Even if they didn't know what to do with their prize, holding it ransom would deal enough of a blow to the government.

"We'll expect to hear from you daily," Grandfather went on. "I like to know what I'm paying for. And I don't enjoy being kept waiting."

He traced idly with his finger a pattern in the table's wood where years of scrubbing had evidently failed to remove the bloodstains from the grain. "Naturally," said Ning. "I am very prompt."

"I should hope so," said Grandfather. "Bring the woman. You'll get your money then."

"I'll need some advance," pointed out Ning. "Information costs."

Grandfather paused, then motioned irritably. Chee came forward grudgingly with an envelope, which he dropped on the table before her.

"She likes the feel of money, I bet," he sneered. "Of course, a girl who's been sold for silver would know about that kind of thing."

Ning said nothing. Grandfather coughed and said, "Thank you for your time, Miss Ning. We'll be hearing from you."

Ning said, "Thank you for the tea," picked up the envelope and walked out. She walked past the dreaming smokers, through the hot noise of the gambling room, out into a street full of early monsoon rain.

~*~

Khairunnisa ran downstairs. She locked and barred the shop door. She did the same to the back door in the kitchen. She drew all the curtains.

There was a crash upstairs. Khairunnisa paused, then made herself turn and climb the stairs.

Khairunnisa's life had not been very exciting since the event of her widowing. Nor had it been before that, but at least having a husband to talk to from time to time made things less monotonous, even if they had not quite succeeded in transcending social awkwardness in the one and a half years of their arranged marriage. This was punctuated by two surprises: first, when an ornihopter fell out of the sky in Batavia and hit, of all people, her husband trying to cross the street to a toy convention; second, when he left her the house and the toy shop in his will despite the simmering unhappiness of his family and hers. Still, she had been better at it than he had ever been. She made beautiful things, and they always worked. So she shut herself up in the workshop while people talked, about her living alone and running her husband's business without a thought for his family; she made it so she could not hear them over the whirring of the gears and the tinkling of the music boxes. And the children loved what she made, and people would come from the ends of the island to Bussorah Street for her clockwork Javanese dancers and wayang singers, her tiny motorcars and rickshaw robots, her intricate mobile of glittering tin dirigibles floating lazily in circles on an engine she promised would last three years on guarantee. And it had been all very nice and calm, until a crazy Chinese woman had come in through her back door, covered in blood and raving in a language she could not understand.

The woman was thrashing in the corner of the workshop where Khairunnisa had left her. "No, please be still," begged Khairunnisa, "someone will hear, I don't think you're even supposed to be here." The woman stared at her, not understanding. She was immense, Khairunnisa realized, hulking shoulders, had to be nearly two metres tall. She wore odd clothes, dark blue and ill-fitting, torn in places through which Khairunnisa glimpsed scars lying thick on her flesh. She began shouting in what was definitely not Malay, but did not sound like Chinese either. Against all odds, it sounded like English.

Khairunnisa tried to make hand gestures to be quiet, which seemed to work until she realized the woman had been pacified not by her hands but by the sight of the Javanese dancer on the workbench, slowly articulating its feet in neat patterns, gently wobbling its elaborate gold foil headdress. "You like that?" said Khairunnisa, relieved. "I have lots. Here, look!" She wound up more dancers, which moved their arms and flexed delicate, shining fingers in uncanny synchrony. The woman was fascinated at first, but then her face clenched and she started to shudder. Her own fingers twitched in something like horror and she began to mutter, to point at Khairunnisa and the dancers and to claw at her own throat. "Please, what do you want," begged Khairunnisa, "I can't understand you, I *can't*—"

The back of the woman's neck had begun to run blood again. There was a nasty open wound on the back of her head, which Khairunnisa could not bring herself to look at. But now she glimpsed something flashing inside the pulped flesh, heard a familiar whirr and click beneath the incomprehensible cries. "Shhh," she said, approaching slowly, trying to get behind the woman without her noticing. She had to stand on tiptoe to reach the wound. "Shhh," she said again, and the woman made a confused expression halfway between a smile and a wince, as Khairunnisa reached deftly inside the wound, found what she knew had been there all along and pulled it, hard.

The woman collapsed onto her, heavy, something she had not been expecting. Blood pumped from the wound onto Khairunnisa's face. She was looking up, into the intricate mess of wheels and discs inside the woman's head, nestled tightly within her living flesh. Khairunnisa thought briefly of her dolls. But this was so much more.

~*~

The smell of food awakened her. Someone was in the room, singing softly, snatches of some song about an old bird. She forced her eyes open and saw the singing woman crouched at a low table, laying out dishes.

"You're awake!" The woman put the food down and came over to her; she flinched, and the woman paused, then got down on her knees and put out her hand tentatively. After a while she allowed the woman to edge closer, touch her face, feel the back of her neck. "Is there pain? Can you hear me?"

"No," she heard herself say. "No pain."

"I reconfigured the language punch-cards in your head." The words made no sense. "I didn't understand anything you wanted, I was worried. Your punch-card was in English for some reason, but luckily I had a Malay sample I was trying out on some of the dolls. It's not very developed, there are lots of things you still won't understand."

"There's something else I should be speaking. Some other tongue."

The other woman looked away sadly. "Chinese, yes. Or your home dialect. I don't know. It was overwritten when they programmed you, I think. I'm sorry."

Overwritten?

"My name is Khairunnisa," continued the other, rising and moving over to the table. "Or Nisa, if you want. Yours?"

She shook her head. "Don't know."

"I feared so." Khairunnisa knelt by the table and beckoned. "I got us some food from the padang stall. Lucky they were still open. I thought you might be hungry, you slept so long after I fixed your head."

Nothing made sense still, but the food smelled better than anything she could remember eating. Not that she could remember eating, or remember anything. Khairunnisa pointed out chicken rendang, jackfruit curry, vegetables in coconut milk. Uncertain, she tried to copy Khairunnisa eating expertly with her right hand.

"You don't remember where you came from? Who you are?"

She thought hard, trying to get a grip on a slithery chunk of unripe jackfruit. "I was in a box. Moving. I was trying to get out."

"A hearse crashed into the cemetery near here," said Khairunnisa. "I think you were in it. But why they were taking you to be buried I don't know. You're not dead. You can't...I don't think you would die in the normal way."

"I'm like them." She pointed at the clockwork toys that watched them eat from the bench. "Inside."

"No," said Khairunnisa. "You're better than them. You're better than anything I've ever seen. I don't know, of course, I haven't really looked inside you. But you're talking to me. You're eating my food. I don't know if you're a living person whose inside has been entirely replaced by clockwork organs, or if you're a machine who somehow does living people things. Or both. It's incredible. Have you tried the sayur lodeh?"

"You knew how to fix me."

Khairunnisa shrugged. "It was simpler than I thought. These things make sense to me—more than words, or numbers, or cooking—gears always speak the same language."

"If I sleep tonight will you fix me again?"

"Do you want me to?"

She thought about it. "If somebody has to open me up, better it's you. But I don't like it."

"Then I won't fix you unless I have to," said Khairunnisa, getting up. "I'll have to open your sternum to load some coal in, but that won't be for a while, and anyway I can teach you so you can do it yourself."

"Thank you," she said. "Thank you, Nisa. For this."

Khairunnisa laughed lightly. "It's nothing. You can sleep in here. I'll get a mat."

She waited alone before the food-stained dishes and the silent toys. A bottle of red saga seeds on the windowsill kept catching her eye. The colour reminded her of something, she just could not think what.

~*~

Ning did not enjoy speaking Malay. She had been forced to learn Baba Malay during her years of bondage in a Peranakan house; it had been over a decade since, but the sound of it still left the taste of beatings in her mouth. However, the language was now part of her stock-in-trade, and here in Kampong Glam she chatted up perfume-sellers, shisha smokers, anyone who might have seen a six-foot-tall Chinese woman with scars running around after the hearse crash. People were hesitant towards this uncanny woman with one eye, for all she might joke about in their tongue, but Ning was known to some and charming to others, and above all assured money under the counter for the good stuff. The old men at the teashop had maybe seen one such woman heading for Bussorah Street, though as they had been afternoon-sleepy they could not say which household she had graced. The owner of the Sufi bookstore on Bussorah allowed that perhaps some screaming had been heard from the shophouse of the late toymaker Al-Jazari, may Allah rest his soul in peace. A sweeper at the nasi padang stall on the corner recalled the widow Al-Jazari making a late-night trip to their premises to buy food for two. "But what to expect, her living alone like that?" she lamented to Ning.

"Bound to be trouble sooner or later. You know what I mean?"

Ning watched the toy shop, waited till dusk when she would be less visible, and then did a little climbing until she sat straddling the roof of the Al-Jazari domicile. Delicately, she reached up and pushed two fingertips into her right eye, her fingernails found the faint grooves in the glassy surface above the irises. With a pop, the eye came loose from her head.

From her waist pouch, Ning pulled a device that seemed to be composed of multiple tiny abaci. The first two rows she deftly manipulated with a hairpin; this set the rest of the wooden beads snapping into motion of their own accord. With the same hairpin, she pried open a panel on the bottom of the eyeball and flipped a few minuscule levers, then replaced the panel and dropped the eye in the roof gutter.

The eye began to roll. It rolled along the gutter and dropped down onto the parapet below, where it swivelled rapidly to regain its balance. From there it rolled on industriously out of sight.

Ning got off the roof and went round the corner to the drinks stall, where she sat drinking black coffee for an hour.

Then she strolled back to a grassy patch near the Al-Jazari house, where the eye lay, slightly grimy.

Ning polished it on her blouse. Then she sat down, braced her back against a tree for good measure, and pushed the eye back into its socket.

The kickback nearly floored her. Her back arched from the shock of it, as volleys of images jittered through her brain, an hour's memory registered in a second. Ning tried to ignore the resultant headache, piecing together what the eye had seen on its reconnaissance.

"Oh yes," she said aloud, to the eyeball if nobody else. "That's the house."

~*~

The women get up at four in the morning to walk to the fields. The road is not well-made, but their feet are hard and they no longer feel it when the cracks bleed. When the sun rises, they are already hauling rock, shovelling coal, watching the great machines as they hiss and pummel the earth and vent columns of steam into the grey, humid dawn.

These are the dirigible fields of Changi. Vaster yet than anything the island has raised from its virgin swamps. Every day they call for more workers, more hands, and the fields seethe with blackened figures roaring work commands in half a dozen dialects. Among these masses, the women always know each other by the red headdresses they wear, bobbing brightly here and there across the treacherous walkways like saga seeds in the mud.

The oldest among them is well over fifty, the youngest just shy of her sixteenth birthday. Still unused to balancing her yoke while navigating the flimsy walkways, she stumbles sometimes, little Chai Sum, and the others watch her like hawks because if one falls, they all fall.

They only stop once, at mid-day, when the sun beats down so hot it seems to blister the very soot flakes as they cloud the thick air. Over their lunches of rice and pickles, they chat—about home, mostly, about the seven younger siblings Yip Soh left in her village, who she needs to send money to this week. About the unreliability of men: Man Lai, as usual, bares her bicep to show the burn scars from where her husband struck her with a boiling kettle, after which she fought her way onto a slow boat for the Straits of Malacca and never looked back. About the machines, how they get bigger every day, how they eat more coal. "If they keep bringing more in we'll be out of a job," grumbles Cheuk San. Yuk Hong, the tallest and broadest among them at over six feet, laughs. "They'll never get in machines that work faster or better than us. They'll have to keep paying us for all the crap they need done." Ah Lei, the oldest and their de facto leader, does not laugh with the rest of them. "I don't trust them, those machines. I hear they had an accident in Field Five the other day. Valve blew on a pumping engine. The men on the platform with it, their own mothers couldn't recognize them now if they brought them over from the old country to sort the bits that are left."

The women finish their meals, fill their bowls with water and slurp them clean so that they don't leave a single grain uneaten in the bowl. They tighten the straps on their sandals, patched together from old car tyres, and head back to work. Today they are carrying coal to one of the giant drilling rigs, which makes a racket so deafening the women cannot talk; instead they follow Ah Lei's quick hand signals with the ease of long practice.

It's Cheuk San who sees the leak first. The engineers on the rig have not spotted it yet; they do not hear her shout. Ah Lei senses something is off; the women all down the line see her mouth open in a silent scream, see her slide the yoke from her shoulders and turn to run. What they do hear is the sound, the unmistakeable rumbling thunder, that seems to pour forth from her mouth and through their heads and

into the hot, still air above them.
And then everything goes white.

~*~

She woke with a start to Khairunnisa shaking her. "You were crying. Bad dream?"

"In the dream," she said slowly, "we are speaking. We are speaking but the words are lost to me."

"You don't know what they're saying?' murmured Khairunnisa.

"I know what they mean. I don't know how they said it. The language —it's gone."

She rolled up her sleeve. There, the burn mark. She had known all along, in the incongruous moles and birthmarks, in her impossible height, in the scars that mapped her body in the uneasy badlands between memory and skin. And the memories, the memories, of her sisters skipping in the yard and the sun in the mountains and early rheumatism and weak rice and the sounds she made when the boiling kettle seared her skin. Of the ocean. Different boats, same ocean. The dozen moments she set foot on Singapore for the first time. She knew what she was.

She began to moan, rocking back and forth. "What, what," begged Khairunnisa, trying to hush her before someone heard. She could not tell her; knew if she told that Khairunnisa would not want to fix her any more, would not lay a finger on her ever again. She wanted to tear her limbs from her shoulders, hands from wrists, heart from steam chamber, to put everything back in the charnel heap from whence it came. Somewhere out in the night, the rest of her lay festering, unburied. The ashes never to be sent back to the dozen villages she knew as home. And this body, this abominable patchwork of flesh and metal that should never have been. She dragged her fingernails down her collaged face and screamed. Khairunnisa bit her nails and did not know what to say.

~*~

Ning waited till all the lights in the house had gone out again. Then she scaled the drainpipe again and deftly unlatched the workshop window using a hairpin.

It was dark in the workshop. Ning trod carefully, but the floor betrayed her with a drawn-out creak.

Something moved, rose, silhouetted against the window. Ning stayed still. The sound of a match striking, then the flare of a candle.

A huge woman was staring at her. Her face odd, something off about it, like someone had described it to an artist who had never seen a woman before. Ning knew this was the woman she wanted. She levelled her crossbow at her.

"Easy now," she said. "We're just going to take a little walk."

The woman moved towards her.

"*This is a crossbow*," hissed Ning. "I will *shoot* you!" A lie: the kongsi would not pay for a dead woman. "Oh, for—"

The woman slapped the crossbow away. Ning turned to dive out of the window again, but the woman hauled her back. Then she punched Ning in the face. Stunned, Ning watched the world turn upside-down and bloom into agony.

~*~

This is the dream from before she was Ning. Ah Mui is the name they call her in the dream.

Ah Mui thinks she should leave. She should leave the house now, because she has scratched the tempat sireh. The bibik has said before that if Ah Mui ruins any more of her things, she will beat her to death. And the tempat sireh, with its delicate gold leaf, is a favourite of the bibik, who likes to have her friends admire it while they chew betel until their mouths are red as if they have drunk blood.

Ah Mui thinks she should leave, but where will she go? She has never been outside the house, from as long as she remembers. She has barely even been allowed upstairs. And now the bibik is coming, she is coming down into the kitchen, calling for Ah Mui. From where she is hiding in the woodpile, Ah Mui sees her feet first, in their beaded slippers, then the print of her sarong, then her beautiful kebaya. The bibik has seen the scratched tempat sireh. She stops in the middle of the kitchen. Then she begins to shriek and overturn the kitchen to look for Ah Mui. The kitchen is not large. Ah Mui is dragged sobbing from the woodpile and the bibik begins to slap her, crying stupid girl, bastard girl, I'll kill you. I'll kill you and nobody will notice. You are not anything to anyone. Your parents sold you for money. Even then they charged too much and I should have got you for cheaper because you are not worth the food I have to feed you, you get nothing right.

Ah Mui is trying to curl up, to hide her face with her arms. The bibik pulls her hair to force her head up. Ah Mui sees herself reflected in the polished sides of the stove, the bruises rising to her skin, the tears leaking from both her eyes. Then the bibik smashes the right side of her face into the corner of the table, over and over. Pestle and mortar. When she comes back up, Ah Mui can no longer see anything of herself. There is nothing left to see.

~*~

Ning swam in and out of consciousness, hovering above the horror of the old memory. Someone was talking. A young woman in Malay.

"...this is incredible. It's European make, I think, but there have been so many modifications it's hard to tell what it used to be—the lensing is marvellous, you don't get that sort of work anywhere off the black market. Where on earth you would get something like this—"

"I got if off a Bugis pirate," mumbled Ning. She was sitting down, she realized, tied to a chair. Her head felt like it had been mined for tin ore. "He couldn't pay me, but luckily for him I'd taken a liking to his eye. Most of the extra work I got done by a watchmaker in Geylang. I could give you his address, if you liked."

The Malay woman—Khairunnisa Al-Jazari, if she wasn't wrong—was staring at her open-mouthed. She seized Ning's crossbow and aimed it at her. "Tell us who sent you!"

"You don't even know how to take off the safety catch," said Ning. She tried her hands, but they were well and truly bound behind the chair.

The other woman rose from where she had been squatting in a corner. She was truly immense. Closing her fingers around Ning's throat, she rasped, *"Who sent you?"*

"The people who stole you," Ning choked out. "Surely that's obvious."

From the expression on both their faces, neither woman had any idea who that was. Ning attempted to change the conversation. "How come you speak Malay?"

"So? *You* speak Malay," pointed out the tall woman.

"I am gifted beyond your wildest dreams," said Ning. "But I'm guessing you picked it up even quicker than me, no?"

Both of them ignored her. "What do they want her for?" demanded Khairunnisa.

"I actually have no idea," said Ning. "I'm just the delivery girl, right? I hand you over. They pay me. Nobody needs to lose any eyeballs. Speaking of which, can I have mine back now?"

"No," snapped Khairunnisa, hiding the eyeball somewhere in her sleeve.

"Oh well," said Ning. "You should let me take her, you know. Not one, but two surprise Chinese women appearing in your house. Headache, I tell you."

This earned her a slap from the tall one. Ning's head rang with it like a bell.

"We're doing this the wrong way," Ning went on blithely, ignoring the risk of being throttled. "Let's be nice. Hello, my name's Ning Lam. What's yours?"

The other stared at her a moment, then walked off brusquely. She returned holding one of the dolls, a Chinese bride in scarlet robes. "You speak the language I'm meant to speak, yes?"

"Chinese?" hazarded Ning. "Cantonese? Probably."

The woman pointed at the doll's garments. "What colour is this? In that language."

"Red? Um—hong, I suppose—"

"Right then. That's what I want to be called."

"That's nice," said Ning. "Hong. Ah Hong. Nice to meet you. You too, Khairunnisa. We're going to get along so well."

"There'll be more like her coming," said Ah Hong to Khairunnisa. "We ought to kill her. I can carry the body, easy."

"Oh for your mother's sake," muttered Ning.

"I would really rather not kill anybody," whispered Khairunnisa.

"Me too," added Ning. "I wasn't going to kill anyone to begin with. I was just going to bring you to these nice people, they don't want you really, they just want to have you so that the British or whoever made you get mad."

"Look me in the eye," said Khairunnisa. "Look me in the eye and tell me they won't hurt her."

Ning tried to hold her gaze. "Well—"

Khairunnisa turned away coldly. Ah Hong said, "I won't be given away. I won't be taken apart like a dead thing. I won't be bought and I won't be sold. You don't know what that's like."

Ning was silent for a while. Then she said, quietly, "You'd be surprised."

Ah Hong squatted in front of her, till she was almost nose to nose with Ning. "If you had even the slightest idea, then you wouldn't be about to do it to someone else."

Ning said nothing.

There was a knock on the door.

"Don't open that," said Ning, instinctively.

Khairunnisa hesitated. "Maybe... one of the neighbors..."

"At this hour?'

"I'll just go see..." The knock came again. Khairunnisa headed for the stairs. "Don't make any sound."

She was at the foot of the stairs when the door crashed open.

"Untie me," hissed Ning. "Untie me now." Ah Hong stared at her, wordless with panic.

From downstairs Khairunnisa screamed. "I have to—" gasped Ah Hong, starting for the door. Khairunnisa's scream was cut short. Ah Hong froze as footsteps sounded on the stairs.

Ning began, without subterfuge, to scratch at the rope with the tiny blade hidden in her fake jade ring.

A man came through the door. A Gurkha, judging from his uniform and the curved Kukri blade he held lightly before him. "Number 24," he said in English.

Ah Hong had begun to shake. "No," she said. It was the first time Ning had heard her speak English. "You will not call me that."

"Number 24," repeated the Gurkha, "everything is fine. I'm taking you home."

"Where's Nisa?"

"She's fine," said the Gurkha. "She's just unconscious. We want her alive too."

Ah Hong howled. Lowering her head, she charged the Gurkha. She was at least two heads taller, but the Gurkha did not flinch. Moving fast—faster than anyone Ning had ever seen—he slid out of Ah Hong's path and dropped her with a blow to the back of her knee with his kukri handle. As she stumbled, he was suddenly behind her; with a flash of his blade he opened a huge gash at the back of her head before she could grab for him. Ah Hong screamed. Grabbing her in an expert armlock, the Gurkha reached inside her head, feeling about, and ripped something out.

"No," gasped Ah Hong, "n-n-n-n-n-n—" She crumpled face-first into the ground.

The Gurkha ignored Ning and called a command down the stairs. Two other men entered nervously and carried Ah Hong's body out. The Gurkha walked over to Ning and calmly removed the ring from her finger.

"I know who you are," he said simply. "You're like me. The hired help."

"I expect I'm paid a damn sight better than you," snarled Ning.

"It's not about the money. And you won't be paid this time." The Gurkha leaned over her. "Take this message from my master to yours. Don't come for her again. We know how they did it. We know who they are. There will be blood. You understand?"

Ning bit his ear.

The Gurkha yelled in pain and backhanded Ning so hard she flew across the room into Khairunnisa's workbench. The chair legs snapped under her. Teeth buried in her lip, Ning scrabbled behind her till she felt a file in her fingers.

The Gurkha came on, his kukri a blur. Ning barely ducked the first blow and rolled under the bench, the remnants of the chair crunching. The file clenched between bleeding fingers, she scraped furiously. Little clockwork dancers went flying as the Gurkha upended the bench to get at her. She felt the last strand give just as his blade caught her in the thigh. Ning hissed, tore herself free of the chair and sprang for her crossbow, lying in the debris of the bench.

The Gurkha only just eluded the first volley of bolts by diving to the ground. Ning rocked up and fired again as he scrambled for the door. Lights came on in the neighbouring windows, and people were shouting.

The Gurkha made it down the stairs, Ning storming after him, and leapt into the waiting motorcar at Khairunnisa's door. It clattered off down the street and out of sight before she even cleared the threshold.

Ning swore profusely in Hokkien, the dialect she favoured for profanity. Then, as the neighbours started flooding into the street to see what was happening, she too had to slip away.

~*~

"Extraordinary," said Dr. Horace Bradford. "Simply extraordinary. You're quite sure it was her?"

"Her alone, sir," replied the Gurkha. "I was watching the house. They had no visitors till the Chinese agent. When I entered to retrieve 24, it had been reactivated and was speaking Malay."

They were in Bradford's laboratory, staring down at the prone form of Khairunnisa on one of the operating tables.

"But such work from a native," marveled Bradford. "And a slip of a girl, at that." He removed his goggles and began to polish them absent-mindedly with a fistful of his coat. "Why, I doubt my so-called colleagues in Bencoolen could get 24 to even twitch a finger. We'll have to keep her around, this girl, see what makes her tick."

"Her disappearance will have raised some alarm," said the Gurkha. "I fear that in retrieving them I was... indiscreet."

"Ah, someone will take care of it, I'm sure," muttered Bradford. "A pity you had to disable 24 though, Narayan, I'll have to cobble together its spinal cord all over again."

"Apologies, sir."

"Astonishingly tenacious though," went on Bradford, "the bodies of these, er, samsui women." He had turned to where Ah Hong lay in shambles on another table, peering into her various ruptures. "I must say, they are eminently suited as subjects. We'll have to put in an order for some more."

Khairunnisa had begun to stir. As she took in her surroundings, she let out a whimper.

"The girl's awake." Bradford donned his goggles and advanced upon Khairunnisa, who flinched from him and began to call desperately for Ah Hong. "Have you a clue what she's saying, Narayan? I haven't the faintest."

"I believe it's the name she has for 24, sir."

"How quaint," said Bradford, trying to keep Khairunnisa pinned to the table. "Women have such funny ways. I say, my dear, *would* you keep still a moment? Narayan, do give us a hand."

A bell started to ring. The Gurkha went over to the speaking tube on the laboratory wall. "Yes?" After a while, he said, "Sir, somebody to see you."

"I have no appointments," snapped Bradford, as Khairunnisa toppled off the table and scrambled behind a cabinet. "Tell them I'm indisposed."

"It's Mr. Stroud and Mr. Murchison, sir."

"Well, that's bloody tedious of them." Bradford fumbled irritably with his goggles and leather apron. "See that you lock her in."

They left, the Gurkha bolting the door after them. After a while, Khairunnisa crept out from behind the cabinet.

She tried the door first, but of course it would not give. Then she checked the lifeless Ah Hong, running shivering fingers over the ruin of her. She cast her eyes around the laboratory, and froze.

There were other bodies. Lying on slabs or in glass drawers, stacked on top of one another. Some of them, like Ah Hong, had machinery worked into them. Some were in pieces.

Khairunnisa turned to look at the cabinet she had taken refuge behind. When she opened it, it gave off an icy gust. Inside, packed in ice like cuts of meat, were body parts sorted neatly in rows. Arms, thighs, livers, tubes.

Khairunnisa fell back against the table. Her trembling hand brushed against Ah Hong's limp one. Slowly, unwillingly, her eyes moved from the cabinet of flesh to the scars on Ah Hong's body, multitudinous. To the odd discolorations of her skin. Khairunnisa clapped her hand to her mouth and was sick on the laboratory's smooth white tiles.

~*~

Ning limped stubbornly through the night. Her lip was split; her trouser leg was stiff with blood. Occasionally she pulled out the abacus device and checked it, before hobbling on. When she passed under gas-lamps, her eye socket gaped harsh and empty.

~*~

It was a warm night. The black-and-white blinds in Bradford's living room had been raised to admit the weak breeze, along with the flying ants and tiny night moths that lived in the bungalow gardens. Stroud and Murchison, despite the heat, had not shed their coats.

"I do apologize, gentlemen," Bradford was saying with obvious discomfort, "I'd offer you refreshments, but you see the servants have gone for the night... this is quite unexpected..."

"So were your recent escapades," responded Stroud.

"But that's all sorted," Bradford hastened to add, "the subject's been retrieved, you know..."

"An explosion in the Malay cemetery." Murchison wore strapped over his coat a slim aether tank, the nozzle propped on the arm of Bradford's chaise longue. Bradford's eyes kept flicking anxiously to it. "A midnight house raid. Neighbors' complaints. Police reports. And on top of that, the secret societies nipping at our heels. I would be worried, old boy, really I would."

"We give you top-notch equipment," went on Stroud. "Fresh supplies. Your own personal guard. And you're still letting the side down."

"I beg your pardon," exclaimed Bradford, "the project's really making unprecedented leaps—why, 24 is fully integrated and utterly functional—"

"Functional?" scoffed Murchison. "Derailed a fully-powered hearse, rampaged through Kampong Glam—your man had to put it down."

"We wanted tame golems, not a time bomb," remonstrated Stroud. "Look at Narayan there. Why go to all that trouble if your creations won't be half as tractable as he and his lot are? We've barracks of them, after all—boys who, when we say 'jump', say 'how high, sir?'"

"I need more time," pleaded Bradford, "it's just a defect in the cognition engine, I'll overwrite it in a jiffy..."

"Face it, man, you're through," Stroud said. "All this uproar has got the attention of the... shall we say more *liberal* factions under the Governor. There's already been talk of an investigation."

"You're to be repatriated immediately," added Murchison. "The rest of it will have to go, of course, the lab and all. The higher-ups want a full clearance report tomorrow. Where do you think you're going?"

Bradford had got up and was fumbling in the liquor cabinet. "Do excuse me, I'm quite—something to steady the nerves—"

"Sit down, Bradford," barked Murchison.

Bradford swung round. He was holding an antique shotgun. "Narayan, please see the gentlemen out."

"Bradford..."

"I'm almost there," Bradford shouted, "if you pull the plug now, you—"

Stroud shot him in the chest. It was a small, gleaming pneumatic pistol that slid easily back into his sleeve. Bradford dropped to his knees.

"Frightfully sorry it had to go this way, old chap," continued Stroud, "but you see how it is. No hard feelings."

He and Murchison rose. Stroud beckoned to Narayan. "The servants are gone, you said?"

"Yes," said Narayan. His eyes were fixed on his master choking on his own blood.

"Take us to the lab, there's a good fellow," called Murchison. "Do step lively, we haven't got all night."

In the lab, Khairunnisa was elbow-deep in blood and metal springs. Ah Hong lay with her back to her. "Come *on*," whispered Khairunnisa through gritted teeth, "come on..."

"What's this then?" said Stroud cheerfully. "Our Dr. Bradford had himself a taste for the local flavour?" Murchison powered up the aether tank and aimed the nozzle at the drawers of bodies. Flames licked the blackening glass. "Oh well," said Stroud, "she'll have to go too. Narayan, you know what to do."

Narayan stared at him.

Stroud gestured impatiently. "Everything has to go. Dispatch her first, then we'll do you. Hare and I weren't for it, you must know, but— orders. They're saying you've lost your touch, what with that fiasco in Bussorah Street. You understand, of course."

Narayan stepped towards the table. Khairunnisa's hands kept

moving. Her lips too, in prayer.

The flames were spreading. Murchison moved on to torch the ice cabinet, which resisted stubbornly. "Get on with it," Stroud said irritably to Narayan.

Khairunnisa was crying, getting blood in her eyes when she tried to wipe away the tears. Narayan turned away from her.

"You can do your own dirty work, sir," he said calmly. "There comes a time when a man tires of asking *how high*."

The shot made Khairunnisa drop her instruments. Before her, the Gurkha collapsed quietly. He had made no move to dodge the bullet. Even in dying, his face did not change expression.

"Bollocks." Stroud was angrily reloading the pistol. "Bloody natives. Can't rely on them for anything." He lifted the pistol again, meeting Khairunnisa's frightened eyes.

On the table between them, Ah Hong sat up and tore the pistol from his hand.

Then she was on him, blow after blow to the face, pulping it against the tiles. The wound on her neck still gaping, the mechanisms within whirring furiously. Stroud's hands scrabbled ineffectually against her broad back. Ah Hong crushed his lower jaw, then strained until it ripped free from his face.

Murchison turned in alarm, the nozzle flaring. A crossbow bolt thudded into his hand.

Ning limped into the room. She fired another bolt, which bounced off the tank. The nozzle, which Murchison had lost control of, was spilling flame wildly across the room. Khairunnisa scrambled out of its path.

Ning tossed the empty crossbow aside and went for her butterfly knives. Murchison pulled out a gun similar to Stroud's, but could not fire properly for his wounded hand; Ning ducked his shot easily. Murchison tackled her. They went down together in a pool of blood and vomit, Murchison's good hand landing blows where he could. Writhing to avoid him, Ning managed to force a knife up and stabbed Murchison through the eye. Ning clutched the hilt for dear life as he died above her face.

Across the room, Ah Hong was pounding what was left of Stroud into the floor. Ning got unsteadily to her feet. "Eh," she said, "he's giamcai already, you can stop."

Ah Hong took a muzzy swing at her. Ning stayed well out of range. "Will you stop it? I'm not your enemy."

"Still want to sell me?" snarled Ah Hong.

"I'm not sure you've noticed," retorted Ning, "but trying to do anything with you is stupidly exhausting. And I've had it up to here with this night."

"Everybody," said Khairunnisa from the corner, "this room is on fire. I would really like to go."

Outside the black-and-white bungalow, they took deep, welcome breaths of the night air. "Didn't you stop working?" Ning demanded of Ah Hong.

"I fixed her," said Khairunnisa. "Easier the second time round, actually. Didn't you get left behind in my house?"

"Wasn't hard to keep track of you," panted Ning. "Speaking of which, please give me my eye back now, because I can hear trouble coming and I would like to be able to look it full in the face."

A group of men was approaching. Ning recognized Chee in their lead. Chee was scowling. "Grandfather wants to see you."

"Are you joking," groaned Ning, "can a girl not get cleaned up first."

"Grandfather said *now*," repeated Chee grimly.

Ah Hong had her fists clenched, ready to attack. "Just go with them," Ning told her in Malay. "Let me do the talking, it'll be fine."

"And if it's not?" said Ah Hong through gritted teeth.

"Then you can punch them to death, whatever you like. Come on."

~*~

Grandfather was eating a pre-dawn breakfast at a dimsum bar attached like a parasite to a garment factory. A great knot of pipes siphoned steam from the factory and vented it onto small columns of bamboo dimsum trays, which then went rolling out on little mechanical trolleys through the breakfast crowd. Everyone glanced at the stinking, bloodied women as they entered, but said nothing.

Grandfather picked up siewmai with his chopsticks. "Miss Ning," he said without preamble. "You have not been discreet."

"In my defense," said Ning, "I was not the one who set fire to everything."

"You have also worked too slow," said Grandfather. "The tide has turned. The woman is now worthless."

"Wait, wait." Ning cocked her head at him. "You mean you don't want her now? And I went to such trouble."

"What for do I want her?" demanded Grandfather. "The only man who would pay ransom for her is dead. Now, if the British even realize she is still alive, we won't see any money from them, just an extermination squad. This whole thing has been a waste of time."

"I think it was more of a waste of *my* time," snapped Ning. "I'm not getting paid?"

"You have the audacity, Miss Ning," thundered Grandfather, 'to ask for payment at this stage?"

"Grandfather," said Ning with dangerous calm. "I have had a very bad day. I have been shot at. I have been punched in the head. I have been stabbed. And I smell like vomit. With all due respect, Grandfather, I think I should be paid."

"That's too bad, Miss Ning, because you won't be."

Ning gave a bark of laughter. "How far the secret societies have fallen indeed. Can't even pay those they contract. Thought you were old school in this kongsi, but you're cheap as any upstart crook."

A ripple of anger ran through Grandfather's retinue, stationed around the restaurant. "Perhaps a compromise," said Grandfather. "We'll cover the medical bill for whatever wounds you sustained."

"And I get to keep the advance," said Ning.

"Yes."

"And I get her." She pointed at a startled Ah Hong.

Grandfather raised his eyebrows. "Why would you want her?"

Ning shrugged. "You don't. I'll take her elsewhere. Maybe somebody else will be willing to pay."

"The British will come after you for this," pointed out Grandfather. "Be it on your head."

"I'm not scared of the British," said Ning. "Unlike some."

She turned on her heel and strode out, Ah Hong and Khairunnisa following uncertainly. Nobody made to stop her.

"What happened?" Ah Hong wanted to know.

"Nothing much. I bought you. You were damn expensive." Ah Hong stared. "I want breakfast," Ning continued, "and then I want to never wear these clothes again."

They ended up at a roadside coffeeshop. Ning drank black coffee and mashed liquid eggs with soy sauce in the saucer. Khairunnisa opted for milky tea. The whole ritual confused Ah Hong, who drank whatever Khairunnisa ordered for her and consumed mountains of thick toast smeared with coconut jam.

"What do I do now?" asked Ah Hong.

"I'm in the market for an associate," said Ning. "I've begun to think that if I had a partner, preferably one who can squeeze out a man's eyeballs with her fist, then I would spend less time bleeding and more time watching other people bleed. Also people would think twice about not paying me. That happens depressingly often."

Ah Hong considered this. "Would you teach me back my language?"

Ning gazed at her thoughtfully. "I'd try."

"We could put you back in touch with other samsui women," suggested Khairunnisa. "Find people who knew you... knew the people you were from before..."

"No," said Ah Hong quietly. "Nobody will come near me. Not when they know what I am."

Khairunnisa stared into her tea. "What I saw down there. At the house. Allah will not forgive it."

"He's dead," said Ning curtly. "The man who made her. He's probably having a great time explaining it to Allah or whoever right now."

"They'll come looking for me, you know," remarked Ah Hong. "They'll always be coming."

"When I ran away from the people who took my eye," said Ning, "they kept trying to get me back. Eventually I proved to them it was more trouble than it was worth." She looked at Ah Hong approvingly. "You're going to be a lot more trouble than I ever was."

Ah Hong smiled.

In a companionable silence, they finished breakfast and watched the sun rise over the island.

Spider Here

Robert Liow

[I]

Dai Ji skittered into the Jurong Central Wet Market, pushing through the crowd. The walking-chair strapped to her waist splashed through a wet spot, and a middle-aged woman turned to scowl at her, unhappy that her pants had gotten wet. Dai Ji smiled and apologized in Malay.

"Sorry, auntie! My fault."

"Aiyo, girl. Careful a bit lah. Go, go."

There was a loud crunch. A fat rodentlike bearing a message listed to the right, its gears squealing as it attempted to right itself. It sparked and spurted a strange green fluid, but limped on, reasonably mobile, towards its destination. Dai Ji looked at it with a frown, but didn't stop. She couldn't help it, anyway; everyone could Shape, but this thing had been locked down tight, all its functions tuned to its owners' Shape by whoever made it. She could barely feel its threads. Besides, it was almost one, and she had to be on the roof early to set up. Towgey and the rest of her crew were already there.

Dai Ji walked out of the wet market and into the Reconstruction Trust block behind it. The slablike postwar buildings, replacing the kampungs obliterated by years of fierce back-and-forth fighting over Singapore between Nanyang and British Malayan forces, each housed thousands of people in blocks thirty stories high and the length and width of football fields. A Thai woman in a Reconstruction Trust uniform supervised a walker as it sprayed the ground in a sweeping arc with a high-pressure hose. Dai Ji waved at her as she nimbly sidestepped the water-jet. She rushed to the lift lobby and jabbed the call button with her umbrella. Decades-old hydraulics and gears began to grind as the lift descended from the fifteenth storey, and then abruptly halted as it paused at the fourth. Dai Ji sighed and folded her arms.

She wondered what her brother was doing now. Kian Boon was the Officer Commanding of a company of mechanized infantry, stationed near the Causeway. He'd been busy recently, with the Malayan Federation making war-noises across the border in the papers, and he hadn't been home for the past two weekends. She strained to remember Kian Boon's call, the night before. He usually made his daily calls from his office, but yesterday had been different. His voice was hushed, the sound of steam and hydraulics and the metal footsteps of walkers in the distance. He was out of breath, his personal radio kept falling to the floor and he had spoken as fast as one of his gasguns. He had used the words "Confrontation" and "riots". He didn't know what was going on either, or why. He couldn't tell her where he was going. Something big was about to happen. She could hear the steel in his voice as he had said that, and the slight smile when he told her to take care. A harsh, drilling bell rang, and someone shouted "Captain Wong, sir!" He swore, rushed a farewell, and shut the line off. Silence.

Dai Ji was sure he'd be alright, though. Her Dai Kor was good. He'd studied biology in Chulalongkorn University on a Nanyang Forces scholarship, and spent two years on the border with Sarawak with the Sultanates' Army, defending the Sultanates from the White Rajah's incursions. He'd find a way.

The lift finally opened to a cloud of kretek smoke and several batik-clad Sultanate women, their tiny pet birdlikes buzzing happily behind them, stepped out. Dai Ji shifted back a little, letting the little metallic fliers hover around her and play with her hair as their owners wiggled into the lobby. She whistled at one that stopped in front of her face, calling up and tweaking an unsecured thread, and it flushed red for a brief second before reverting to its natural, iridescent green. It flicked its tongue out, catching beads of sweat dripping off her forehead and chirping in glee as it twirled in the air.

Dai Ji loved birdlikes; she'd seen her brother work with the larger mail-delivery versions before he'd joined the Nanyang Forces; watched him feed them concentrated sugar-water and smooth their feathers of metal and keratin back into shape after each flight with the Sultanates' Postal Service. She preferred spider casings, though. Casings were easy and cheap to build. Unlike lifelikes, they didn't have an integral live brain, instead using that of an animal "pilot", and so required much less maintenance and life-support. More importantly, though, they were a decent source of income for any young, skilled Shaper. She'd made a few spider casings over the weekend, easily ten dollars' worth; there would certainly be willing buyers after Chalerm's demonstration. The Sultanate women whistled, and the birdlikes returned to their shoulders as they left. Dai Ji stepped into the lift and let the old gears take her up.

~*~

[II]

Dai Ji climbed the final steps to the top floor of the building, where the lift did not go. Approaching the ladder that led to the roof-access hatch, she reclined in her lifelike walking-chair and called up its threads. The goat-brain inside bleated as she forced the tarsal claws of its pneumatic legs to latch onto the rungs of the ladder. She undid the hacked padlock and chains, gave the hatch a rough push with a chair leg and pulled herself through the opening. She inclined her seat and dusted herself off, watching her crew climb in after her. There was Towgey, her twelve-year-old cousin and bet-collector; Ridzuan, the backup host and spider-seller with his Sultanates' Army-surplus load-bearing vest packed to the brim with spiders in their containers; the Chong twins, there to break up the occasional fight, and Chalerm.

Chalerm was the newest member of her crew. He'd replaced her old casing tester after the latter had been bought out by a ring from Clementi a couple of weeks ago; Dai Ji had personally locked them out of their meeting place with a few dead rats and a bicycle wheel, but she'd had to find a new tester. Chalerm wore the uniform of the fancy Thai school that replaced the old Singapore Institute after the British were expelled. His head was shaven, and his shirt had been deliberately left untucked. He palmed the casing he'd asked for as part of his fee; "Kiet", he'd named it. "Honour" in Thai. He reached out to shake hands with his new boss, but she merely nodded at him.

"Chalerm, your first time for me right? Don't fuck up."

Chalerm grinned and chuckled. "Can, boss. Can. This spider," he flourished, "I catch myself. Put in my special container. Confirm win."

~*~

Dai Ji heard the knocks. Thrice, twice, then thrice again. She checked her watch. It was one-fifty. Someone was just in time. She returned the pattern with a chair-leg, tapping sharply against the metal of the hatch, and then tapped twice. The almost-latecomer repeated the pattern, and Dai Ji reached out to open the padlock. The lock slithered open as she pulled its threads aside, and a lean, sweaty Chinese boy eagerly clambered up. She scowled.

"Oi, Rotan. What time already?"

"Dai Ji, one fifty only! Still got time lah."

Dai Ji sighed and waved him in, watching him disappear into the crowd. Towgey was running from one person to the next collecting bets. The first half's fighters were gathered in the middle of a circle of children and teenagers, parading their casings. There was a couple, two young Nanyang Forces officers on home leave; Chai, the cocky fifteen-year-old with a tiny, badly-done dragon tattoo under his left armpit; Margaret, the Eurasian convent-school girl who wore a jacket, even in the heat, to cover up her pinafore; and Aminah, who helped Shape Ridzuan's spider-containers and was pretty handy with casings herself. The match-list drawn up on the board pitted Chalerm's "Kiet" against Margaret's "High Spirits" as the first match of the day. Kiet was heavy and energy-hungry, but fast and optimized for short, fluid movements. High Spirits, in contrast, was light, slim and covered in cockroach-based sensor hairs, designed to outlast its opponents and whittle them down.

Dai Ji checked her watch, then rang a bell. The circle quietened as the Chong twins brought out a large folding table from behind a cistern and opened it in the middle. Chalk lines drawn breadthwise marked the distance from the centre, and two chalked semi-circles on either end were labelled "spider here" in Chinese, Thai and Jawi. A cardboard barrier down the middle shielded each side from view of the other. Chalerm and Margaret laid their empty casings in their semi-circles.

Kiet opened with a pneumatic hiss at the touch of Chalerm's hand. Chalerm removed a container from his bag, a jam jar with holes in the top nestled within a slightly larger jam jar filled with water and sealed with waterproof skinfilm. The spider inside seemed rather lethargic as Chalerm tapped it out into his hand, but livened the moment it touched the warmth of his skin. Blowing gently, he coaxed it onto the spongy padding in the casing's head. It stopped moving as the padding enveloped it. Kiet's lateral lines, lifted directly off a mackerel, iridesced blue and green as it stirred. Chalerm stroked its abdomen, feeling the threads fold in around the spider and its mind settle into the casing's circuits, and it raised its forelegs in response. Taking a small phial of sugared water and a needle from Towgey, he pricked his finger, squeezed a drop of blood into the phial and poured the mixture onto the padding. Across the table, High Spirits was fuelled up and ready to go, with one of Margaret's favourite spiders inside and preening itself with a hairy foreleg. Chalerm tapped Kiet's head, and it hissed closed.

Dai Ji made one last call for bets. A small group of Malay children, no older than ten, ran to Towgey with a total of five dollars between them to put on Aminah for later. Towgey looked around briefly, saw nobody else and nodded at Dai Ji. She announced the contestants and their casings, then rang the bell. The two challengers stepped away from their corners. She rang the bell twice again, and the barrier was lifted.

~*~

Kiet and High Spirits spotted each other immediately and threw up their forelegs. Kiet strode towards the centre in smooth, measured steps, waggling its abdomen in the air, and tapping its long, thick forelegs on the ground. High Spirits made a zigzagging advance, darting from side to side, and suddenly leapt forward when less than a chi remained between the two; Kiet thrust its face forward to meet the charge, clinching High Spirits' fangs with its own before the latter could dart back. Dai Ji stole a glance at Margaret, whose lips were tightly pursed. As High Spirits attempted to jump, Kiet snapped its forelegs shut around its pedicel and tugged in the opposite direction. There was a small crack, and High Spirits' second left leg fell off. Steam puffed from the wound as it sealed itself, but High Spirits was already in motion, leaping not against the pull, but into it.

Kiet reared up onto its hind legs, balancing against the push. Its chin resting on High Spirits' fangs, it marched forward on its third and fourth pairs of legs, forcing High Spirits to support its weight while pinning its jaws open. High Spirits' fangs were stuck in Kiet's chin, trapped in the tough carapace. It wrenched its body, trying to topple Kiet, but the heavier spider shifted its weight in time with its opponent's movements. Both spiders staggered around the arena, searching for a weakness.

The crowd was shouting; most of them had bet on Margaret's seasoned spider trouncing the new tester who had paired Dai Ji's casing with a spider unused to it. The few who had bet on Chalerm were cheering loudly. High Spirits' fourth left leg snapped and buckled, and it slipped. Taking advantage of the situation, it pushed off to the left with its right legs, sliding free of Kiet. It was leaking steam in a few places, its carapace cracked and its fourth left leg dragging uselessly on the ground. It retreated, hampered by the damage, towards the side of the table. Kiet waited, forelegs open, in the middle, as its defeated opponent surrendered. Chalerm glanced at Margaret, his mouth curling into an apologetic smile.

As High Spirits crawled under the table, Dai Ji rang the bell. The cardboard barrier was lowered. Chalerm and Margaret retrieved their casings and bowed to each other before switching them off. Margaret opened her casing and gently shook her spider free; it limped around uncertainly for a moment, then hopped with glee back into its box. The sugar water drained out of High Spirits' rear end in a thin line onto the ground. Kiet's reserves were almost dry; with a little prompting, there was a brief stream, then nothing. Chalerm's spider slipped back into its jar, where it curled up in its leaf. The fight was over.

~*~

As Towgey distributed the winnings, Rotan sighed. He looked at his new casing, Heavy Jumper. Its neural circuits, built from scavenged chicken heads and the brain of a macaque that he'd found killed by a roadwalker, sang at his touch, but he didn't know if their construction was anywhere close to Kiet's in complexity. If he managed to win enough, he'd save up for one of Dai Ji's casings.

The air roared. Rotan felt a wave of heat wash across his back, and he almost dropped Heavy Jumper in surprise. He ran to the edge of the roof, peering over to see what had happened; below him, the wet market had caught fire. A plume of dark smoke was rising from a crater in the ground, where the butcher once was. Several shop-carts close to the explosion had been shredded, their contents scattered burning on the ground together with the bodies of several shopkeepers, while the survivors fled the burning market on foot. Already, the Nanyang Fire Corps' sirens were wailing, and their red, armoured elephantines thundered out of the nearby Jurong District Fire Station.

Rotan screamed in Malay, "Bomb! Bomb! Downstairs got bomb explode! Run!"

~*~

Five seconds after the blast, Dai Ji was already in motion.

The rooftop access hatch was wide open, lock smashed by the twin officers. She skittered across the rooftop on her walking-chair, looking for her crew. She sent Ridzuan to watch the hatch and keep people moving in an orderly fashion, and then jabbed Towgey, cowering on the floor, with a chair leg. She shouted just to be heard. "Go! Help them get out!"

Dai Ji grabbed Chalerm and Margaret, who were standing shell-shocked, and shoved them towards the exit. Rotan ran past her, a pale-faced Chai clinging tightly to his hand, while Aminah led the crowd of Malay children who had bet on her ahead. Towgey picked kids older than he was off the ground, sending them scurrying for the access hatch. The crew who laid out the table were busy folding it up and keeping it behind the cistern. Dai Ji ran past them with a curt nod. She found a boy, barely seven, hiding behind a vent, and screamed at him.

"Want to die is it? Then? Don't hide here, go! Go!"

Her fury shook the little boy out of his fear, and he ran. She made a final tour of the rooftop before heading for the hatch herself. Her walking-chair reclined all the way back as its legs latched on to the rungs of the metal ladder; she descended vertically, strapped in, into the top floor of the Reconstruction Trust block.

Forty-odd children, young men and women waited in the lobby. Dai Ji looked at them, and they looked back expectantly. She shouted, "Oi! Stand here for what?"

The crowd scattered, heading down the stairs. Dai Ji waited until they had gone before she began to make her way down. Her chair-legs quivered slightly; noticing this, she focused, steadied her grip on the threads of the walking-chair's brain and forced it down the stairwell.

[III]

Dai Ji sat in her room. Her homework lay blank in front of her. Mathematics, Chulalongkorn-Ministry of Education Joint Advanced Level. Normally it would have been done by now, but she had merely scratched the paper with her pen. Her radio played the latest chart-toppers from China and the Sultanates. The Nanyang band Gwei Ngeow was on, and the crisp guitars dislodged her.

There had been military men at the wet market after the blast. She had seen them as a pair of medics looked her over. Police officers, manning the cordon in their neat brown fatigues, had waved them through. They had been unarmed, but wore thick, segmented armour with the Nanyang insignia but without a unit crest. They picked through the remains of the butcher stall, fishing out a rodentlike which leaked green fluid. Dai Ji saw two of them pass an organic wand over it, and then drop it into a skinfilm bag. They lifted a large, red object out from beneath the rubble and attempted to transfer it into a second bag. It was slippery; one of them dropped it on the floor, and it shattered, spilling grey matter and green fluid. Dai Ji turned away to vomit. A medic caught it in a bucket and wiped her mouth with a clean cloth. She watched a team of medics load body after body into an ambulance; later, she learned that there were twenty-seven dead, the bomber included.

Keys caught in the front door, and it opened with a creak. There was a rustle of bags. Dai Ji's mother dropped her packed dinner on the dining table and rushed into her room in a tight embrace.

"Siew Gim..."

Dai Ji returned the hug. She breathed in the smell of her mother; river and rust, barely hidden beneath sharp medicated oil and the dull stink of her Civil Utilities Board uniform. Her father's heavy boots came off at the doorstep and he walked in, gave them both a squeeze, and headed for the shower, saying nothing. Gwei Ngeow continued to riff in the background.

~*~

Dai Ji could not sleep. She'd been allowed to take a day off from school; her mother had called her form-teacher Mrs. Oon to explain the situation. Lifting herself from her bed, she lowered herself into her walking-chair, parked next to it. She felt its straps, specially designed by her brother, automatically cinch around her waist and the three stumps attached to it. She could feel it bleating, and realized she'd forgotten to refuel it earlier.

"Shh."

She grasped for its mind, found it, and twisted the threads she felt there, calming the goat-brain and silencing its bleating. She popped open the cap on its left armrest with a flick of her fingers, pouring in the sugar-water she kept on her nightstand, and it vibrated a little. Taking hold of its reins, she headed for the kitchen. If she could not sleep, she would work.

There were chicken necks in her personal cooler, as well as a small reticulated python she'd bought off a gardener the day before. Dai Ji removed the snake and a pair of chicken necks, checked them for freezer-burn, then returned to her room with a scalpel, a chopper, a spoon, a sheet of skinfilm and a bag for the scraps. She switched on the nightlight and shoved her homework to the side, spreading the skinfilm and her materials across the newly-cleared workspace. Inspecting the scalpel, she drew the edge several times along a small whetstone and tested it on the chicken neck. It fell away easily to reveal the spine. Satisfied, she started to work.

She started with the chicken necks. She felt for the threads she knew were there, bringing them into view and rubbing them between her fingers to assess their viability. The material was relatively fresh, and would stand up to reconstitution well. Dai Ji carefully separated the head and spine from the rest of the chicken flesh with her scalpel, unmaking the stubborn bits of tissue and vein that clung to the spine into raw cell-matter. She defleshed the skulls with a hard pinch of her right hand, liquefying the eye but saving the optic nerve. Merging the muscle scraps into a clay-like lump and discarding the fat, she broke the skulls with the flat of the chopper, pulled out the brains and set them aside. Cracking the spines, she extracted the nerves within and discarded the bones.

Next, she moved on to the python, which she gutted and reduced to spine and skull again, before extracting the nerves and brain. The skin and eyes she kept intact, as well as the tongue and Jacobson's organ. She'd use those to build sensors. Her brother had installed the same kind, made from the heads of several mangrove vipers, a few years back so her walking-chair wouldn't bump into things; he'd playfully refused to teach her that trick, so she'd gone through his university notes and figured it out herself.

From a cupboard on the desk, she removed a block of cartilage plastic. This was the basic building block of a casing; her hands tingled with anticipation just holding the thing. She could feel the threads extending in a uniform grid pattern, waiting to be shaped. She traced the outlines of the parts she wanted with her fingers, liberating them from the block one piece at a time. Soon, she had in top and bottom halves an abdomen, a cephalothorax with a hinged lid and a pair of thick fangs, the pedicel joining the two and eight hollow, multi-jointed legs. The rest of the block she coaxed back into shape, leaving it next to the chicken and snake parts. She carved channels into the casing's outline, where she'd put the muscles later, and pinched out holes for the casing's eyes and lateral line. Inspecting her work, she carefully set the top and bottom halves of the casing together and persuaded them to join at the seams.

The next step in building the casing was filling it in. She loved this part, working intimately with the flesh and blood of her components, feeling each cell sliding into place and knowing the intended purpose she had given it. She started with the snake muscle; liquefying and spooning the cells through the hinged cover of her casing's cephalothorax, she animated it, guiding the little muscle-worms to their destinations individually and convincing them to settle down, organically fusing with the cartilage plastic. Next, she reconstructed a venous and arterial network that would keep the casing alive and mobile without her intervention, coaxing the cell-matter to shape itself into the blood vessels it once remembered. This required some prodding, stern jabs and a little thread-pulling where the cell-matter was stubborn or not entirely present yet, but Dai Ji could feel the blood vessels branching and spreading throughout the casing. She grinned as she felt a flicker of life taking hold. Taking the snake tongue, she briefly merged it with the Jacobson's organ in a brown-and-purple slurry, then Shaped it into dozens of delicate purple hairs, each as long as an eyelash and complete with follicles. These she implanted along the lateral line of the casing, integrating them into the existing circulatory system. The snake eyes, kept intact, she placed behind protective cartilage plastic coverings in the eye-holes. The casing was pretty much done, with only its brain remaining to be constructed.

Dai Ji sighed as she brought the snake and chicken nerves and brains together. She felt calm now. Separating out cells from each, she gently laid a network of inter-species nerves that connected each of the muscles to the casing's eyes and sensors, and tied the network together in a spongy padding at the centre of the spider's cephalothorax. This was the brain, where the spider would go, taking control of the casing with its augmented sensing and cognitive abilities. Dai Ji sealed the casing again and layered snakeskin on top of it, bonding it to the cartilage plastic. She used her scalpel to peel off errant scales, sweeping them into a corner of the table, and reapplied the snakeskin in layers each time. When she was done, the casing resembled a tarantula, with scales instead of hair and the cold, yellow eyes of a baby reticulated python.

She swept the remaining raw material and skinfilm sheet into the scrap bag, save the snakeskin and the cartilage plastic she hadn't used. Sighing, she let the bag of flesh and bone fall down the rubbish chute in the kitchen, listening as it clanged against the sides on the way down, loud at five in the morning.

[IV]

Dai Ji woke up at eleven, flopped into her walking-chair and stumbled to the bathroom. Towgey had gone to school, and her parents had left for work hours ago. She brushed her teeth, scrubbing the staleness from her tongue.

The newspaper that day had Nanyang President Li's face on it; tearful and furious, he raged, open-mouthed, against the Federation's crimes in black and white print. Dai Ji pushed it off the table to make room for breakfast.

There was one egg left in the kitchen. Dai Ji boiled some water in a kettle, poured it into a large porcelain mug and then dropped the egg in. She grabbed a cold mantou from the refrigerator and shoved it into the steamer while she waited. After a couple of minutes, she fished the egg out with a spoon and let it cool in a saucer. The steamer dinged, and she lifted the mantou out with Shapable wooden tongs. A large crow landed outside the open kitchen window, eyeing the meal hungrily; Dai Ji closed to arm's length, brandishing her tongs, but it refused to back off. Scowling, she searched for its unsecured threads, pulled, and at once rent a handful of new feathers into black fluff; the crow took flight, alarmed. Dai Ji looked at it, flying towards the next block, and turned to crack the egg into the saucer. She tore the mantou in two, dipped it in the egg, and took a bite.

Dai Ji cleared the plates when she was done. She watched the sink slurp the soapy water down greedily, stripping and breaking down the harsh chemicals and organics so they wouldn't contaminate the water supply. She looked at the time; it was almost twelve. She returned to her room, picking up her personal radio, and dialled Chalerm. The radio whirred for a while before he finally came through, whispering.

"Hello, boss, what you want? I in school, must go toilet pick up you know..."

"Chalerm, I got new casing today. For special match, me and you."

"You coming today? Thought Ridzuan host."

"Of course I coming lah, Chalerm. Bring extra spider for me. One thirty, usual place. We go first."

"Can, boss."

Dai Ji shut off the personal radio and picked up her new casing. In the afternoon light that streamed through her curtains, it had a bluish-green sheen on top of its scaly exterior. She ran her hands over it, feeling its smoothness and the buzzing of its circuits beneath her fingers and seeing the hard, beady stare of its python eyes. It was violently beautiful. Dai Ji carefully packed it into a shoebox with two more unsold casings in it and lowered it into her backpack. Pulling it onto her lap, she unlocked the door and stepped out of the apartment.

In the lift, her Thai block-mate greeted her, and she politely nodded back. He fished for a pack of chewing gum and offered her some. The lift doors shut, and the old gears rattled.

~*~

The circle was smaller than usual today; maybe about thirty kids, with the rest either spooked by the blast or forbidden from coming. Still, Dai Ji could see Towgey darting around, collecting his bets as usual, while Rotan fussed over Heavy Jumper in the middle. Aminah was entertaining her little gang with what looked like a home-made birdlike; the size of a mynah, it repeated her words in a tinny voice and hopped from one leg to the other. Chalerm and Ridzuan were playing capteh, their spiders and casings left in a corner with the Chong twins. The Nanyang Forces officers were conspicuously absent.

Dai Ji looked at her watch, and rang her bell. The Chong twins once again set up the folding table as the circle closed in. Dai Ji waited for them to settle down, and then spoke.

"Today got something special for you. Who see me play before?"

A few hands went up.

"The rest of you, today your first time. Today I challenge Chalerm and Kiet!"

Chalerm raised Kiet in the air as he strode to his side of the table. Dai Ji brought out the casing she'd made the previous night, trotting around the circle so everyone could get a look. She tugged on its threads discreetly, and it reared up, baring its fangs.

"This is Khuai Boey. Ask you, who last night cannot sleep?"

People tittered, and some of them yawned.

"Ya. Me too, so I made this."

She set it down in "spider here" and stroked its back. It opened with a deliberately loud hiss that trailed off only after a few seconds. Removing one of Chalerm's water-cooled jars from her backpack, she coaxed the spider into the casing. Towgey passed her the needle and sugar water, and she fuelled up. On the other side of the table, Kiet was already preening itself.

Dai Ji passed the bell to Ridzuan and took a deep breath. She turned to look at the circle and smiled.

"You all watch."

Ridzuan rang the bell, and the cardboard barrier was lifted. The two casings stared each other down for the briefest of moments, and then charged.

The Chamber of Souls

z.m. quỳnh

Today it is announced that our quarantine is over and our refugee camp sufficiently detoxified to enter the Waterlands of Lạc, the home of our rescuers. Cheers and song rise in the air as the airship descends from the sky. A magnificently carved rồng on the bow of the vessel glistens of lacquered red, orange and gold scales, as its body, decorated by gems, wraps under the hull to reappear in a long curved tail on the other side of the vessel.

Heavy plumes of vapor expire from fangs framed by long whiskers made of copper metallic strips. Along the side of the vessel, large rotor blades whip the air as two enormous orange balloons, hovering higher than the tallest building in Sài Gòn begin to deflate, pivoting to form triangular sails.

Thirty days ago, our sinking fishing boat cramped with a hundred refugees fleeing Việt Nam had emerged from a hidden corridor of the South China Sea. We were rescued by the Guardians who had descended from a similar vessel that barely skimmed the surface of the water and we, arms waving and voices strained in desperation, failed to observe what should have been obvious—that our rescuers bore an element of foreignness that we were wholly unprepared for.

"Where do you hail from? Are you in need of assistance?" a Guardian had called down to us. The language spoken was Vietnamese, but it sounded as if the tongue of the speaker had been wrapped around a poem and restrung in curves back to us. A slight echo of melody lingered after each word.

Silence had spread among us at the strangeness of the dialect and though we could make out the gist of what was spoken, it was interwoven with words and tones we did not recognize. Whispers of warning spread that our rescuers may be agents of the very government we had fled.

Tentatively, mother had stepped forward to speak what many had waited ten years to voice, "Yạ, greetings, we are refugees, fleeing our homeland of Việt Nam because of the cruelties we experienced there. We respectfully request asylum."

At that, three Guardians had leapt onto our boat, their long black hair, arranged in motley styles that interlaced colorful braided metallic strands with feathers, flapped in the wind as they examined us in our squalor and malnutrition. Their speech clearly carried Vietnamese tones, but their eyes and skin, the features of their faces, their height—they were as tall as the tallest American soldiers, if not taller, and their strange dark tunics, decorated with metallic accouterments, that sheathed one arm and left the other arm bare spoke of a culture completely unfamiliar to us.

Approaching the eldest among us, my aunt who had made the journey at sixty-seven, a Guardian with jet-black hair spiced with metallic blue had bowed deeply.

"Yạ, greetings, grandmother," the Guardian had said, "The sea has brought you to us and we will care for you. Come and we will brew tea and rice for you. You are under the protection of the Waterlands of Lạc, we grant you all sanctuary."

Despite understanding only bits and pieces of the Guardians' words, my aunt's face had broken into a grimace of blackened teeth and sobs, the Guardian's message of granted asylum unequivocal.

"What are you called, dear one?" she had said, wiping her tears on her sleeve.

"What I am called, you cannot express, but you may call me Jzan Nguyệt after the moon that once carried the tides of our Waterlands. And it is in my hands that you will rest the security of your people, for I am jzan who is the protectorate of these Waterlands."

Jzan Nguyệt, as well as all of the Guardians, referred to one another as "jzan." At first this was confusing, making learning their names challenging. Once in quarantine though, we quickly found this highly convenient since the title was enough to convey respect while eliminating the need to know anyone's name.

~*~

As we board their airship, I notice that our steps, frenzied and awkward when we entered quarantine, are replaced by lightness as children skip, lovers hold hands, and elders stroll side-by-side. My own mother is all smiles, her arm crooked unevenly through the arm of my aunt as they board together. Despite all of this, I can't help but feel an odd mixture of excitement, anxiety, and remorse about journeying to a land that will become our new home—to replace the one we had lost.

As we board, a Healer tells us to grip a sanded bar that runs along the deck. Unlike the heavily muscled Guardians, whose faces and limbs are almost entirely covered with intricate drawings much like our ancient fisherman who drew sea monsters on their bodies, the Healers' skin is free of any markings and their heads are completely shaven. In quarantine, they were tasked with providing us with food, shelter, clothing, and herbal medicine. Like the Guardians, they also had a title, "nan," which they use to refer to each other.

We had been delivered into quarantine soon after our rescue. It was the Guardian, Jzan Nguyệt, who had brought the news to us: "You will be taken to an atoll island where we will prepare you for entry into our Waterlands."

Mother's forehead had furrowed instantly with concern. I had known what she was thinking; I could see it in her eyes - the fear of incarceration. So many stories had carried their way back to us from people who had made it to refugee camps in Mã Lai, Thái Lan and Hương Cảng. Stories of starvation, sickness, and festering away like prisoners while waiting for dreams that never materialized.

"Are we prisoners?" Mother's voice had quivered.

"No."

"Then why-?"

"Because in our country, your senses are severely impaired. You must acclimate. Because you carry toxins and you must detoxify lest you bring death and illness to our people." In that moment, in Nguyệt's voice, I did not hear the graceful generosity we had all become accustomed to, but a fierceness that seemed immovable.

Despite our fears, though, our "quarantine" was more like a paradise vacation. Instead of barbed wire fences, rationed food, and poorly ventilated stalls, we had been surrounded by miles of green coral reef, a never-ending buffet of rice, nut dishes, and fresh fruits and vegetables, and cool bamboo mats to sleep under the rounded canopy of the sky.

Quarantine reflected the imagined freedom that many among us had dreamed of. The freedom I had envisioned was somewhat different though. I wanted inclusion, to belong somewhere—to be valued—to be more than the label Việt Nam gave to me—the untrustworthy child of a political dissident. How that freedom will look in the rescuers' land, I do not know. Would we be equal members of their society, or a relief effort from some war-torn country?

~*~

The airship picks up speed, rising into the sky and the Guardians begin to pull on ropes and equipment, preparing for flight. I hear sobs break out as we watch them. It is not what they are doing that is disturbing; it is how fast they are moving. Our eyes can only catch their faces and limbs momentarily before they are in different locations on the airship.

In quarantine, they had moved with languor and ease. The thrill of our trip is foreshortened as it becomes apparent that wherever we are going, we will not be among peers.

"What is happening?" someone wails, "how is it that they can move so fast?"

I reflexively dig my fists into my eyes to block out the movements of the Guardians. The sound of balloons filling with hot air and the smell of thick plumes of steam dominate my senses and I breath in the warm humid air wishing I were back home. When I finally lift my fists from my eyes, the vessel is surrounded by a blue film behind which the clouds move by at such a tremendous speed that they are just a blur.

I not only see the movement but I also feel it in the gut of my stomach. It begins as a slow nauseous churning that becomes pain seizing my entire body. I fall over, buckling on the deck, collapsing alongside my countrymen whose kicking legs and flailing arms bruise my sides.

In the din, I hear the gruff shouts of Guardians in their twisted tongue as the vessel decreases markedly in speed. Healers rush to our side, bringing their palms flat on our head and our chests. Sharp pangs of pain jolt throughout my body, causing my eyes to water. Then as quickly as it had came, the pain subsides. It is not just the immediate pain that dissipates, but every cramp, injury, or discomfort I have felt since leaving Việt Nam—the constant hunger in my belly, the rawness of my bowels, the sharp nagging headache—all gone. Instead I am left feeling renewed as if the past ten years had just been erased. Momentary ecstasy befuddles me.

"Your people cannot travel at our speeds—it appears to result in severe internal degeneration," a Healer says to me and immediately my spirit sinks. *What was it? What was it that makes us so different from them when they look just like us? When they speak our words? When they bear our faces?*

"We must leave you behind. At this decreased acceleration, we will be open to attack. We are charged to take Nan Ngọc swiftly back to the Guardian compound. We will leave behind sufficient Guardians to protect you."

"Protect us from what?" But the Healer has already moved on to help someone else. That sinking feeling lodges deeper inside me and I find myself wishing I were back on my dilapidated fishing boat where I felt, at the very least, human among human beings. I rise in search of Ngọc. Of all our rescuers, it is Ngọc that I feel the most connected to. Ironic since it was Ngọc that all of us had feared the most at first.

We had all met Ngọc shortly after our rescue as it distributed tea and rice into our wearied hands. I had been instantly dumbstruck by its beauty. Underneath its skin, which wavered between translucency and unblemished coppery bronze, were several layers of rotating gears that intertwined with leafy vines and moss that made up the substance of its body. Its eyes, twin orbs of jade, were fanned by small turquoise and deep blue feathers that added softness to its human-like face. From the top of its head trailed braided branches and vines from which mahogany green leaves, mushrooms, and dark flowers emerged.

"Yạ greetings, Nan Ngọc," I had said as it handed a warm gourd of rice to me, "that is also our family name."

The automaton had made no acknowledgement of my attempt at familiarity.

"Yạ, Nan Ngọc," I had began again, "please tell me again what it is that you do so that we may know what to call on you for?"

"Yạ, I am here to provide you with food, water, and all that you require while you detoxify. And to collect your souls should you perish."

Its words had silenced me and I was afraid to speak to it further. Many of us had avoided Ngọc for fear that its intention was to take our souls like a demon. But Ngọc was boring for the most part, and I saw in its actions nothing mystical or magical.

During our quarantine, it had spent most of the time cycling through the preparation of nut dishes. Within its limbs were various sharp instruments that revealed themselves once its appendages were removed. With these, Ngọc chopped, diced, crushed and blended nuts with noisy vigor.

When nightfall fell in the quarantine camp, Ngọc had not slept. Instead, it sat in the middle of camp, surrounded by four Guardians, as if in a meditative state. I had laid silently on my bamboo mat studying with relish its every detail, the way the firelight bounced off its gears and the braid of vines down its back graced with small black flowers.

"Is it a custom of your people to gaze at others for long periods of time?" it finally asked one evening.

Startled, I had blushed, feeling the heat of embarrassment from being caught.

"Yạ, apologies, it's just that—we have nothing like you in our country."

"I am the only one of my kind."

"What are you?" I had asked, slowly inching my way closer to it.

"I am an automaton created to hold souls."

My face wrinkled in confusion. "Hold souls?"

"Yes. In the catastrophes of this world, souls have been lost to the dark void that surrounds our world—never to return—the void from which you emerged."

"You mean the Biển Đông?"

"If that was what it was for you. Our alchemists believe that the void is a transitory medium between universes."

"Universes?" I remember straining to understand Ngọc, feeling slightly abashed to have no knowledge of the world beyond my own country where I had spent most of my youth serving in the army. All that I knew was of war and fighting—not of other worlds and universes.

"In this void, we have lost valuable lineages, many of our people becoming ancestorless. I was created to preserve souls within the Waterlands until a new life is conceived."

"How can that be possible?"

"Within the core of my body is a chamber made of the searing of air, fire, molten metal and the tears of the kin of those that have departed. When someone passes, if a new vessel is not available, those that guard over death ensure the soul's safe passage into the chamber where it awaits rebirth."

Its words were a mystery to me and I had stared uncomprehending at its chest, searching for the chamber that it spoke of.

"It is protected, you will not be able to see it, try as you might."

"So if one of us dies..." but I had left my question hanging, afraid to complete it and Ngọc offered no answer.

~*~

As usual, I find Ngọc surrounded by four Guardians.

"Perhaps this will calm the nerves of your people," Ngọc says, deftly pouring tea into small gourds. I have always thought it a bit funny that the Guardians would be entrusted to guard someone whose main function is to brew tea and prepare snacks.

"Can I help?" I offer, finding immediate comfort in being near Ngọc. A tray of gourds filled with hot tea is pushed my way. Lifting the tray, I follow closely behind Ngọc to the chaos of the upper deck. My people are huddled sobbing and shaking, some still writhing in pain while Healers move swiftly through them.

Without warning, their screams of pain are suddenly replaced by terror as a loud explosion tears through the air. Beside our vessel where once there is empty sky, a large ebony creature appears roaring like madness, encircling our vessel, its long body oscillating in waves of shimmering green.

I am so filled with astonishment that I forget to be afraid, marveling at the sheer beauty of it. Its large red eyes glow as it circles the boat with a large ocular device on its left eye. From its serpentine back, several people flip and rotate onto the deck, transforming into flashes of light that flit about in all directions.

Immediately I find myself thrust against Ngọc as Guardians press their backs to us. My tray tips over spilling hot tea onto my chest and I howl at the scalding water, falling to my knees at Ngọc's feet. The Guardians spring into motion, forming layers of protection around Ngọc.

Their movements are so fast that dizziness besets me. Above me Ngọc's arms cross into a protective stance. The air moves around me and I feel something graze my side. The Guardians dance in rapid spins, jabs and thrusts, slashing at a force I cannot make out. The shine of blades I have never seen them carry send sparks into the air.

In the distance, I hear my mother scream and I attempt to dart out from under Ngọc towards the sound of her voice only to find myself slam against an invisible barrier. For long moments I claw and pound at the blue aura that surrounds Ngọc.

Only when I feel Ngọc's body fall hard against me, am I finally able to move. Then it is the circle of Guardians that serves as my obstacle. Around me, Guardians continue to clash their swords with an enemy whose face and body I can only glimpse, metallic gears in segments on their limbs and their naked torsos. I cradle Ngọc in my arms, quivering in fear at the bloodshed all around us.

Then a Guardian howls, landing on the deck in front of me, leaving me face to face with a person whose chest and torso is torn, frozen gears underneath flesh instead of muscle, tissue, and blood. The person lunges at Ngọc, moving faster than I have ever seen anyone being move. I crouch, bracing myself for impact.

Light surrounds me and I feel the brace of a death grip on my arms. I cling tighter to Ngọc, feeling its softness give way to a cold hard outer shell incapable of responding to my embrace. Pain rips through me as if I'm being torn molecule by molecule and darkness engulfs me.

~*~

When I awake, I am laying in a corner of an unfamiliar dark room. Voices swirl around me, echoing indistinctly. I attempt to rise but vertigo grips me as a sharp pain throbs in my head. My stomach begins to rumble dangerously and bile rises in my throat making me keel over, vomiting to my side.

I hear scuffing near me. Above me are stalactites and I realize that I must be inside a cave. I feel the splash of cold water on my face, startling me. Beside me kneels a woman, gears and pulleys curl within her right eye, sliding down her neck and shoulders to her torso, the blue and red of veins snaking around the gears. I reel at the sight of her, hitting my back hard on the rock wall behind me.

Sounds of a blade slicing into metal come from behind the woman where, on a table lit only by a few torches, lies Ngọc, still as death, a man hovering above it with a round swiveling blade in his hand. I call out to Ngọc, but my own voice comes out hoarse, barely audible.

The man at the table turns towards me, diving down towards me faster than I can catch my breath. He pulls my head back and stares at me, his eyes boring through me. On the left side of his bare torso are gears that run the length of his chest and down his left arm. He shakes me violently and I attempt to push back at him only to find my wrists and ankles bound.

"Who are you?" he asks me, "why can't we map you?"

"What?" I respond, confused.

Then the sharp sound of blades begin again and I can see that the woman has resumed their attempt to cut into Ngọc's chest.

"What are you doing to it?" I demand.

The man shoves me against the wall. "Why can't we map you?" he yells.

"Map me? I don't know what you are talking about." He strikes me hard, flat across my face. I spit at him in frustration, unsure of whether I understand his odd accent correctly. I draw back and flail my body attempting to strike at him, but I only manage to tumble over, sliding down the slippery rock floor causing my rubbery bindings to tighten.

Waving an impatient arm my way, the woman calls out, drawing the man back to the table where together they pry open Ngọc's chest. Sobs I cannot control pour from me as Ngọc's beautiful braided vines and gears are torn from its innards leaving its hull barren, protruding with jagged edges of cut metal.

Over the next few days, frustration and anxiety begins to build between my captors as they dig with more and more ferocity into Ngọc's chest. Watching its dissection piece-by-piece kills a part of me. Its chest is now completely bared, its side panels torn aside to reveal a thick inner metallic cylindrical core.

"It's too thick, it's impossible to cut through," I hear one of them say.

"Maybe there is a way to bring jzan soul to prominence," the other replies.

Their arguments are punctuated by moments when I am dragged to the table and thrown over Ngọc. Their movements are as swift as the Guardians, and every time I am moved, I feel as if I am being torn from the inside out, my vomit becoming filtered with my own blood.

"Open the chamber!" they demand, pointing to Ngọc's chest.

"I can't!" I say over and over but their eyes show only disbelief before flinging me against the wall.

~*~

Days I cannot track pass. Perpetual darkness shrouds the cave. Dehydration causes my lips to crack while hunger continuously tears at me and I have soiled on myself more times than I can remember. My stench must have become ripe because one day I awake to being dragged across the cave floor and thrown into water. I startle awake to find myself drenched and sitting in a pond of water in the shadows of the cave. In its depths I see what looks like an opening into an underwater tunnel.

Underground caves! Near our fishing village, we had an entire vast network of them. From time to time I swam through them. I had never swam more than a mile—but if that was the only route of escape I had...

A thought comes to me. I cannot move as fast as they can, I can never outrun them, but I can swim. I can swim as far as my strength can take me. And I can disappear into the water, into mud, into dust. I have done it time and again in the war—and when I fled my country.

I begin watching Ngọc with more vigilance. The woman often takes to napping, laying her head on the table, as the man continues to tinker with Ngọc. From time to time he too would doze, leaning back in his seat and crossing his arms. Then they'd wake and circle around Ngọc, fervid expressions on their faces.

On the fourth observation of this cycle, I decide to act. I wait until the woman lays her head down in exasperation. The man always follows soon after her. When he lifts his legs to the table and his chin comes to rest on his chest, my heart begins to beat wildly in anticipation. When I hear his light snoring begin, I roll quickly to the table and reach up to slip my bound arms around Ngọc's neck.

Pulling Ngọc towards me, I brace for its weight, but it is not as heavy as I predicted; it has been severely hollowed out. With it resting on me, I writhe to the edge of the pond and slip silently into the water.

Through the opening of the tunnel, I swim like a dolphin, my arms and legs still bound, holding Ngọc at my side in a choke- hold. Where the tunnel will lead me, I do not know. How much I will have to swim before I find air, I do not know. At this point, I no longer care.

I swim as far as I can, allowing the opening to pull me. Darkness surrounds me and my lungs begin to burn but still I swim. My instinct is to go upwards so I undulate my body, pushing water around me as much as I can until my head hits the top of a rock ceiling. I search for air pockets and find several small ones where I swallow mouthfuls of air.

Time begins to fail me and after a while I begin to feel as if an eternity has passed as I meander through the water endlessly, desperately searching for air pockets. I do not know how long I have been swimming, whether it has been hours or days—I only know that my endurance is beginning to fail me as the slow creep of panic begins to inch its way through the membranes of my lungs.

A few more circles through the tunnels and I begin to get dizzy, feeling as if I have been turned around, afraid that I would swim back into the cave that I escaped from. Time and again I find myself slamming my fists at finding the same pocket of air—feeling the crude markings I had scratched with my own nails on the rock ceiling.

Then the moment came, as I knew it surely would—when my bound ankles cannot pump any longer, when my arms begin to resist pushing through the water, when I am too weary to hold my head high enough to breathe. I feel myself sinking, Ngọc still locked in my arms. Weariness from somewhere deep in my bones overcomes me.

Stranded in a large air pocket that I seem to keep coming back to, I begin to sob. My bound fingers feel all over Ngọc's shorn jagged parts. There is no button that I can push, nothing to flip, nothing to switch on or off. Frustrated, I throw myself against it, banging its head against the top of the air pocket.

"Wake up damn it!" I sputter, water beginning to seep into my lungs. Then I laugh. I laugh at the absurdity of my journey. At the flight in the dead of night from our fishing village, at the days lost, dying of starvation in the South China Sea, to being rescued and stationed in an island paradise by the oddest people I had ever met, to being taken by an air serpent and machine people and bound wallowing in my own filth in a dark cave with an automaton made of pieces of a clock and leaves. I laughed at how ludicrous it all was.

"I am unsure whether you expressing happiness or grief."

Ngọc's voice startles me and I turn it over. Its eyes light up and for the first time in what feels like days, light painfully dilates my eyes. The gears along the side of its head, which had been sliced open, rotate a few clicks.

"Ngọc!" I say, excitement and adrenaline rushing me.

But then its jade eyes fade and I am left in darkness once again. My fingers fumble along its head, searching for the gears I just saw. Once I feel them, I manually rotate them.

"It appears that we are situated in a very precarious position." The air pocket illuminates with the green glow of Ngọc's eyes.

"We're in an underground cave system. We need to find a way out." I watch as the gears on Ngoc's head rotate.

"I can map us, but it will make our position known." Its last words wind down slowly and I immediately rotate its gears.

"Map us? What does that mean? They kept asking me why I could not be mapped."

"In our world, all living creatures exist in a vast Fabric." I reach out to wind its gears before they slow down.

"I am equipped to connect to a wavelength that is receivable upon the Fabric. It is not a direct link because only those who follow the jzan path can open a direct channel. I will use the organisms in this pond to relate us."

"Jzan Nguyệt will be able to receive it and locate us?"

"Yes. You cannot be mapped because you are not from our world."

"Not from your world?" That same sinking feeling came back to me. Am I a ghost?

"I can instruct you on how to enable it but once it is on, I will be open to both the Guardians and the Machinists."

"Machinists?"

"Those that brought us here."

"What choice do we have? We will die down here."

"You will die."

I sigh.

"But what I hold is of great importance. I cannot remain here lost in this cave."

"How do I turn it on? But first, tell me how I can get one of your blades."

~*~

After I enable the mechanism, Ngọc directs our course through the tunnel until we reach a river. Relief fills me as I roll onto my back and swim with Ngọc strapped onto my belly. Inhaling deeply, I can taste the difference in the air.

"Who are they? The Machinists—they had machines in their bodies."

"They are not made of machines. What you saw were brandings that were inscribed on their bodies."

"Drawn on them?"

"Yes, for their beliefs, in opposition to the Guardians' markings." I hear a hint of resentment in Ngoc's words and I wonder if that is even possible for an automaton.

"What are their beliefs?"

The river narrows into an enclosed tunnel.

"This is a question better suited for another time. This will be your last swim before we reach the opening of this cave. Beyond it is a waterfall."

"How long will I swim?"

"Approximately two minutes."

"Two minutes Ngọc? I can't hold my breath for two minutes!"

"Midway through, the current will strengthen, increasing your speed."

Ngoc's words are not reassuring. "I don't have two minutes," I say sadly.

"If you activate my chamber, I will be ready to collect your soul."

I turn toward it horrified. It registers my horror without response. Closing my eyes, I prepare myself. I can swim, I tell myself. If nothing else, I can swim.

Then I grab Ngọc and propel myself off the top wall of the cave. Making broad strokes, I scale the length of the tunnel as fast as I can. My unbound hands and legs move water past us with all the velocity I can manage. I cannot move as fast as them, I cannot see, hear, nor speak like they do, but I can swim.

The current does begin to pull us forcefully, but not soon enough as the burning in my lungs begins to give way to darkness. Consciousness begins to leave me and my arms and legs slow down, unable to respond any longer. Just as water begins to fill my lungs, blinding light stings my eyes and air rushes at me, clear beautiful fresh air. Wrapping myself around Ngọc, I brace myself as we plummet down a waterfall.

A load blast ruptures the air followed by a flash of light that whizzes past us. Jzan Nguyệt's airship appears and beside it, the Machinists' enormous raven beast carrying several Machinist's on its haunches. Both trail beside us as we plummet. Tumbling through the air, Nguyệt leaps from the ship to seize us, side-sweeping the blows of three Machinists who also plunge towards us.

Guardians fling themselves from the airship after the Machinists who twirl in the air as they are falling. In flashes and streaks their blades meet as I am catapulted back onto to airship in Nguyệt's grip, landing in a painful thud on the floor of the deck, my limbs still wrapped around Ngọc. Immediately I feel my insides resist the speed of the movement and I dry heave onto the deck attempting to grasp onto a reality that refuses to remain still.

Pain cleaves through my mind, searing my body as the ship maneuvers towards the waterfall below the tumbling Guardians. Deflecting the Machinists, the Guardians tumble onto the airship and, before I can even register their appearance, the ship spins wildly and leans sharply to the left. A hand grabs me as I rocket down the deck and Nguyệt's palm comes to rest flat against my forehead, flooding me with calmness, taking my pain—and my consciousness.

~*~

When I awake, Ngọc is beside me, its face and chest barren. Jagged cuts jut from all angles of it where the Machinists' blade has sawed through it.

"We have arrived," Nguyệt approaches me, bowing, "You have our deepest gratitude for returning Ngọc to us."

Around the ship is the sea and in the distance along a foggy horizon is the outline of a mountain with the vague rings of a city encircling it. Near it are a dozen or more narrow mountains that jut above the fog, some connected by a thin bridge.

"It looks just like Vịnh Hạ Long," I say, marveling at the beauty of the landscape.

"You will have to tell me more about your bay one day, it rings familiar."

"Is that where we are going?" I ask, referring to the mountain directly in front of us, bracing myself as a brief wave of nausea washes over me.

"We will return to our compound." Nguyệt points upwards towards the right. I look up, confused, seeing only the sky and clouds.

Beside me Nguyệt is flanked by several Guardians whose entire faces are covered with intricate drawings. Unlike them, only the left half of Nguyệt's face holds a delicate pattern that twists and turns, weaving some unique tale. I want to ask what story is hidden in the drawings, but Nguyệt interrupts my thoughts.

"Yạ, please accept our apologies for your troubles. It was our intent to acclimate your people slowly to our world, to find ways to address the limitations of your senses. I regret the difficult introduction you have all had."

"They are safe?" I ask, ignoring jzan inferences about my abilities, feeling a twinge of humiliation.

"Yạ, yes, and awaiting your arrival."

"The black beast..."

"Rồng, our living ancestor, from whom we are descended. In our world their transcendental form can only be achieved with the assistance of alchemy and the ocular tool."

"Their transcendental form?"

"At a cost. Day by day this world ties them to human form."

"And the Machinists—they were tearing Ngọc apart—why?"

Nguyệt turns to look at me, jzan eyes thoughtful with concerns that stretched far outside the scope of the question. I can feel the ship rise gradually and I cannot help but wonder if we are traveling slowly for my benefit. Chagrin fills me.

"The Machinist have attempted many times to take Nan Ngọc. It is the chamber within nan body that they seek."

"The one that holds souls."

"Yạ, yes, Ngọc carries the soul of one of their deceased, a truly gifted alchemist and warrior. We believe they are attempting to secure certain reincarnation of that soul."

"That," I hesitate, "Can be done?"

"It *cannot* be done, but there are those that believe it possible. The Machinist believe many things that are not... Some among them believe that a world exists where machines dominate, a world completely unlike ours. They believe that we, that I, have abandoned our own there and that we are burdened with the obligation to search for and return to this world."

"What do you believe?"

"I believe that our world requires all of our focus. And now that your people are among us, you too are a part of our world."

The clouds part and we pass a mountain of elegant green rice terraces. I feel as if I am returning home, nostalgia thick in my throat. Turning from the majestic countryside towards the mountains looming in the distance, I expect to see meandering rivers, urban roads and the signs of a civilization.

But instead what I see is each mountain island, unconnected to each other, standing solitary, floating by itself surrounded by nothing but the air. Turning reflexively to look back at the helm of the vessel, I see not the sea, as it should be, but a colossal waterfall that spans an entire horizon. Between the waterfall and the mountain is neither miles of cliffs nor the roaring lapping waves of the sea. Between them, there is nothing—absolutely nothing but the emptiness of the wind.

"Where..." I turn to Nguyệt, "Where is the rest of the ocean?"

~*~

No matter how sharp my combat maneuvers are or how well synchronized my movements through the Bronze Drum choreography is, it is evident that I lack the basic abilities for candidacy as a Guardian. The taste of my own blood from hitting the ground after missing the inaudible cue of the young Guardian leading the entrance trials still lingers in my mouth. I was disqualified immediately, as were about a hundred and fifty other natives.

I walk slowly back to our home, ignoring as much as I can, the world around me that I fail to fully experience. To rebuild our community, we had been given a small circular hamlet adjacent to the Guardians' compound in the center of the largest mountain island of the Waterlands of Lạc.

A short walk away from all of the amenities of the island, mother views the hamlet as an extension of the generosity of the people, especially since those that once dwelled there willingly vacated the hamlet for us. To me, though, it is just an acknowledgement that we are far from being self-sufficient. In the most unexpected moments, Nguyệt's words come back to haunt me, "in our country, your senses are severely impaired." I am only beginning to brush the surface of the meaning of these words.

The fragmentation of the Waterlands was the final shock that sent many of our people into denial, whistling about their days focused only on acclimation to their hamlet life as if the thousands of floating islands of Lạc did not exist. They consciously ignored the fact that these islands are completely inaccessible to us except at a snail's pace on board airships that only hover at minimal speeds for our benefit. On a daily basis, the pace of life in our new world far bypasses our natural abilities. Yet we all pretend that we do not care. Most of all mother.

Returning to our hamlet, I find her bent over the hearth at the center of the ringlet of homes designated as ours. Focused on her current obsession, mother lays before her the exotic spices that she has collected from the air-market.

Determined to create the right concoction of spices to create phở, her favorite soup, I find her scribbling notes with a twig using a thick savory sauce that tastes like a combination of soy and coconut sauce as ink.

Mother smiles as I approach. Despite my unease at our situation, it does bring me comfort to see her happy.

"Almost there. I just need something that is close to Sài Gòn cinnamon and none of these come close." Mother's fingers jab at the spices in front of her.

I study her notes, impressed at her dedication.

"It's so strange, mother, how can they have ships that fly through the sky unlike anything we've ever seen, at speeds that defy the best airplanes, and still run around nearly naked, can't read or write, and live in these." I look around at the circular homes built of mud bricks, lacking completely of doors. The only entrances to the homes, which circled into one another through oval openings, are bamboo thatches on the roofs that also double as the streets of the hamlet.

Mother laughs as she nibbles on different spices.

"Do not underestimate what you cannot understand. Tell me, how were the candidacy trials?"

I turn away, hiding the tears that fight to come to the surface. I feel mother's eyes hard on me.

After an awkward silence passes between us, mother says finally, "Soon I will find the right mixture of ingredients and our soup can be traded in the air-market. If people like it, we will be very busy. Already your aunt and uncle have been trading the áo dài they've fashioned. Have you seen them? The fibers the Guardians gifted to us are so soft! They have gained much favor among the people—especially after

Jzan Nguyệt wore jzan áo dài uncle made of trailing feathers at the ceremony."

Mother had fallen to using their titles and already I could feel the language of our people slowly changing and the dialect of our rescuers intermingling with ours, usurping it. I sigh feeling the disquiet within me simmering.

"The trials were difficult. What it is that they see, I do not know and I can't figure out fast enough to respond. I cannot hear what they are saying half the time and they have to make special hand signals just to make sure I can detect the nuances of their speech. Only those that move like lightning have a chance and even they have a second trial to undergo." I cannot finish, feeling frustration welling inside of me. I rise instead, and retreat to my bamboo mat, feeling the weight of my mother's sympathy behind me like an unwanted embrace.

"Dinner will be ready soon," mother calls behind me. I slump onto my mat.

"Child," mother calls to me, "Remember, all that we can do is give the best of ourselves."

I sigh, my heart falling at her words. I had managed to pull Ngọc out of the depths of this world's hell. I just cannot believe that my "best" is selling soup or hocking áo dài like some flea market salesperson.

I lay my head down only to hear moments later a familiar voice at our rooftop entrance. I rise instantly, walking quickly to the courtyard where I am met by Ngọc, fully restored and followed by four Guardians who graciously entertain mother's discussion of our region's dishes. Upon seeing me, Ngọc excuses itself to greet me, leaving the Guardians behind to sample mother's experimental recipes.

"I have come with condolences for today's trials."

I feel embarrassed at its words.

"You did not need to do that."

"It is only reasonable that someone capable of escaping the Machinist, even given your limitations, would aspire to be a Guardian."

I don't know whether to take its words warmly or to be offended.

"I have something to show you. Somewhere private?" I am confused. I have not known Ngọc to ever require discretion; nevertheless, I direct it to my bamboo mat.

"What you have, no other Guardian candidate can match."

"What's that?" I asked, unconvinced.

"Your knowledge, your memories."

At these words, Ngọc taps its chest and a small panel slides out.

"What do you remember of this?" it asks as I stare at the handcrafted instrument in the middle of the panel. It is made of the finest bamboo embellished with an intricate metallic circular design; its handle displays ornate carvings and its series of bronze gears are polished to a shine. An intricate eyepiece is mounted on top of it to increase its accuracy.

Though its machinery is different, the addition of gears and gadgets here and there adding some element of functionality I do not understand, it is, in essence, not unlike any other pistol I have ever seen or fired, though the barrel could probably stand to be improved to increase bullet speed. I do know about this. I knew about when it had been pointed at me and when I had held it in my own hands in the war.

I turn to Ngọc.

"Is this something the Guardians want? Or Jzan Nguyệt? These can bring death and violence. I thought they were all about non-violence and peace."

"It is for neither."

"Then who—?"

I stopped mid-sentence and drew back from Ngọc, wondering for the first time at what I had rescued.

"It is time for a new era, a new focus, one that will bring us back where we belong. Your memory and your contribution will be priceless, and your place among us cemented."

"Us?" I ask.

Ngọc makes no reply.

I reach for the pistol then, feeling its weight in my hand, stroking its intricate gears, and its handcrafted eye scope. With the exception of Ngọc, it is the most beautiful thing I have ever laid eyes on.

Petrified

Ivanna Mendels

Biwar was a big man. Compared to his Sumatran and Javanese crew, his Papuan origins made him taller and more muscular than most of them. These traits, along with his tattooed face and thick, frizzy hair, uncommon around the western part of the Indian Ocean, usually made him look fearless and formidable. Today, however, he was feeling neither, as he sat in front of the two military officers who were going to question him.

Dealing with military officers was never his area of expertise. Despite being the first mate of the famous air ship, the *Sweet Water*, he had always left this particular activity to his captain. Biwar had no choice today. The captain was nowhere to be found.

He placed his sword on top of the table, between him and the officers. The sight of the sword always had a calming effect on him. "So you really want to know what happened?" He let out an involuntary shrug. He didn't want to be here; he wanted to go and rest somewhere. "To tell you the truth, I'm still not sure what really happened either," Biwar said.

Since about five years ago, the *Sweet Water* had been patrolling the Indian Ocean, the Strait of Malacca and the Java Sea—helping out the new Republic Nusantara against the threat of returning Dutch colonials, and the ever presence threat of Portuguese and French invasion.

The newly independent archipelago gained its victory recently, thanks to the ingenious giant steam automatons created by Professor Adipati Dewanto. In 1874, the twelve steam titans—now in display at the professor's school in Batavia during these times of peace—took the Dutch colonials by surprise in a decisive battle on the coast of Atjeh. Never in their years of colonizing the archipelago had the Dutch seen any hint of technological advances. In just a couple of years that followed, the professor lashed out his geared titans upon them, wiping out every trace of Dutch outposts all over the archipelago.

Nobody seemed to really know where the Professor came from, nor where he had gained such advanced knowledge on steam engines. Given his contributions to the archipelago's independence, however, no one objected when he was appointed as the new presidential advisor. The Republic had since prospered under his watch. Adipati's steam ships also patrol the waters, securing new trade routes with neighboring countries as far as Siam.

The *Sweet Water* did not operate under the new government; they also sort of began their career looting other ships like pirates. After learning the word from some French traders, however, Captain Mal had preferred the term "corsair." They only attacked the enemies of the nation, after all. Biwar was very proud to be part of the *Sweet Water*. He actually felt patriotic most of the time too. Unfortunately for him, after last night, the majestic *Sweet Water* was no more, and Biwar was the only known survivor of the strange event that had befallen its ill-fated crew.

He stared uneasily at the two officers in front of him. Something was really strange about these two. They claimed to be from special units in the military, but one of them actually looked like a fifteen-year-old girl. They also both wore dark, hooded jackets, despite the fact that it was almost thirty degrees out here by the beach. The jackets were bare; none of the usual military insignias were visible.

The other one introduced himself as Buto. He was taller and almost bigger than Biwar, which was quite a surprise, since Biwar was seldom shorter or smaller than anyone around the western parts of the republic. Biwar remembered the boy, though. Last year, he had somehow managed to combine hot air balloon technology with train piston mechanisms, and added the strange contraption to the *Sweet Water*—making it the first ever airship to patrol the new Republic.

Although Buto seemed to be slightly older than the girl, the only time he spoke was when he introduced himself. The girl took charge of the questioning right away, and she spoke with certainty, with the air of authority of someone who had already known more details about the events than Biwar himself.

"Take your time," the girl said, "Tell us what you remember. Everything you can remember."

Biwar inhaled deeply. *All this mess began about two weeks ago.*

"We tracked them down all the way from Sunda Kelapa port to the West Sumatran coast of Teluk Bayur. You know who I'm talking about, right? Because I'm still not sure who they really are. All Captain Mal said was that this trip had to do with military secrets..." Biwar waited, wondering if the girl would confirm this. She stared at him patiently, quietly. Almost as quiet as a lion watching its prey, Biwar thought. Her eyes seemed to give off a faint green glow under the shadow of her hood.

"Anyway, two weeks ago, after receiving a message from an unknown source in the port of Batavia, the Captain seemed to mistrust us. He barely ordered us to do our duties anymore, preferring to do things himself. I naturally took charge of everything else, as was my duty as his first mate, but I cannot deny that there was general uneasiness amongst the crew. We all felt that our Captain was keeping a terrible secret from us."

The girl raised an eyebrow. It was the first time Biwar noticed a change of expression in her face.

"Uh..." Biwar scratched his head, feeling suddenly anxious under her gaze. "Well, we didn't know whether the secret was terrible or not. I did try to confront him. Told him his attitude was bringing everyone to the edge. He dismissed it. Joked about it, really, blaming it on the bad oysters we had before we left the port." Biwar sighed, "But everyone could tell something was making him uneasy. He was acting strange. When he was not doing most of our usual duties by himself, he kept to his own cabin, but then wandered the decks alone all night... Once, we received reports on a Portuguese spy ship along the coast of Bali, and he totally ignored it, even barked at one of the crew for pursuing the matter. This was not the Captain we knew. With the modified ship, we could have gone to Bali, taken care of the spies and got back on route towards West Sumatra only a few days behind schedule."

Biwar realized he was leaning on the table, too excited with his own story. He had talked too much. He always talked too much when he was nervous. He cursed under his breath. "This is why I don't handle military officers," he muttered, barely audible. He never knew how much he should tell them. The captain always knew exactly how much to tell. He always played his cards right, helping the military as demanded, using them as much to his own advantage. It was all a game, and Biwar was not good at games. Making his crew obey him was easier. Seamen respect his strength and his excellent navigation skills. He never needed to elaborate his orders.

He leaned away, not wanting to upset the girl. Something about the way the girl stared at him made him really uncomfortable. He could have sworn she had not blinked even once ever since he began telling his story.

"He wasn't himself, not since two weeks ago... He got a bit worse before we arrived at the port."

"Worse?"

"Fidgety, tense." Biwar waved his hand, as if dismissing the details, "Anyway, it is a bit hard to land the air ship on small harbors, you see, so first of all, someone had to go down the rope ladder to secure it to the ground. We can"t just randomly throw an anchor from an air ship." He grinned sheepishly, "Might hit someone on the head, eh?"

Behind the girl, the Buto mumbled something, nodding to himself while furiously sketching and writing on a small leather-bound notebook. He had taken off his hooded jacket. Despite only wearing a thin white shirt, he was sweating profusely. The girl did not seem to be bothered by the heat at all.

"I'll work on the anchor system," Buto said, still slightly mumbling without looking up from his sketches.

"Yeah, sure... I'm sure Captain Mal would..." Biwar stopped himself. No one had seen Captain Mal since yesterday night.

"Go on," the girl said after several seconds of awkward silence.

"Oh, yes. Well, anyway, the captain decided he should be the one going down to the shore. He used to help his old master dock, but it had been several years since he had done this himself. He also decided to dress in his old pirate... uh... I mean... corsair..."

"That's okay," Buto interjected, there was no judgment in his tone. "Everybody has to start somewhere."

"I see." Biwar gave the boy a little smile, "I, uh, I asked him about the attire. It was his famous signature blood red! I didn't see why anyone would have wanted to be recognized as a pirate... especially since the Dutch had been continuously trying to gain back access to the land, you know how most of them disguised themselves as traders, riding in with pirates from the coast of..."

"We know how it is with pirates." The girl sounded like a judge pronouncing a final sentence. Biwar was used to Captain Mal becoming slightly exasperated with his ramblings, but there were always signs when someone became exasperated. Eyes rolling, deep sighing, fingers tapping on the table. The girl showed none of this; there was only that certain finality in her tone.

Probably sensing this, Buto cleared his throat, launching Biwar back into his story.

"Well, he ignored my remarks on his attire and then, when I volunteered to go, you know, to help with the docking? He actually snarled at me as if I was offering to burn the ship or something. He also specifically told the crew to stay on board.

"Now I've travelled for more than four years with the Captain, some of the crew even longer than that. Do you know we would gladly follow him, to even the end of the seven seas despite his young age?" Not many people knew, nor believed, that the Captain was actually the youngest person in the *Sweet Water*.

"Before the *Sweet Water*, we were all low life scums. Pirates, ex-slaves, beggars—but he made us believe we could be heroes. We were always a team, an unstoppable team. We just could not understand why, at this particular mission, he did not want any of us to come down."

"So you came after him despite his orders?" asked the girl.

Biwar nodded firmly, he did not regret his decision. "I guess when he went, I followed him anyway... I mean, look, the whole place almost felt idyllic, yeah?" Biwar gestured out of the window, only to realize that it was closed tight. "I don't know." He shrugged. "It looked as if it was untouched by the war. Clear water, no real ports, small fishing boats, you know what I mean." He paused, taking a deep breath, preparing himself for the next part of his story. "And yet... something felt wrong. I just felt it. I have been hunting a lot in my life. There are just some tell-telling signs when there was a bigger predator nearby.

"And I was right, as soon as his feet touched the ground, all hell broke loose. There was a loud bang from a nearby fishing village, followed by screams and wailings. At first, I could only see smoke and fire, then someone was running down the beach towards us.

"I said run, but actually that old woman was not really moving that fast," Biwar added, now remembering a little bit more details of the event. It was not that easy to remember everything, given how it all happened so fast.

"There were two... things... behind her. I think they were chasing her, but they were not moving fast either."

"Things?" The girl prodded. Her voice changed a little bit, sounding more interested, but he could have sworn she was still not blinking.

Biwar could not help it. "I'm sorry, what did you say your name was?"

"Kat," Buto answered for her, "You can call her Kat."

Cat? Biwar thought it was a very strange name, but Kat herself didn't even seem to notice the question. She repeated herself, "Why did you say they were *things*? Are they not men?"

"I..." Biwar began, then paused, looking for the words. "First of all, they were grey. I mean I know they were dressed in all grey but their skin too look grey and dull, like stone. They moved like... they were dragging their feet. Their arms hung heavy by their sides... Have you ever been to those picture shows?" Biwar said, suddenly remembering the last time they had docked in Batavia. There was a technological fair by the port and the captain, fascinated with these pictures shows, had paid for all his crews to join him.

"Cinematograph shows?" Buto asked.

"Yes, well..." Biwar never heard that word before. While the western part of the new republic was thriving with new technologies, his own hometown in Papua was so far on the eastern side that it was more or less cut off from the rest of the archipelago. He might be one of the best sailors in the whole Nusantara, but new engines still baffled him. In fact, without wanting to admit it, he was still quite upset about last year when Buto modified their ship to fly.

"When I went to see one, the... errr, cinematosomething machine was not working properly and whole thing slowed down. These... things... they moved like that... like still pictures forced to somehow move. Like there was an interval, a fraction of their movements that was missing."

Kat frowned, looking suddenly concerned. She stole a glance towards Buto, who nodded silently.

So they didn't know everything, thought Biwar.

The girl shook her head, as if dismissing her own thoughts. "What happened then?"

"The old woman was saying something about the children, something about those grey things trying to take all the children. We didn't see any children around though, just her. Those grey things followed, and the Captain shot at them. Not really at them, he started with a warning shot, at the ground by their feet."

"He did not shoot at them?" It was Buto again, sounding amused.

"No, he kept his aim on their head after the first warning shot, though, and asked them about the children and a certain professor." Biwar paused, suddenly realizing something in his own story. He searched the faces of his interrogators, "We are not talking about the same professor, are we? Is he in trouble? Is the New Republic in trouble?"

"You knew the professor?" Kat asked.

"Of course! Who doesn't? Adipati Dewanto, right? *The* Professor? The national hero?"

"No!" Buto's voice sounded a little bit too harsh and loud.

"I... uh... is there another professor? Ah, yes, Captain Mal once told me." Biwar nodded, recalling the old tale, "When he rescued me from being sold as a slave... He said he was once a victim like me, that he was once a slave to someone he only knew as the professor. He said the professor damaged his arm badly. You know about his right arm, right? Of course you do, I remember it." Biwar turned to Buto. "You gave him the mechanical glove, the same week you came to fix our ship. Ah, I remember that particular year, everyone had a problem crossing the Java Sea."

"The currents were particularly strong during those years, yes." Buto nodded.

"Strong? I would say the water was sentient! It would be calm for days and then as soon as a ship was drawing near, it would go crazy. Well, anyway, you sure fixed that problem by making us fly. Thank a lot!" Biwar didn't try to hide the sarcasm in his voice.

"I'm sure you'll get around to learning all the technical parts, Biwar." Buto smiled. "You are one of the best sailors I've known, and a flying ship is still a ship, after all."

Biwar couldn't help but take pride at that comment. The boy was right, of course; there wasn't any ship in the world that Biwar couldn't handle. Flying or not. Except for one obvious problem. There was no flying ship anymore. The thought soured his mood, "Anyway... The captain said your glove really helped him move his slightly paralyzed fingers. He never used his old glove ever again."

"I think it's only fair that you know," Kat said, after glancing sideways at Buto as if seeking permission. "This very same professor kidnapped your Captain from this very beach when he was just about fifteen, and did some terrible experiments on him. He had been doing experiments on other people, too. Your Captain, however, was the youngest test subject, and the only one who survived the test. How he even managed to escape after being subjected to those experiments... we could only imagine. He never really wanted to talk about those days..."

"Experiments... Is that what happened to his fingers?" Biwar shook his head. "He never told me... They did experiments on him? What kind..." He stopped. If the captain had wanted him to know, he would have told Biwar already.

"Anyway, while aiming at those grey men, the captain seemed to almost forget the woman, who was now hiding behind us. She said something then, something about him being her long lost son. Captain Mal ignored her, but those grey men suddenly turned back towards the village, ignoring the captain's gun-blade that was still pointed at their head... and the Captain shot them both in the head. No hesitation. Blood oozed from the wound on their heads."

"Oozed?" Buto interjected.

"Yes, I said oozed, not flowed. Their blood looked reddish grey, like mud," Biwar confirmed.

Kat frowned, she glanced sideways at Buto, as if waiting for him to say something. When he did not, she nodded at Biwar, "Then what happened?"

"Perhaps hearing more than one shot, more of those strange men emerged from the village elder's gadang house. I assumed the children were kept there while they awaited the ghost ship we have been following from Batavia. We didn't see the ship when we arrived. It has a way of disappearing when we get close to it.

"The Captain shot them too. Then he turned to me, and we both knew he didn't have many bullets left in that gun. He hadn't planned to use the gun at all. Whatever he was thinking when he came down in his pirate's attire, he hadn't thought of fighting. I got myself ready to fight, pulling out my own sword." He glanced at the table where the darkened bone sword, with shark teeth carefully sewn around its edges sat. "But the captain shook his head at me."

"And then there were just so many more of those feet-dragging, dangly-armed men coming out of the gadang house. By this time I honestly wasn't paying attention to numbers anymore. They were shooting at us. The Captain was shooting back while yelling at us. So much confusion in so little time.

"He told us to go back to the ship. Naturally I refused. He had once saved my life. How could I leave him to fight those strange men alone? The old woman refused too. As the Captain repeated his order, she said, 'I'm your mother, Malin, why don't you remember me?'"

"Those were her exact words?" Kat asked.

"You know, it's weird, everything else was a bit of a blur to me, but I remember those words clearly, there was just something in the way she said those words. So much... pain... and I think she had somehow grabbed his hand as she said this, because the next thing I know, the Captain was shaking his arm so hard the old woman was actually thrown back towards me.

"He told her he didn't know her. He told me to drag her away. I... I didn't have time to reflect on any of this at that time, but now, now I think that it was strange to see the Captain like that. He could be fearsome in battles, but he had never treated women and children this way. He was even honorable towards prisoners of war... mostly... It was what set him apart from the other pirates. You know that, don't you?"

Buto nodded, "Malin has been working with us these past two years. I know how honorable he can be."

Biwar smiled, feeling a certain camaraderie in that last statement. He also noted how Buto had slipped and called the Captain by his real name, and without the title.

"Well, anyway, as she fell towards me, she accidentally pulled the glove off his arm. She saw his arm. I saw his arm too. I never saw his arm without his glove before and well, it was all grey, like those men... You gave him the mechanical glove. Do you know this?" Biwar looked at Buto but the boy avoided his gaze, preferring to make more notes in his book.

"I didn't know what to think, but she clearly did. She threw the glove hard towards him and started to actually curse at him. She said that he was just like those stone men. She asked what he had done to her real son. And the Captain actually raised that heavy petrified arm towards her. He told her that her son had died a long time ago."

"How did you get separated from Malin then?" Kat asked.

"I told you I didn't want to leave... but then he grabbed my shirt and looked me directly in the eyes. He said that he had saved me, so that now I owed it to him to survive." Biwar paused, remembering that moment. "I decided that whatever was going to happen, it was wiser to go up the ship and call our men. I ran back to the ship with the old lady."

"If you were at the ship..." Buto began.

"You don't understand. When I turned around towards our ship, it was already gone! I sorely remembered that we had not had the time to tie the ship nor drop the anchor. With those men shooting behind us, I ran to the water, got into the first fishing boat I could find, all the while dragging the lady, and rowed as fast as I could. The last thing I saw at the shore was the captain running towards the village." He stopped. Somehow feeling exhausted now that he managed to recall the whole event.

"It was daylight when we left the shore, and following the sun, I was able to go further down to the ocean without straying too far from the coast. The boat had no real shelter though, the noonday heat was enough to make the old lady pass out. She must have been exhausted. Sometime during the afternoon, lacking fresh water, I decided to rest. I woke up much later, when the boat shook violently. It was already dark, so I looked up to check the stars to get our bearings. That was when I saw the chunks of rocks falling out from the sky!

"Well, you found me afterwards. You probably already knew more than me..."

"I see." Buto said, and when Biwar just stared blankly at his own hands, he added, "Thank you for your time." It was Kat's turn to be quiet now. Buto stood up and saw Biwar out the door.

~*~

"Should we send in the lady now?" Kat asked as Buto closed the door behind Biwar.

"Do you know you didn't blink once while you were recording?" Buto said. "You scared the poor man to death!"

"I didn't?" the girl asked, blinking in a sudden, rapid succession.

"Did you send the transmission to the headquarters?"

"Yes, I just did."

"I thought so. You were suddenly quiet towards the end of the questioning. You really do need to work on those skills, you know. No one should be able to guess that you are an automaton."

Kat frowned. She frowned like a fifteen-year-old girl, not an automaton.

"There you go. You look more human that way."

"So should we send for the mother then?" Kat asked again, still frowning.

"No, no need. She has suffered enough already. Better she thinks her son died a long time ago at sea."

"So what do we know until now?" The frown remained. Buto wondered if she had forgotten how to turn it off. Ever since her last modification, her human emotion module seemed to be completely dysfunctional.

"Well, we know that Adipati has been trying to create new, invincible soldiers. He could not recreate my mother's automatons, so he tried chemistry instead... Those things on the beach sounded very close to what Malin told us about the experiments he was subjected to."

They had been chasing Adipati for several years now. The man was hailed as the Father of Steam Engines in Republic Nusantara when his steam powered automatons helped the country win their victory against Dutch colonialists. Buto and Kat's unit, however, discovered that the man had been secretly trading technologically advanced weapons with the Portuguese, French and the Dutch as well. It seemed that his goal was to cash in as much as he could from the war—selling technology that would keep all parties equally powerful, thereby dragging the war for as long as possible. Unfortunately, due to his high connections in the government, it was not easy to bring Adipati down. The team had been forced to stop Adipati's trades through secret operations instead, hoping to gain enough evidence to make his case public.

"The Basilisk Serum." Kat nodded. "So now we know Adipati had perfected them further. Between rounding up the children and fighting Malin, those new creatures at least remained mobile hours after creation. Malin, however, is still the only test subject who has gained stone-like skin, without his muscles and bones turning likewise into stone, even after eight years. You said it yourself: when you first met him, despite the slight rigidity, his fingers were definitely still moving. What if Adipati was in this port to capture Malin so he could draw his blood and try to replicate the result? Do you think he was going to use Malin's own mother as bait?"

"Which explains why he didn't want to admit that she was his mother," Buto agreed.

Someone walked into the small room inside the gadang house. "It goes further than that."

"Putra." Buto greeted the newcomer with a nod. He didn't know Putra was supposed to join them in this particular mission, but Buto guessed the headquarters must have called for all the help they could get.

Unlike Buto, who was tall and muscular, Putra was lean, though almost as tall as Buto. All three of them had known each other for several years, but Putra had only joined their team a year ago. Well-cultured and fluent in many languages, the young man quickly specialized in intelligence gathering missions.

Kat's frown turned to a bright smile when she saw him. "Hello," she said cheerfully, "I hope your night was better than ours?"

Putra stood in front of his friends, his arms dramatically spread to show his torn vest, bloody lips, and the cuts on his expensive-looking pure linen pants. "What do you think?"

Buto noted that despite all that, Putra still managed to have a certain flair, as if he was a hero who just stepped out of a storybook. "I think you've certainly had more fun," Buto scoffed, "When we got here, there was nothing to fight. All we got were the screaming mothers and lots of very frightened children. We were basically babysitting all night!"

"Someone actually went back to clean up the mess before we got here. We didn't even know Adipati was testing more of his Basilisk Serum until we heard the story from our witness. We found none of the golems he mentioned." Kat added.

"Lucky for me then!" Putra said with mock enthusiasm, "I did. I located the *Sweet Water* last night. It was not easy to spot, the mirrors you installed on the ship's hull were actually turned on, camouflaging the ship. I went up the ship thinking I could ask it to patrol the ocean and find Adipati's submersible ship.

"About twenty of those golems were already aboard. I fought them as best as I could, and then about fifteen more came up. These were fresh golems, the ones that just got their skin hardened. It was the first time ever I have seen them fresh like that. They were really fast. I was hoping Malin's crew could help me..."

"And you did not put two and two together at that time? Fifteen fresh golems?" Buto interjected.

"I was busy, remember? Fighting thirty-five golems all by myself while you were busy babysitting." Putra rapped his knuckles quickly on Buto's head. This made Kat smile, and Buto thought her smile was worth the slight pain on his skull.

"Anyway, I hate to admit it, but I was not doing so well. Then, Malin came out of nowhere. Seems like that winged pirate vest you gave him worked like a charm. I knew he could fight, but I never saw him fight in a rage. When he saw what had happened to his crew, he went berserk.

"The first golem that came close to him got stabbed by a keris right in the eye. Malin finished off the slower golems first with that keris. Then a pair of kerambits came out to take care of his own crew. Those were his favorite weapons during raids, remember? He was fast. Dodging his crew before any of them could land a hit, slashing at spots he knew were still untouched by the serum: a cut through the neck, a slash across the heels to incapacitate movements. I really need to write down all those weak spots. It could be useful if Adipati somehow succeeds in creating his army. If all those golems are as fast as Malin..."

"Did you see Adipati?" Buto asked.

"No..." Putra shook his head.

"Didn't you say you found something worse?" Kat asked. Buto was surprised to see her clutching at the hem of her jacket, so tightly that her knuckles turned white. Some of her humanity seemed to be coming back after all, he thought, making a quick note on his leather-bound book.

"Yes, we found something before I set out from Japan," Putra said. "According to the intelligence reports I gathered, Adipati promised the Japanese army a batch of new, improved soldiers. I believe those children were not bait. Adipati was going to use them for his new experiments. Perhaps he thought age was the key, since he was only successful with Malin, who remains, to this date, his youngest test subject."

"He's trading with Japan now?" Buto raised his voice in disbelief.

"But we are safe, for now. Knowing we are chasing him and his submersible ship, Adipati moved all of his experimental Basilisk Serum into the *Sweet Water*. The forged paperwork that we found along with the cargo, made it quite clear that Adipati was planning to take the hijacked ship to Japan—probably thinking he could rely on the camouflage to get out of the republic unnoticed. Malin... well... he saw the box leaking as it fell off the cargo during the fight. Parts of the ship were actually affected by it..."

"He injected his already transformed crew with the serum?" Buto shook his head, troubled by where this story was going.

"He loaded the ampoules into his blade-gun and shot them with it... and the other twenty golems as well. The effect of overdose turned them to stone almost immediately. It was almost unreal. Like being with Medusa from Greek mythology."

"Yes, we all know you read a lot of antique books in many languages." Buto stood up. It had been a very long night and day. "Cut to the chase. Where is Malin now?"

"When it was over..." Putra's voice went low. The excitement of the battle suddenly left him as he was forced to face the reality he had been trying to avoid. "When it was over, I told him about the children. He just looked at the remaining two ampoules. We believed those were the last of the ampoules batch. Thirty-five were spent on the golems, now all turned to statues, and thirteen ampoules broke on the ship, turning several parts of the *Sweet Water* to stone. I told him we should bring the ampoules back to you so you can study them, develop a cure, or at least..."

"He... injected himself with those ampoules?" Kat asked. Buto placed a hand gently on her shoulder.

"The ship was turning to stone, he was turning to stone... I had to leave him there. He told me... He said no one must ever endure what he went through. Perhaps he thought this was the best way to prevent Adipati from continuing the Basilisk project. Well, you saw the rest... I got out just before that whole ship became too heavy and dropped like a rock down into the sea."

"He died a hero," Buto said. "Just as he always wanted to..."

"A hero!" shouted a woman from outside of the gadang house. "Did you hear that? My son is a hero!"

"Wait, rangkayo! Wait!" There was a sudden loud noise from outside the house.

The three officers went out to see what the commotion was all about. An elderly lady was waddling into the sea, chased by several villagers.

"My son, my Malin Kundang. A hero. And I... What have I done... My son..." the old lady cried, going farther into the water.

There was a blurry movement beside Buto and Putra. Before they could do anything, Kat was already in the water, helping the lady out.

"No, no, let me go to him. My sweet son. All alone down there..." she said weakly. Her body hung limply in Kat's arms.

"The lady has a point," Kat said, "We should probably go search for the bodies..."

By sunset, however, they were forced to call out the search due to the low light conditions. Using his own giant automaton, Buto managed to carry as much as he could from the ruins of the *Sweet Water*. All thirty five bodies were accounted for. They left the parts of the ship and the petrified golems by the shore as a memorial to the *Sweet Water* and its crew. There was someone still missing of course. They still could not find the body of Captain Malin Kundang.

It was very late when the team finally finished all their reports. The moon was high and full, giving an eerie silver shine to everything its light touched. Buto left the small cabin before the others. It was too hot in there. He needed some air. He was walking in the general direction of his ship when he saw the statue.

A beautifully carved statue of Malin Kundang now stood on the shore, where his mother had first seen him on the previous day, just a couple of steps away from the ruins of his ship and the silent figures of his crews. At a glance, Buto almost mistook it for Malin himself. It was about the same height as his friend, a remarkable representation of the Captain. They even captured his spirit, Buto thought. There was always a certain tautness in the way Malin stood, as if his muscles were made of spring, ready for any action. This statue felt like that. Like it would move any minute if Buto did not watch it carefully.

Buto approached the statue, marveling at the exceptional details put into the work. The villagers certainly didn't waste time in honoring the hero. He smiled at the thought.

"Ah Malin," he said, as he saluted the statue, "Why do you have to go ahead and be a hero? Were you not the one who taught me the science of thinking straight? You made fun of me each time I charged ahead, you scolded me for relying on brute force alone... We could've done so much more with you in our team. I could've done so much more with your ship..." He glanced away at the sea where some new rock formations had formed a protective barrier around the beach. Buto sighed, seeing some features of the modified ship still quite easily recognized on the surface of those rocks.

Kat came up slowly behind him. She could be so quiet when she chose to, but he could always tell when she was close by.

"Look," he said to Kat, "They even got the nose right." Malin's otherwise perfect nose was slightly crooked when he broke it several months ago in a fight. Buto himself had helped the Captain straighten it back into place. He could still recall many of the new curse words Malin taught him that day.

Without saying a word, she reached out and held his hand. Her hand had been so cold ever since he upgraded her systems, but today it felt warm. Could it be that her humanity had really seeped back in? He did not want to think about her as an automaton today. He simply wanted to enjoy that warmth of her hand as they both silently mourned the passing of a great friend.

He remembered the first time they met Malin, specifically that moment when Malin casually winked at Kat and made her smile after he miraculously (or as Malin put it, dashingly) maneuvered his ship away from intense cannonball fires. Buto thought about telling stories of their adventures with Malin tonight in their own airship.

As if reading Buto's mind, Putra, walking towards them said, "We shall be telling stories about him tonight. Remember the first time we met him? How he rescued us after you crashed Shiva?"

Buto groaned, Shiva was the name of his giant automaton. Putra was right, though; they were lucky Malin was in the area when they crashed. They will definitely be telling more stories about Malin's daring deeds tonight. Buto even thought of writing those stories down, perhaps send it to Malin's poor mother? *Can she even read?*

"The water was murkier all the way down there," said Buto, more to himself than to his friends. He still could not believe Malin was gone. "Perhaps we could try again in a couple of days? I could probably fix a few more lights on..."

"I shall come back with you," Biwar said, coming close to the three officers. Biwar had volunteered to come to the headquarters in Batavia to help out with the special unit. He saluted the statue as well. "They have really made him a hero!"

"An excellent likeness," Putra noted, "From his roguish half smile to the way he always stood with one hand behind his back."

"A befitting monument." Biwar nodded.

Kat placed her hand gently upon the statue's face, "Good bye, dear friend," she said, and then she stared at her hand, slightly bewildered. "It's... dripping wet..."

"It was raining," Putra said.

"Was it?"

"It's October! Name one day since last week that hasn't rained?"

Kat shook her head, peering close at the statue. Buto pulled her towards their own aeroship, "Come, we need to locate Adipati as soon as possible."

They walked pass the statues and the ruins of the *Sweet Water*. Kat turned back once, but then, as the other three started the rockets on their vests, she too got herself ready to board.

~*~

The statue of Malin Kundang blinked. He watched his friends as they all flew up towards their own camouflaged aeroship. "Good bye, my friends," he said in a voice that sounded as hollow as an empty grave. "I wish I knew how I survived, but for now, perhaps it is better that Adipati thinks I'm dead."

Malin also didn't know how he could ever be a pirate again, sky or sea, with a body that would sink the second it touched the waters. He wanted to curse, but he was out of curses. He had used them all up as he forced himself to walk all the way from the bottom of the sea to the shore. It had taken him forever.

He did have one thing clear in his mind, however: he had a village to protect, and a mother to take care of. With heavy steps that left grooves in the sand, he walked slowly towards the village.

The Insects and Women Sing Together

Pear Nuallak

As Kaew pounded chilli relish for the midday meal, she daydreamed about her mother.

This is what she saw: Amphon, with her ever-serene face, piloting a great nak with bright scales and a noble crest above its great windowed eyes.

She imagined the machine beast winding through the sky, powered by engines whirring like cicadas, an articulated metal body that dazzled pavonine in the sunlight. A fin of ixora-bright silk stretched tight over bamboo frilled the considerable length of its spine. The nak's progress through the air matched its dignity in native rivers, comfortable with its power, its sleek beauty.

Inside the head of the beast was Amphon at the dashboard, her fine firm hands and strong knees steering the metal nak with the same concentration as she rode an elephant. Marking the roof above her mother's head were symbols in white and gold, blessings from a monk necessary for any vehicle. Her mother the hero, the adventurer!

This is the kind of great machine beast which is worthy of her mother, Kaew thought, and a creation that would have to reside only in her imagination. Not even the engineers in Krungthep, the capital of Siam, had yet reached the sky in a vessel of such advanced size and power—flight meant a person strapped to bamboo wings, gliding from mountain tops. If they were to build a nak, why then, they'd place it in the water where it belonged.

Every creature has its place in the world. Kaew paused before her pestle and mortar to consider this carefully: her own was far away from Krungthep. Nong Ngu Saeng Athit, so named for the gleaming snakes one encountered in the rice paddies, fell within the governance of Khorat city but remained a quiet village an hour's walk away from this provincial capital. Mountains shouldered its way across the landscape and the fields were lush and full, pregnant with Phra Mae Posop's gift to humankind, rice which whispered its blessings as it swayed in the soft breeze.

Despite the progressive road-building and puttering steamboats along the waterways which connected Siam together, the village was still quietly tucked away, unremarkable, a little sleepy. It was better this way, said Amphon and Grandmother Jampa, though each woman had her own reasons for desiring solitude.

"Child, what are you doing?" said Auntie Muk, noticing the thudding behind her had paused. She looked over her shoulder, draining the just-cooked rice from its milky water. "Roast the aubergine and look after the rice as it steams, won't you? And don't forget to add the chillies and salt to the mortar. I want everything complete when I return from feeding the dogs." She set off for the yard, a bowl of rice milk in hand.

"Yes, Auntie," Kaew said to her moving back. Auntie Muk loved her dogs, calling them Chaba and Mee Noi, Maphraow and Toong Ngeun, feeding them from her hand and praising their elegant ridged backs. There was no need, then, for Kaew to hurry.

When the coals finally burned low, she returned the clay pot to the stovetop, the rice murmuring to itself as the heat further perfected each grain. With a pair of tongs, she pushed the slender purple aubergines into the open maw beneath, where the dark heart of charcoal flickered patiently. Auntie Muk was contemptuous of gas-powered fires; food simply wasn't the same without the lingering richness of smoke and ash, even if it did set you coughing.

A sudden puff of steam came from the hair-thin gap between the rice pot and its lid. This bringing together of fire, water and air was the same power which moved whole boats, she realized—power which could be harnessed to bring people higher and faster through the sky.

Kaew remained deep in thought as the meal cooked itself. Perhaps a metal khrut, with its noble beak, deep chest and broad wings, would be a more suitable vehicle for her mother. She giggled, feeling as if she'd picked one quarrelling suitor over another: though both nak and khrut were allies to Phra Phutta Chao, they were enemies of each other.

The last projects in Krungthep she'd heard of were faster steam ships and the beginnings of a war elephant with legs that marched and an armored trunk which spewed shot. Kaew wondered when the engineers in the capital would consider the merits of heavenly creatures—those who had come to the aid of man, at least. In addition to desirable qualities like impenetrable scales and wings that levelled mountains, they had a beautiful form. That much was evident in stone carvings and murals on temple walls finely detailed and utterly still. To realize them in motion would be glorious.

Such thoughts of machine beasts and brave women pillowed Kaew's head as she dreamed at night, after she'd pulled up the stairs to the upper floor and settled onto her reed mat next to her grandmother. (Old woman Jampa, meanwhile, dreamed of regrets, a man who had seemed so good at first, and her family darting away from her like so many fish.)

Kaew snatched secret moments of the day to trace pictures in the dirt, copying images from temple murals in her memory. A person wasn't supposed to put pencil to paper until properly apprenticed lest the spirits of the old master artisans overwhelm the untutored mind, but her love of drawing made her reckless: she reasoned that pushing a sharp stick through dry earth could hardly count. Even with these crude materials, her lines were already smooth and finely controlled, and she wanted to know where her skill would take her.

Yet the girl understood messages both loud and quiet which told her that most of her family wouldn't understand how her heart shouted for this craft. She wanted this and nothing else, even though weaving, planting rice, courtship, marriage, a child in the belly ought to be her life's richest work.

Perhaps her mother would advocate for her. Amphon was ostensibly a maid in Lady Boonluea's household, a role which for some reason meant travel and gentle, quiet smiles when Kaew pressed her for detail after detail. Those long trips away made frail Grandmother Jampa weep with anger while clinging to Kaew.

"She leaves home as if she were a man! What's wrong with rice-pounding and water-fetching that runs a house? Is that not enough work for her?" Jampa shouted at no-one in particular. "Who will winnow the grains and cook the meals? Who will guide you, my little Kaew, when it's your turn to marry? Who will lay my ashes to rest?"

Later, Kaew overheard Auntie Khajee talking to Auntie Muk while they worked on the family garden. "If you ask me, Amphon is a fine sister, a good woman'" she said.

Auntie Muk nodded. "It's no fault of hers she was widowed so young. Who can predict the comings and goings of husbands? And you can see with your own eyes that Kaew is precious to her. Let Mother rage as she wishes. Amphon has done her duty as a daughter."

Kaew swept the chilli and salt into the mortar with a sigh. There were expectations of womanhood that went deeper than the roots of a takhian tree. No matter how much wealth a woman accrued, or the number of rai she owned, the world turned its usual course and the day always came where she knelt before someone else and carried out their wishes. She felt suddenly vexed by this life, a narrow path crammed with too many things she didn't want, and put her heart into pounding the chilli relish forcefully until it became so smooth and fine that not even Auntie Muk could find fault with it.

As she finished, a tiny fleck of chilli landed in Kaew's eye, fierce pain which burned away coherent thought. She'd later reflect it was unjust that, out of all the ingredients, it was somehow always chilli which jumped so precisely into her face.

Auntie Muk returned to see her niece flapping her hands ridiculously with one hand and clutching her face with the other.

"I've told you at least a hundred times, child, you need to concentrate," Auntie Muk said to Kaew as she wailed, "You want to eat soon, don't you? Go and rinse your face and eyes."

~*~

I know, well and truly, that I've committed many misdeeds. I don't love as women are supposed to love. My daughter Kaew is precious to me all the same, my best secret and light of my eyes. Lady Boonluea presses me to bring her in but even now, after so many years of service, I hesitate, knowing the danger. I keep my girl in Nong Ngu Saeng Athit for a reason.

Still, I recognize the same restlessness in her as I knew in myself. I'll tell her our stories, women's stories, so that she may learn the words to sing and shout what she already knows in her heart—and to plumb the depths of dreams she's never even thought possible.

I will sing her the song I learned in my sixteenth year. Even now there are those who disbelieve Grandmother Mo's resistance against the Lao, claiming the impossibility of a fifty-five year old woman taking up arms and commanding warriors because of her age and gender. Some even say she simply did not exist, a story spun by Khorat officials to appease Krungthep of their loyalty to His Majesty in the capital.

Of course I disagree; I expect the quality of my bones, heart, and intellect to be preserved for at least the next two decades, during which I may go from woman to man and back again. I do not command as she did—the Lady is real, life-changingly so—but I slough off my skin, creep softly, and take on the guise I require to find and capture secrets.

As a child I learned from my two sisters to spin lies and act perfectly when mother pinched my lip or father roared at us to ensure our obedience. What were children for, after all, but to gift them with work and riches in return for the life he'd created within us?

We were good daughters to the outside world, happily laboring away, smiling, saying the right words with soft, high voices. Yet our bida and manda still raged at us. What terrible misdeeds had we committed, in this life or ones past, to merit this treatment? We turned to the wisdom of our elders, begging for succor and the knowledge of how to make our parents happy. From the kindly luangpor to our oldest cousin, their responses were one and the same: "You must love and respect your bida and manda."

Our father ignored us, keeping his vicious behavior for private moments behind closed doors. Our mother fed and clothed us, but no matter how much we worked on the farm or completed our home duties, she hissed that we were deceitful and ugly and would be reborn as maggots.

We quietly understood the truth of our parents' household, a truth that has never passed our lips for fear that the weight of such a sin would plunge us straight down into hell. This was our secret: that the order of the world had gone awry within those walls. Neither of my parents truly knew how to conduct themselves with true righteousness, which is the duty of our elders so that we may follow in their example.

But there was wise Aunt Lerm, my father's older sister, and her gentle husband, Kamon. She had watched over us closely since the birth of Khajee. The couple had no children, and so asked us to stay for a day, a week, months, until we had become a part of her family.

"I appreciate the laughter of children and their helping hands within my household," was all she said to her younger brother when he complained she was keeping his children away, and to the village headman when he intervened. Lerm was a formidable, intelligent woman, her authority governed by a deep sense of reason. The headman backed away from the set of her jaw and the matter was settled.

Lerm patiently taught us good manners and a handful of numbers and letters. We knew the obligation to our elders, but our Aunt spoke also of commoners to nobles, nobles to kings, small rulers to great ones. This was how the world turned; I was burdened with the knowledge that life had an order of things. And yet a soft dark place inside me, which remained no matter how much I prayed and made offerings and had quiet reflections, told me that order did not necessarily mean fairness.

Still, under Lerm's kindness and reason we grew into ourselves: Khajee loved to tend the garden, Muk made the finest meals, and I wove. We all loved to sing.

When the villagers gathered after a day's work to enjoy each other's company and a boy called out his first line of song, I was the quickest to respond in greeting. My lungs and mouth together made a charming instrument. Khajee and Muk would speak with longing and irritation about the other gender, and I would mimic their words. We performed the roles of Woman or Man, Girl or Boy, so to sing with daring wit didn't mean that I, Amphon, truly wished that the boy Klahan would ask for my hand or any such thing, no matter how fine his tattoos were. I was simply interested to hear whether he would sing back intelligently or else lose to my skill.

This was my secret: I knew from late girlhood that my interest did not lie with men. Each night I would play at wooing a different boy while feeling absolutely nothing. I enjoyed their shame when they could not answer my song.

When Khajee asked me to accompany her on a trip to the city on a clear morning in the third month, I gladly agreed. She wished to seek trade and perhaps suitors, and I wanted to see the land beyond the village, perhaps glimpse the curious remains of the copper and bamboo water buffalo they had built in Khorat. Uncle Kamon, returning from a trading trip, said the spirit workers had quarrelled with the engineers over the lack of payment for their work; the latter had only managed to build four useless legs before fleeing in abject terror, which failed to impress my uncle. A water buffalo of bright metal and useful magic would be invaluable come rice-growing season, if one could afford it and it was warded against the damp.

"Have a good day," said Auntie Lerm as she pressed her nose to our cheeks. Muk gave us satchels of food and told us to come home safely.

By the evening, I was with thousands of others on the northbound road to Wiang Chan flanked by Lao soldiers. I did not know where Khajee was. My mouth burned with anger.

~*~

Kaew brought the coconut shell dipper to her face again and again, sighing and wincing. She was thankful for the water; plentiful rain that year meant round-shouldered terracotta jars brimmed in each household across Nong Ngu Saeng Athit. There was also a new water tank nearby, one of several in the region gifted by His Majesty in Krungthep, recognising Ya Mo's deeds decades later.

She was curious about it. If such great water tanks and machine beasts were being built, why couldn't they invent a tool that made chilli paste without this level of pain and suffering?

"You can never wash chilli out of your eye fast enough, can you?" came a voice at Kaew"s shoulder.

"Oh, Lek! How are you today?" said Kaew, turning to greet her best friend, pulse fluttering, suddenly self-conscious of her red eye and sodden head.

"I'm well, thank you," said Lek, "look much maenglak we've got. They're growing wonderfully! Your Aunties will be so pleased." She held up a phakhaoma bundle stuffed with fuzzy green leaves and tiny white blossoms. "But I think they're less fragrant exactly because of all the rain. Herbs are more potent when they're starved of water. What do you think?"

Lek crushed a leaf between her forefinger and thumb, offering them to Kaew. Kaew breathed in the citrus-bright scent of maenglak and noted the lovely taper to Lek's fingers.

"Well," said Kaew, "they're beautiful."

Lek raised her eyebrow. "They... smell beautiful?"

"I mean... that is to say, it smells as usual to me, but I'd rather weak herbs than all the trouble that drought brings to the land." Had she been too obvious? Had she been too abrupt? Lek's sprightly manner and broad shoulders jolted Kaew's heart so, sending jumbled phrases out of her mouth.

Lek frowned, then brightened. "Oh, I see. Well, the rains have been so good these past months. I hope the new water tank's caught it all..."

Kaew took a deep breath and said, "Would you like to go and see it? They say it's vast, like an old monument."

~*~

If I married, I feared taking leave of my aunt's home for unfamiliar rooms where I'd be judged by a sharp-eyed grandmother. Aunt Lerm's house, with its sweet-scented wood and tall stilt legs, was safety and comfort to me. I'd simply assumed that my home would be as permanent as the mountains.

Standing amongst the Khorat townspeople, we were told Krungthep was under threat of attack from the white-skinned island-dwelling Angrit, and that King Anouwong of Lao had arrived in Khorat to take the city into his care. He'd generously offered us, the people of Khorat, a haven in Wiang Chan across the river, but only when he'd ensured each citizen had been divested of any weaponry, confiscating even humble kitchen cleavers.

He sent us on our way, escorted by soldiers who kept our knives and axes safely in their care. Guns and cannons and carts laden with gunpowder trundled along with us.

Well, I could not be comforted. It was then I realized what I desired most of all was the freedom to take myself where I wanted, and my shame about the first and my denial of the latter made me so furious I was beyond tears.

"Who are you, child?" an older woman asked me. Her cheekbones were higher even than mine, the jaw severe. I heard people calling her Lady Mo; I knew this name, the wife of the Khorat governor. She was treated with respect even from the Lao commanders. Curious, then, that someone as humble as myself should fall into step beside someone such as her; surely she would sit proudly in one of the carts. I noticed the tall handmaidens flanking us, pha sbai fluttering over broad shoulders, finely wrought metal bands encircling solid yet sinuous arms. From the look in their eyes I knew I had to answer quickly and speak well. What did Lady Mo want with me? My chest was tight, my throat dry.

"My name is Amphon, my lady," was all I managed to say.

"And who are you?" she pressed. "All around you there are Lao and Jeen, Tai and Khmen. Much of them are glad to be on their way to Wiang Chan, preferring the rule of King Anouwong to His Majesty in Krungthep. The ones who weep bitterly are Tai. You do not weep; you look angry, and the music of your speech is unique. So, child, who are you?"

"I am Khorat."

Lady Mo laughed softly. I heard she too was Khorat-born, living in the region's capital across from the great temple. "Little Amphon, what do you like to do?"

"Weave. I weave, and I sing."

This seemed to interest her. "And where would you like to go, my child?"

"Home," I said, "I have no quarrel with my neighbor, but I want to weave my cloth and sing my songs on my side of the Mekong river, and not be herded like cattle to where my new master pleases."

She laughed again; there was a coldness to her voice which made my stomach writhe like an eel pond. I couldn't tell what it was about my answer that pleased her. Something at her waist caught my eye. Like mine, her chongkraben was fastened with a segmented silver belt, but hers was a row of beetles each the size of a coin, their shells embossed in complex patterns, each of their bodies linked together with a fine chain. I'd never seen this level of craft before.

As Lady Mo and her attendants moved away, I could have sworn that one of the insects fluttered its wings. The light could play such tricks with your eyes, I thought.

We marched under the glare of the sun. There were families who anticipated their new beginnings in Wiang Chan, others still who had made their first home there and were gladly returning. Auntie Lerm once told me how the civilian Lao men were branded and forced to labor in Siam, so far from their homes for many months of the year. My heart should have gone out to them for their plight was greater than any I'd ever know, yet I desired only to find my own kin and my own home. I couldn't bring myself to hate the Lao, nor could I turn their want into mine. Desperation grew inside me, knocking against the walls of my chest, my eyes darted and fingers itched.

I knew what my single self wanted: I'd return to my village somehow, to sit before my loom and feed the chickens, and I'd leave only when I wished. There was fire in me as I had never known it, my heart dark like burning coal. If the Angrit attacked Krungthep before continuing north east, so be it. I wanted to die in my home.

Twice I untied my chongkraben and squatted by the side of the path to piss as modestly as I could, holding the fabric up as a screen and peering over the edge to watch those who passed. Each time, a soldier always ensured I fell back in line. I'd already glimpsed what I wanted.

Lady Mo easily moved through the crowd with her attendants and a girl a little older than me. I'd heard through Muk that the lady had adopted a child called Boonluea, nursing her back to health after the baby's parents had been struck by illness. The girl seemed only to speak to her mother and her attendants with any measure of affection, haughtily ignoring all the townsfolk around her while behaving with careful politeness towards the Lao soldiers. The commanders treated Lady Mo like a fussing aunt, humoring her, granting her requests for axes to chop firewood or repair carts. How could they miss her calculating looks, the conversations with her husband and the nodding of his men?

When we approached the border jungle of Thung Samrit, Lady Mo appealed to the Lao men.

"Do you see, sir, how your people new and old have slow and aching legs from their journey? Even the strongest soldiers grow weary, longing for a good meal cooked by wives and daughters," she said. "Resting here for the night would help us reach Wiang Chan in the highest of spirits, ready to celebrate and be welcomed by our new capital."

"I understand your concerns, good lady," replied one of the Lao commanders, gracious and sincere. He turned away and talked to his men before announcing that we were to stop and make camp. The soldiers left their carts of gunpowder and cannons amongst the trees like a gathering of strange beasts, each man relieved that they no longer had to haul these things over the increasingly difficult terrain. The wheels sunk in the soft, sandy ground up to the spokes.

As we laid out rattan mats in the clearing, I exchanged pleasantries with some Khorat girls. They were not from my village but I recognized them by the weave of their chongkraben and the rhythm of their sentences. Before long, Lady Mo appeared, ushering us to another part of the camp where the rest of the women were preparing a meal. After granting us permission to use knives and handing over a limited number of blades, the Lao soldiers left us; as with any men, they didn't bother listening to so-called women's prattle as we did our women's work. We could speak freely.

"Little Amphon, what do you know of kings?" Lady Mo said, as we chopped vegetables and stoked fires. The other girls and women attended to their own share of work, but I knew they were listening closely.

Auntie Muk had told me how the Lao king, like our governor, sent tribute to His Majesty in Krungthep, men and money.

"There are great and small kings as there are great and small gods, and all rule over us," I said.

She nodded. "And which king would you serve, the greater or the smaller?"

The question startled me. "These are decisions I do not make, my lady."

"What if," she said, "you could go home if you made the right choice? What do you think will happen to your homes now that Khorat is in the hands of a new ruler? Not even the smallest village escapes conquest. There's always one more babe to snatch." She turned to face the women around us, arms spread wide. "King Anouwong will have us taken to Wiang Chan, and I have no wish to go on a journey I didn't ask for. Why should I leave the house I was born in and forsake the trees of my garden? Why should we be herded like cattle to where our new masters please? Women of Khorat, join hands and return to our city!"

She told us of her plan. What choice did we have?

Our men arrived in our makeshift kitchen hefting a wild pig over their shoulders. While we drained its blood and butchered its still-warm flesh, Lady Mo spoke to her husband, one hand on her belt, the other making precise cutting motions in the air.

"I can tell you that the farang will not attack Siam. King Anouwong's intelligence was mistaken, rooted in his assumption that Krungthep's treaty with the white-skinned Angrit makes Siam weak. I hear, too, that our neighboring towns have been taken by the Lao; King Anouwong's claiming of our people and their capitals gives strength to his nation for now, but there are thousands of Siamese troops approaching the north east as we speak," she said. What kind of woman knew such things, and spoke of them with such certainty to influence men?

"We will go ahead as planned," her husband replied. "Prepare the dinner and bring out the rice wine."

Boonluea sat with the two handmaidens under cloth tied over bamboo. Lady Mo fiddled with her belt, removing one of the fine metal beetles.

"You're a farmer's girl from a small village, but I can see you are not uneducated. Someone must have taught you well." Lady Mo's contempt stung, but I was curious.

She held the beetle flat on her palm, showing me its parts. It was half-machine, half-creature, with a basic intelligence that knew ally from enemy. Its belly contained tiny chains and gears which controlled the whirring of legs, wings and biting mouthparts. There were two compartments in its body, one for medicine and the other for messages. These malaeng-yon, insect automata, were astonishing to me; I wondered how she could have a belt full of these contraptions when a team of engineers and spirit works had not even managed to build a single water buffalo.

All my life I had paid my respects to the many spirits of the land, propitiation granting us rains and full harvests, had witnessed the witch doctors dancing in ritual to call back protective spirits to encourage health in my ailing neighbors, but I'd never seen how one could ask machines to understand us.

"Those fool engineers and spirit workers know nothing about the proper songs," Lady Mo said when I told her about the abandoned water buffalo. She whispered fast in my ear. "Child, this is my secret work, my woman's work. My malaeng-yon roam the country and hum their secrets to me. Oh, men can speak of women's gossip, but what is gossip but knowledge, and what is knowledge but power? Any wretch can hammer parts together, but great engineers and artisans are few and good spirit workers fewer. All metal holds memories of earth which was once its mother and cradle. You have only to sing to it, make it remember, satisfy it with your knowledge of the world, teach it to understand the scuttling creatures of the earth and the delight of a smoothly turning engine. Approaching it as master or supplicant will do us little favor: we must, instead, partner with spirits."

She leaned close to me, her face a yaksha, terrifying in its glare. "You must never tell anyone of this, or I will ensure your line is cursed for generations untold. Only I will decide when others know of this."

I understood, then, why the fool engineers had fled, and there was no telling what kind of power Lady Mo truly had. But I had no time to tremble. Truth be told, my desire for knowledge and to see my home once again went deeper and harder than fear.

Boonluea taught me how to administer colorless medicine in the malaeng-yon and wind the creature with a tiny key concealed at the bottom end of the beetle.

"This medicine hastens drunkenness and causes a heaviness of the limbs," said Boonluea as we filled and wound the malaeng-yon. "It's a family recipe."

I stared at her, wondering what kind of family would need such a thing.

"Perhaps I may teach you someday, clever farm girl. I know medicine well. Machines, too. Subjects close to my heart." She laughed, amused by herself.

We spoke of what we loved about our homeland, and I was glad of her company. She was nothing like the cold girl from early that day, the one who had walked so stiffly.

Boonluea was fond of me, promising me gifts of knowledge, glad that she had found someone whose mind was as curious as hers, even if I was a simple farm girl. At that last remark I decided to laugh at her, rather than with her. Still, I liked her soft voice, even if she did tease. My heart still ached for Khajee.

The Lao commanders complimented us on the food we served for the evening meal. The stewed finger root, dried chilli, sliced vegetables and pork was so hot that it chased the rice into our mouths. We shared the same taste for boldly-flavored dishes which made the tongue burn and eyes water. People hardly noticed the insects which buzzed over through the air in the flickering shadow of firelight, releasing droplets of medicine into each Lao soldier's portion of rice.

Afterwards I sang with Boonluea under the starlight, our voices smooth and sweet like the rice wine we served to the Lao soldiers. It was past midnight, then, and the Lao men were delighted to find we knew some of the same songs.

A woman's words can never be trusted, a soldier sang. My heart thudded but my lips smiled. *A blooming flower found far from its tree can hardly be named.*

This is what men think of us: that we change when out of their sight.

As long as the jik tree has branches and the sugar palm has fronds, my promise shall never be broken, we sang in return. Lady Mo tilted her head and laughed.

We implored the Lao soldiers to celebrate their victory, to dip their cups into the pot of wine again and again in triumph, leading them all in a dance farther and farther away from the camp.

I kept my voice lifted in song and my feet light on the soft ground as we wove through the trees before fleeing, letting the dark claim me, hoping that Boonluea would join me. We left the soldiers to stumble about in the forest, knocking themselves over the cannons and carts they'd left there.

Our men and women were waiting for them, monks and merchants, commoners and nobles alike.

They sprung on soldiers with axes, hoes, cleavers, sharpened sticks, taking up arms which had slipped from the Lao soldiers' grasps. Some of the Lao fled deep into the forest, others stayed and fought fiercely, dying in the shadows of the trees.

Since that day I have seen worse violence, become inured to its existence. It is a means to an end. But that was the first day I had seen the slaughter of humans and it marked me for ever. Of course, I had seen animals killed, sometimes helping to butcher them myself and taking on the sin as part of my survival, but it was hard to cleave to those beliefs now. Here, there was only bloodlust. The battleground has its own rules.

An explosion of white light and harsh noise blasted through the thick of the night. We turned as one to witness it, thudding hearts and rumbling echoes sounding in our ears.

~*~

The evening breeze was a cool relief. Walking through the village, Kaew liked to snatch what news she could from the messengers and traders as they travelled across Siam. Paths through the country were easier nowadays, with better roads and small steamboats puttering through the many rivers. The village, though half-hidden, still saw visitors arrive at least monthly, drawn by the fine quality of the cotton cloth and rattan mats, the well-crafted knives.

The farang seemed interested in more than trade, often being very chatty, though the white people's attempts at her language and their general manners were so atrocious that she preferred to ignore them. Whether Portuget or Angrit, they had faces like soured pork, tongues which robbed speech of its natural music, and insisted on wearing shoes all the time.

Instead of the tales of machines that Kaew wanted, the farang were very eager to tell the villagers so-called good news about Phra Yesu, lingering around and making offers to set up schools and teach their letters and their religion.

"Betterment for the village, it would be for," said a farang with eyes as dull as pickled fish. He had made extravagant hand gestures, of pushing forward, upward. Then he peered down at Kaew in a way which made her deeply uncomfortable. The farang seemed as tall as a sugar palm. Perhaps he was a hungry ghost.

Kaew sighed. Like the rest of the village, Kaew paid her respects to Phra Phutta Chao and the many powers which inhabited the land. What else would a person ever need in this world? The succor of the luangpor and the bounty of Mae Posop and all the spirits of heaven and earth were more than enough. She found the farang's presumptions insulting and their proffered gifts useless, and rankled at being told what was good for her.

"If the farang at least offered information about their wondrous machines, then it wouldn't be so tiresome," Kaew had said to her mother before Amphon left for her latest trip. "They have airships. It wouldn't matter if I had to learn their graceless scripts so long as knowledge about gears and bellows and steam filled my head."

Amphon silently noted Kaew's interest in the possibilities of machinery, and said only, "There's often poison in the gift, my child. Knowledge in particular often has a high cost. I hope you'll know that we have much to be proud of, too."

Kaew stood before the new water tank. It was as tall as four elephants balanced on each other's backs. She'd expected it to look more interesting, perhaps let off great puffs of steam and have excitingly complex, whirring parts.

When Lek and Mali arrived, the girls spread a rattan mat on the ground and sat down to an evening meal of salt-crusted fish with rice, chatting idly about the day's events: the sighting of a new steamboat, a neighbor's cat giving birth, how the cotton crop was doing.

Two engineers on secondment from the capital stumbled into the clearing, mildly drunk, boasting loudly about their project and bringing progress to the countryside. The girls ate their pearl-fleshed longan, unimpressed. Even when sober these engineers were exceptionally pleased—and more than a little smug, Kaew thought—with how well the tank caught and held so much of the rainfall in its dull metal belly. She'd glimpsed them striding about and jabbing at paper plans as they talked to the village headmen and headwomen. The tank performed much the same function as the old stone cistern but was considerably larger and made of a new metal compound which had been acquired through trade with the Angrit, which was exciting to the Krungthep people; they thought it generous to share it with us, so that we in return could put more rice in their bellies.

Poison in the gift, Kaew thought. She spat out a longan seed, smooth against her lips.

~*~

My heart may be stone now, but it beats a little faster when I remember the fourth day of the fourth month. It was the day when I knew Boonluea for what she is, the first of the many secrets she showed me about herself.

The smoke from the explosion cleared. All was dark and quiet again, the air stilled with death. The Lao which had not died by our hand or caught in the explosion had fled into the forest.

There was no glorious victory. It was simply that the violence had stopped, and there was nothing left to do but collect our dead and set out on the journey home, where things would never quite be the same.

I saw, then, two tall handmaidens walking out of the forest, bearing a girl in their arms, a girl with soot-dulled skin and red open flesh. I saw her mother, Lady Mo, roaring in grief, refusing to let anyone else near her daughter, not even the healers or the monks, commanding people to stand back as they carried Boonluea back to her tent.

I opened and closed my fists, breathed through my nose and out of my mouth. Later, I would learn that Boonluea had vexed the Lao soldiers as they tried to make use of their canons in the battle. She shouted a warning to our men and swung her flaming torch high, offering herself to the gunpowder.

The dawn was pale gold. My entire self was in deep discomfort, ears ringing and head humming, skin sticky from a long day and night without washing. I had to go home. As I turned, thinking that I perhaps could find the other Khorat girls, I met one of Lady Mo's handmaidens. Silently she led me to her mistress.

"Amphon, child, you did very well," said Lady Mo, standing outside her tent. "Are you on your way home?" The tears had dried on her face. She seemed smugly knowing, somehow.

"Yes, my lady." I knew I should thank her, but the words wouldn't come. She'd blasted open the gates of my world, shown me first-hand how violence and betrayal happened where before I'd only heard them as ideas gently spoken by my Aunt.

Lady Mo tapped her belt. All the malaeng-yon were there, gleaming and perfect and still, merely a rich woman's ornaments. "You will remember what we said, won't you?" She spoke delicately as if she'd requested me to latch closed a shutter. I wondered who'd ever believe me if I told them of her tiny, whirring secrets.

I nodded and said, "I am sorry for Boonluea."

Lady Mo looked at me. Behind us, people called to each other, weary and shaken, gathering up their belongings and thinking of the journey ahead, if it was safe to go back, if there was any shelter for them under the endless sky.

Would Boonluea, would any of these people, have given me so much as a glance without the hand of war reaching for us?

Within the tent there was a screen, and behind the screen there was a body that was once Boonluea.

She lay as if asleep, arms straight at her sides, still wearing her chongkraben. Her lips were pale, she was bound together with bandages, chin to collarbone to waist, her chest was quiet. My knees gave and I slumped down beside her. I'd come to say good bye but only a whining sob came forth from my throat.

"Why do you cry, clever farm girl?" said a soft, strange, creaking voice.

I turned my eyes from my lap to Boonluea and stared, too shocked to speak.

"Well, Amphon? Your voice is sweeter in song than accompanied by tears. It breaks my heart, which is no good, as it must be stout and strong for battle," she said, soft and teasing.

She bid me near and whispered to me her secret, then, of her part-clockwork self. Guiding my ear close to her chest she let me listen to the soft clicks and whirrs, the turning of the engine that was herself, a body which had been saved one from illness and again from war by Lady Mo.

Boonluea had her own malaeng-yon. They scuttled about beneath her bandages, busily healing her copper heart and mulberry paper lungs. I fancied I could hear their whirring chatter.

"It will be a while before I'm well again," she said. "Mother was furious, at first, but I know she's very proud of me. You will visit, won't you?"

I still could not speak.

Lady Mo had her handmaidens accompany me. "Go home to your sisters," she said. "Your village is safe. But you will not hide there, farm girl—I have so much to show you, Amphon. Rest for a week. Then you'll return with my handmaidens to the city."

She was a woman whose heart's fire could consume all, and she would have us know that this mastery of that flame—and of our lives where they overlapped with hers—was for the good of the world beneath her.

~*~

Amphon came back to Nong Ngu Saeng Athit from the Krungthep capital with many secrets. One such secret had palm leaf pages containing the principles of making vast machine beasts and a blueprint for an Angrit airship. Of course, the capital would have the power and resources for a project of this scale. For this Amphon had played the role of lady-in-waiting to the wife of a chief engineer, a man so easy to fool due to his sheer arrogance. It had never occurred to them that betrayal was a possibility that might cost them. It was simply child's play to secret away the documents and keep it warm in her pha sbai.

It was time, she decided, to introduce Kaew to Lady Boonluea. Whether her daughter was interested in secrets or machines, she would surely be well-suited to the household. Amphon tucked the palm leaf treatise well away from the prying eyes of Jampa, who'd grown softer yet increasingly fretful and nosy as time passed.

"Mother," said Kaew one morning, sitting one step below Amphon, "I want to become a chang sin. I want to draw." There. She'd said it.

She looked away for a moment, frowning, then turned back to watch her mother carefully.

Amphon unstoppered a tiny bottle and smoothed thanee oil through her hair. "Oh? What do you like to draw, Amphon? Women, elephants, tewada?" Her voice was affectionate, carefully interested.

Kaew began to draw in the dirt while Amphon watched. Her breath in her chest was shaky but her lines were precise, describing the great proud-crested nak she'd dreamed of, marking out the cockpit as seen through its great windowed eyes.

When she looked up again, Kaew saw something in her mother's eyes which terrified and delighted her, a shrewd calculating look and genuine happiness.

"My child, my dearest Kaew, light of my eyes, come here. I have an idea for you." She took out the treatise from its hiding place and showed it to her daughter.

"You have so much to learn," Amphon said as Kaew lightly ran her fingers over the surface of each page, fluttering over the letters, reverently opening and closing the book.

She turned to her mother, the woman with the eyes that saw so many things, hands which were so deft at the loom, a heart packed tight with so many secrets.

Amphon breathed deeply and began to sing.

About the Authors

Marilag Angway prefers her steampunk taking place in the skies as often as possible, though is not opposed to a good romp on terrestrial territory. She's a writer of science fiction and fantasy and occasionally dabbles in horror and humor (though success at the latter remains to be seen). Her stories can be found in various anthologies, including those published by Bards and Sages Publishing, Hadley Rille Books, Deepwood Publishing, and Ticonderoga Publications. When she's not writing, she's devising lesson plans and activities for a diverse group of rambunctious three-year-olds who she hopes will someday become avid readers of fantasy and science fiction. For her random book and overall nerdish musings, check out her blog at http://storyandsomnomancy.wordpress.com. Don't forget to grab a cookie and a cup of tea on your way out!

Paolo Chikiamco is a Manila-based, Filipino writer whose interests include prose, comics, and interactive fiction. He's the Managing Editor of Studio Salimbal (SalimbalComics.com), a Filipino comics studio, and runs the *Rocket Kapre* blog (RocketKapre.com) to host news and resources about Philippine speculative fiction. He has edited *Alternative Alamat*, an anthology of stories that re-imagine Philippine mythology, and *Kwentillion*, a young-adult focused comics magazine. His fiction has been published in venues such as *Scheherazade's Façade, Philippine Genre Stories, Steampunk III: Steampunk Revolution, Lauriat,* and the *Philippine Speculative Fiction* series. He has also written comics such as *High Society, Mythspace* (a series which uses Philippine folklore as the basis for a space opera tale), as well as an interactive wrestling novel for Choice of Games called *Slammed!* (choiceofgames.com/slammed/) You can find him on Twitter as @anitero.

Timothy James M. Dimacali is a Filipino science fiction author and the Science and Technology Editor of a major Philippine media network. His short fiction "Skygypsies" appears as required reading in select Philippine high school and college English classes, and has since been adapted into a comic book (available for free at Flipreads.com). TJ is also the president of the IT Journalists Association of the Philippines. You can follow him on Twitter: @tjdimacali.

L.L. Hill's fiction has appeared in *Third Flatiron 'Fire' Anthology* (Pushcart nomination,) *Domain SF, Hello Horror*, and others. Her poetry has been published in *Scifaikuest, the Fib Review, Haiga Online, Haibun Today*, and others. L.L. Hill's writing explores relationships in worlds old and new primarily in the genres of horror and fantasy. Her first Steampunk piece, the inspiration for "Ordained" came from Phu Phra Bat National Historic Park and the adjacent Mekong River area of Nong Khai, which she visited in October 2012. www.lauraleehill. com

Alessa Hinlo writes fiction that spans the thriller, fantasy, and horror genres. Born in the Philippines and raised in Northern VA, she's most interested in stories that reflect the push and pull of conflicting cultures and feature people who fall into the spaces between. Her other interests include vegetable gardening, crafting, and yoga. She tweets regularly at @alessahinlo.

Olivia Ho is a writer born and based in Singapore. She studied English Literature at University College London and has just graduated from the University of Edinburgh with a Masters in Literature and Modernity. She owes the inspiration for her work to her parents—her mother, who taught her how to love the history of her island, and her father, whose idea of steampunk is "KILLER ROBOT SAMSUI WOMEN." Besides writing, her other random talents include Arabic belly-dance, stage management, and knitting, and perhaps one day all three at the same time.

Robert Liow, also known as Robert Bivouac, is a Chinese-Malaysian writer currently living in Singapore. An advocate for racial justice and diversity in media, he writes fiction, poetry, and critique from the perspective of a non-Western man of color in a heavily Westernized nation. He has appeared in the inaugural Singapore Poetry Writing Month ("SingPoWriMo") anthology and several publications by Singapore's Creative Arts Programme. He will be reading Law at King's College, London, from 2015 to 2018.

Pear Nuallak was born in South London to two Bangkokian artists. They studied History of Art jointly with SOAS and UCL, University of London, focusing on Thai Buddhist art, hybridity, globalization, and postcoloniality. Since then, they've been an office dogsbody, a community volunteer, a babysitter, home-maker, and now a writer.

They are interested in food, fiction, disruptive domesticity, and textiles. They may be found on a sofa in North London, having opinions while knitting.

Ivanna S. Mendels writes fantasy, science fiction, and steampunk, even children's picture books. Her Opera Dinosaur book was published in France and another of her Asian steampunk short will soon be published in Indonesia. Having lived and backpacked around the world, her adventures often inspired her writings. She is also secretly obsessed with Alfred Russel Wallace, and hopes to follow his trail one of these days. Her steampunk stories are partly influenced by Wallace's descriptions of South East Asia in his books. Ivanna is currently working on another joined project with some of her Indonesian Nanowrimo friends. You can follow her twitter at @ wulfettenoire

Kate Osias has won four Don Carlos Palanca Memorial Awards for Literature, the Gig Book Contest, Canvas Story Writing Contest, and the 10th Romeo Forbes Children's Storywriting Competition. She has earned a citation in the international *Year's Best Fantasy and Horror* for her story "The Riverstone Heart of Maria dela Rosa" (Serendipity, 2007). Her works appear in *LONTAR: Journal of Southeast Asian Speculative Fiction* #1, in various volumes of the *Philippine Speculative Fiction, Horror: Filipino Fiction for Young Adults, Maximum Volume,* and the WFC *Unconventional Fantasy* (2014). Her updated bibliography can be found on her Facebook timeline. She co-edited the sixth and seventh volumes of *Philippine Speculative Fiction*. Kate is a proud founding member of the LitCritters, a writing and literary discussion group. Occasionally, she ventures out into the real world to hoard chocolate and shop for shoes.

Nghi Vo lives on the shores of Lake Michigan, and her fiction has appeared in *Strange Horizons, Expanded Horizons, Crossed Genres,* and *Icarus Magazine*. She likes stories about things that fall through the cracks and live on the edges, and she has a deep love for tales of revolution (personal and political), transfiguration and transmutation. She's a writer by trade, a storyteller by nature, a volunteer by inclination, and a dreamer by design.

About the Editors

Joyce Chng writes science fiction, steampunk, urban fantasy, and things in between. Her fiction has been published in such publications as Crossed Genres, the Apex Book of World SF II, and The Alchemy Press Book of Urban Mythic. She co-edited The Ayam Curtain, a Singaporean anthology of SFF micro fiction. She blogs at A Wolf's Tale: http://awolfstale.wordpress.com. She is interested in social justice, feminism and its intersectionalities, permaculture, and bread-making.

Jaymee Goh is a writer, editor, reviewer, blogger, and academic, of science fiction and fantasy generally, and steampunk specifically. She writes a blog on postcolonialist steampunk called Silver Goggles, and has been quoted in Jeff and Ann Vandermeer's Steampunk II: Steampunk Reloaded, as well as The Steampunk Bible, and has written steampunk-related non-fiction in The WisCon Chronicles 5 & 6 and Steampunk III: Steampunk Revolution. She has an ongoing fiction series across several venues exploring an alternate history Melakan Straits. Beyond steampunk, she is interested in issues of radical womanism, utopia, sustainability, critical race theory, agriculture, and botany.

Also Available from Rosarium...

"... an eye-opening illumination of the full reach and depth of Delany's influence."

The New York Times Book Review

Stories for Chip: A Tribute to Samuel R. Delany
Edited by Nisi Shawl and Bill Campbell
978-0990319177

Stories for Chip brings together outstanding authors inspired by a brilliant writer and critic, Science Fiction Writers of America Grandmaster Samuel R. "Chip" Delany. Award-winning SF luminaries such as Michael Swanwick, Nalo Hopkinson, and Eileen Gunn contribute original fiction and creative nonfiction. From surrealistic visions of bucolic road trips to erotic transgressions to mind-expanding analyses of Delany's influence on the genre—as an out gay man, an African American, and possessor of a startlingly acute intellect—this book conveys the scope of the subject's sometimes troubling, always rewarding genius. Editors Nisi Shawl and Bill Campbell have given Delany and the world at large, a gorgeous, haunting, illuminating, and deeply satisfying gift of a book.

ALSO FEATURING: Christopher Brown, Chesya Burke, Roz Clarke, Kathryn Cramer, Vincent Czyz, Junot Díaz, Geetanjali Dighe, L. Timmel Duchamp, Hal Duncan, Fàbio Fernandes, Jewelle Gomez, Nick Harkaway, Ernest Hogan, Walidah Imarisha, Alex Jennings, Tenea D. Johnson, Ellen Kushner, Claude Lalumière, Isiah Lavender III, devorah major, Haralambi Markov, Anil Menon, Carmelo Rafala, Kit Reed, Kim Stanley Robinson, Benjamin Rosenbaum, Geoff Ryman, Alex Smith, Sheree Renée Thomas, Kai Ashante Wilson

"... may be one of the most important sf anthologies of the decade."

The Magazine of Fantasy and Science Fiction

Mothership: Tales from Afrofuturism and Beyond
Edited by Bill Campbell and Edward Austin Hall
978-0989141147

Mothership: Tales from Afrofuturism and Beyond is a groundbreaking speculative fiction anthology that showcases the work from some of the most talented writers inside and outside speculative fiction across the globe—including Junot Diaz, Victor LaValle, Lauren Beukes, N. K. Jemisin, Rabih Alameddine, S. P. Somtow, and more. These authors have earned such literary honors as the Pulitzer Prize, the American Book Award, the World Fantasy Award, and the Bram Stoker, among others.

ALSO FEATURING: Linda D. Addison, Lisa Allen-Agostini, Joseph Bruchac, Tobias Buckell, Indrapramit Das, Minister Faust, Jaymee Goh, Kawika Guillermo, Carlos Hernandez, Ernest Hogan, Thaddeus Howze, Darius James, Tenea D. Johnson, Rochita Loenen-Ruiz, Carmen Maria Machado, Anil Menon, Silvia Moreno-Garcia, Farnoosh Moshiri, Daniel Jose Older, Chinelo Onwualu, Andaiye Reeves, Eden Robinson, Kiini Ibura Salaam, Sofia Samatar, Charles Saunders, Nisi Shawl, Vandana Singh, C. Renee Stephens, Greg Tate, Tade Thompson, Katherena Vermette, George S. Walker, Ran Walker, Ibi Zoboi

Coming Soon ...

"Carlos Hernandez treats science, culture, and genre with a bracing irreverence. **The Assimilated Cuban's Guide to Quantum** Santeria is a zany, kaleidoscopic whirl of a book that delivers both tantalizing 'what ifs' and moments of true pathos."

—Sofia Samatar, author of A Stranger in Olondria

"A remarkable collection."

—Delia Sherman, author of **Young Woman in a Garden**

Funny, smart, and fierce, these stories are a breath of fresh air in a tightly constricted world."

—Christopher Barzak, author of **Wonders of the Invisible World**